PERSEPHONE'S SEEDS

BY DAYNA HUBENTHAL

Koho Pono, LLC

Persephone's Seeds

Published by Koho Pono, LLC

Clackamas, Oregon USA

http://KohoPono.com

First Paperback Edition 1may2010

Cover Art by Dayna Hubenthal

For general information on our other products, please contact our Customer Service Department at http://KohoPono.com.

Koho Pono also publishes its books in a variety of media formats. Some content that appears in print may not be available in electronic and/or audio media.

Library of Congress Control Number: 2010905179

ISBN: 978-0-9845424-1-3

Manufactured in the United States of America

This book is dedicated to Scott Burr.

I stand in awe at your refusal to be limited and am always touched by your gentleness.

Acknowledgements

I have fashioned my clay self from their great works.

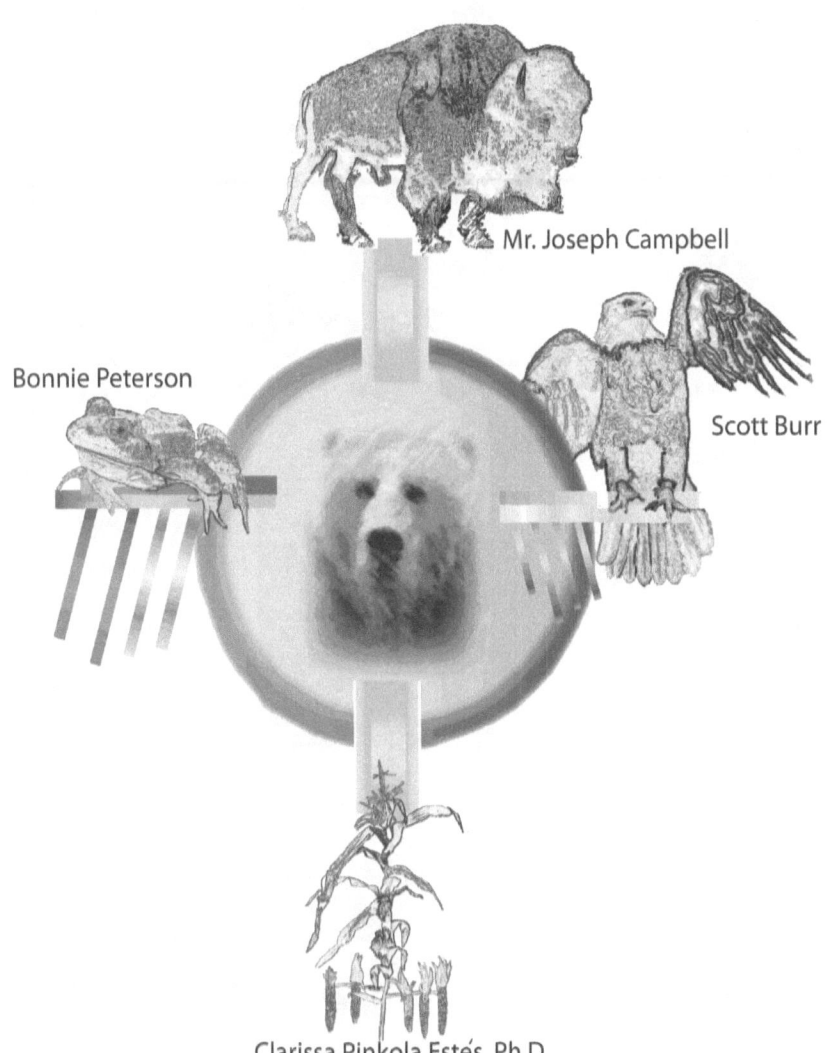

Mr. Joseph Campbell

Bonnie Peterson

Scott Burr

Clarissa Pinkola Estés, Ph.D.

Table of Contents

PART THREE - *"INNAR"*

Prologue

At age 36 I wanted to take a bite out of life. I wanted to chew it, eat its heart; be it. Instead, on May fifteenth, I died - and not for the first time.

May fifteenth is not my favorite day - hasn't been for quite a while. Twice before I died on it and my death today makes death number three. This catapults me-dying-on-May-fifteenth from the realm of freaky accident to nasty habit.

You would think I'd come to dread the day, but I don't. Death is not all that bad. In fact, I quite like it. It's much better than the part just before death. Let me be abundantly clear as I'm an expert on this subject, dying is not an experience worth repeating.

The trouble with being dead twice before … *amm* …is I tend to take death for granted - as odd as that seems. Life, too, I take for granted.

I guess somewhere inside me I know I keep choosing to make life tedious, which is why, against better judgment, I agreed to take a walk in the garden. And that same place inside me, I keep choosing to make death palliative, which is why I died hard for the third time. This story is about choices - Persephone's seeds - and seasons of the heart. But I'm getting ahead of myself. Let me start at the beginning.

Part One – "The Beginning"

"See this, Smudge. It's not for you."

"What is it, Russell?"

"It's a yew tree, Smudge. It's not for you."

"Ammm?"

Chapter 1 – First Years

I am not lordly, I am six.

Just short of crowing and far from regal I shout to the heavens, "I … Am … Six … Today." All the while my proud little feet pound, pound, pound out a cadence raising a cloud inside my self-made hole. Twelve times I trod the circle before my feet feel finished pounding down the dirt. They halt, my feet, in front of a patched bucket. Perfect.

Arms extend outward with hands cupped, all surfaces offered to the last of the kicked-up dust. Swirling clouds settle, lending color to me, thickening my hair. Even the hair inside of my nose gains dimension - dust dimension. At age six I am aware that I need to wear dirt.

"It is time," I pontificate as only a six-year old can to the sky, to the grass and to a baby tree lying on its side just outside the hole I'm

1

standing in. I whisper to sapling leaves and I lean in close to the tree, "Our ceremony continues." Poor thing; needs planting. "Soon, little friend," I reassure the tree, "soon." And then, moving my face away from the sapling I proclaim, "Child becomes dust-child and dust-child becomes ... free."

Excited my heart flutters - trips fast. Utterly still I concentrate on the sky, which is my next goal, and I also notice the heart-tripping-tune that will transform me into flight. *Tha-thump Tha-thump Tha-thump* Today I will fly. *Tha-thump Tha thump Tha ThathumpThathump* My whole body quivers as the blood speeds up.

~

Dear God, I need these old memories to feel alive. Thaaaa ... thump ... Viscous mud creeps in my veins today, but this precious recollection anchors me to the feel of grit on my tongue and gives me hope that if I remember hard enough I can recall what a throbbing heart feels like. Thaa ... thump ... Tha-thump Yes, I can feel it, the mud is creeping faster ...

~

My little six-year-old heart speeds up. *Tha thump Tha thump* Change me, dear beat. Transform me. *Tha thump Tha thump Tha thump* Feathers pop-out along my spine. They itch. *Tha thump Tha thumpThathump* My little bones hollow; feels odd. Weight falls off. *ThathumpThathumpThathumpThathump* The cadence picks up. Balance shifts. My body repositions itself from a vertical creature to a horizontally-centered one on stilts. I stretch my new wings and scratch at the dirt with clawed feet. *Flap, flap, scratch, scratch, ThathumpThathump* My lids close over beady eyes so my imagination can soar and I launch me.

Thick strands of muscle pull my wings down: *flap, lift, thrust.* In jerky jabs I climb out of the hole and mount the sky until I am high above the mansion. There, on warm thermals, I glide with one eye on the sun and the other beady eye looking for what I need to continue my planting ceremony. The wind rustles warm fingers through my feathers. I stretch out my right shoulder and dip just the edgiest tip of my wing and arc to the right with effortless control.

~

My teeth unclench and cheeks relax and I note a hint of warmth along my jaw line as I remember the wild child running circles on the grass arms stretched out and flapping, reality unhampered by inertia. Looking back I can see I was odd. No doubt about it. But was I wrong? Every detail remains as clear as a warm cloudless day. My sixth birthday, the first time I flew to the sun.

~

"Accck," my bird brain reads warm wind, no clouds; eyes bright, far sight. Bird's eyes spies all. I am a far-seer. I beat at the wind and lift myself. Could fly to heaven and back if I didn't have more important things on my brain. Bird brain. Could do it, though. Could fly clear to heaven.

Soar, stretch, lift, glide, spy a seed. Ah. That's what I need. Fly down, beak it and soar it back to dirt. Hop, hop, I hop down into my hole. "Stand back," I chirp at any worms or ants or other creatures. "Bird is back in the nest-hole."

I'm a beautiful bird with a seed in my beak. I bob my head forward and backwards as I fold my wings to my sides and strut once about the hole. It is a good hole. I drop the seed to the dirt and with eyes barely slit to keep the illusion intact. Claw extends outward for the ceremonial bucket.

So exciting. *ThathumpThathumpThathump* Up, up the bucket must rise above my feathered brow. It's heavy, so weighty I shake with effort. *Tremble little dirty bird*

I shake until the bucket is aloft and in position to anoint. I will … in just a moment I will … My eyes pop open. … in just a second I will tip the bucket and … no, wait. Wait. *Thathump Tha thuuummp …*

3

wait. I am not quite ready to anoint us yet, not quite ready for the ceremony to be over. I pause; bird brain searching. Something is missing. Some pageantry still needs expression. I tip my feathered head to one side in consideration.

I have created the birth place. Become dust. Have flown and seen far and found the seed. What is missing?

Ah, I realize. I have not yet shown the sapling that it is safe to burst forth. For the ceremony to be complete, another transformation is needed: child into dust-child, dust-child into bird, bird into … *amm* …

Beady dark eyes close to better contemplate my dissolving feathers, bones, and beak. I collapse into a ball no bird could bend itself into because I am no longer a bird. I am … IIIIII*ammm* … *aaa* … six-year old seed now. That's what I am - a seed ready for birth.

A seed curled up tight.

A seed dropped into a hole.

A dusty seed dropped into a hole by a far-seeing bird.

Dirty, little curled-up seed dropped into a nest-hole by a wise bird. I … am … perfect.

I am coiled inside my hard seed shell with my diaphragm compressed all air squeezed out of my lungs. It hurts yet I will not let my body breathe. Seeds don't breathe. I am … potentiality … at its peak. I stay until my throat's demand for air bites at me.

I won't breathe, I won't …. and then I must breathe or explode and so it is time to break out of my seed-shell and reach for the sky. I uncoil because it is correct, and suck air. Stomach fills, straightens me - nitor - seed, sheath, push, out. My sheath is no longer my sheath. Having done its job, it is done, no longer part of me. I push the shell away; push against the dirt, push against everything, reach for life into air and at the same time dig toes, I mean roots, into the ground. Both

4

ends struggle; one towards the sun and the other for anchorage. Me-seed raises up onto toe-roots and continues to stretch with my stem holding the ceremonial bucket until it is raised high. I suck air until my belly is distended and lungs are topped off and my throat is pregnant and bursting and then, and only then, I am ready to anoint myself and the other sapling with water. I sing out. "With water high and sun in sky I claim this ground for use for my ... ekk."

Heavy is the hand thudding down on my delicate shoot-shoulder. Water surges over the bucket's lip. I, the seed, squeak then peek at the appendage plunked down so heavy it feels like it will push me back into the earth. I consider the benefits of going with the pressure and ducking down into my hole, but gnarled fingers contract - a warning squeeze. "Darn it," my six-year-old seed-brain thinks, but I say nothing because seeds don't talk.

The bucket is lifted away from my grasp. Plunked down. Gnarled fingers twist my shoulder, I mean my tender shoot, and the delicate sapling-me turns in response until I face one of the few people in my world who will not let me use my birthday as an excuse to dig holes in the front lawn.

"Arggggh," says the master gardener, my best friend.

"Darn it," seed-brain thinks again.

"Ya gotta come on up outta that hole now, wee beastie, and walk with me. Yur wanted at ta party." At my downcast expression he lifts his gnarled fingers off my shoot-shoulder and extends them to help me out of the hole. "Look at ya," he gruffs. "Yur as dirty as a sink hole. Smudge, I'm gonna get called to task for it. Ya know that, don't ya?"

My eyes jerk to gauge the stress held in his shoulders. All thoughts of being a seed, a bird, an adventurer flee. I am a child now, six years old today and mischievous, so mischievous that I have once again unwittingly brought trouble to my dear old friend.

Yes, stiff; my friend's shoulders are stiff. He might seriously be worried about this trouble, especially considering all the disorder I instigated this week while in his company. I grab hold of his coat cuff. "When Grandma starts fussing," I offer the advice that never lets me down, "catch Daddy's attention. He sees much better. And, Russell, don't worry. Da doesn't care when I get dirty." I jiggle my friend's sleeve.

Russell clears his throat in that funny way he has...

~

I remember him still, my friend.

~

"Now don't ya go fret'n 'bout me, ya hear," Russell warned. "Last time ya tried to fix somethin' up right-n-tight hardship took tea wiff me."

I screw up my brow in confusion and look a long, long way up to see his face. "What ...?" I start but he interrupts.

"So, yur six today, aye?" And his shoulders drop and his jaw relaxes.

Now I know he is going to be fine. If he's changing the subject, he isn't worried; and if he wants to lead us off into another topic that is all right with me. We don't leave anything unaddressed although we often don't talk about things. Some communication is better than words. Still, I don't want him to forget my little secret so I prompt him again, "Remember, talk with Da. He'll understand."

Russell makes a noise; it sounds suspiciously like a snort. "Right true, Smudge. I remember hauling him outta plenty of holes when he was your age. Your nut didn't fall far from that tree."

And I smile because I can not think of a better birthday present than being told I'm just like my Da.

6

Too soon we arrive at the tea party and Grandma's sharp eyes spy Russell. "What are you doing here?" Grandma asked with her words, but her tone said, "You filthy … man, how dare you show up at my tea party - you, a gardener."

Grandma never did approve of dirt or toil; so odd.

Cousin Rob spies me in my hiding place behind Russell's trunk-like legs and says, "Ah! Dirty brat, don't touch me." His eyes slide towards Grandma to catch her reaction. Waiting in vain for approval, I suspect. No one pays him attention; not Grandma, not his mom or the men or anyone except me. He tries again, only louder.

At the same time the gardener says, "Sir?" taking my advice to address my father rather than my father's mother. "I found the child, Sir." That's what my best friend says.

And the whole family swivel heads and bounce eyes to look for me and that makes me laugh - it looks so silly. As a flock they raise eyebrows and make 'O's' of their mouths. No one notices Rob's magpie finger pointing my way, which makes him furious. No one sees his mouth purse shut or his neck ridges protrude; no one but me. His finger stabs the air in my direction. Three times it stabs at me.

I tilt my head to him in commiseration, but he doesn't want what I offer. So instead I peek around my old friend's legs. I grip his pants, barely able to contain my delight. My Daddy will swing his face around and see me; yes, yes, he is turning now. Eyes catch hold of my position. They light up because they recognize my face. They are surprised yet not surprised at my dirty visage, and finally, the moment I have been waiting for … his whole face lights up in a smile - for me. My Daddy loves me.

And then his face screws into a terrible frown but his eyes dance over my face, drinking me in. "Child," he growls and my giggles burst out. I cannot contain them. I love this game. "Child, step out from behind that good man's legs. And let go of your death grip, for heaven's sake. You are going to wrinkle his pants." That last bit even surprises a snort out of my old friend. I laugh and there is a soft female huff of ticklement coming from the other side of my Da. Soon I will see her face, too. Anticipation rises like thermals on this hot day.

In the background a lady-like 'harrumph' fills the air, which is Grandma's contribution to the conversation.

Cousin Rob audibly grinds his teeth.

The gardener's weather-leathered hand reaches around and cups the nape of my neck. He's not a man who speaks much. Just a gentle pressure against my neck communicates his desire to quit this high-flown affair and get back to the work of filling up the holes I dug this morning. I envy him his task. My coming-job is to make polite conversation at high tea. I release my friend and step out into the open amid exclamations of disapproval.

"Really, my … good man," Grandma's disappointment rings clear, "how did my grandchild get so dirty? I don't believe we see skin through that mess."

It's true. I'm covered head to toe in dirt. But it's dry dirt. It could easily have been mud.

"Russell?" A soft female question - the perfect counterpoint to Grandma's stern tones - stays the gruff gardener's bowing retreat. "Pray tell us …"

Oh tremble sweet tone; glide on laughter precious question, my mother speaks.

"…how did my child manage to get quite this dirty?"

The gardener freezes, then straightens. "Harr, herrm keck," he brings something solid up into his throat and then swallows it back down before answering. Momma has that effect on people. Rough words are never spoken at Momma. "Well, mistress, we was plant'n new trees in the orchard, see. An this one ran off with a sapling when we wasn't look'n." Here Russell frowns at me.

It *was* a bad thing to do. I might have damaged its delicate roots dragging the sapling over the lawn like that.

"Yes, Russell," I admit meekly - and at the same time - "Yes, Russell?" Momma's melodious tone encourages him to continue.

"Well, we follow'd ta trail to ta middle of ta front lawn and found two holes. Tyke must have been work'n on 'em all morn'n. Gotta give credit where credit's due. Them are mighty fine holes. Dug one for the tree and the other for ..."

"My lawn?" Grandma interrupts Russell's story just when it gets to the good part. "There is a hole in my front lawn?"

"Two holes, Ma'am, one for the tree and one for the tyke. Said I was to plant 'em both right there."

Grandma shrieks something incoherent and Rob jiggles with tension so I step past my friend to calm the misunderstanding. "The earth needs something there, not just a big empty lawn," I explain. "The birds need a home and there are lots of animals can use the fruit." Secure in my reasonableness, I continue. "The ground slopes down in that spot and needs shade. And mostly, I wanted to see what a tree felt like when it was buried in the earth. I was going to dig a pond right next to it so we'd have water."

Uncle Eck hustles over to tend to his sister. Grandma looks quite ill at the idea of a pond.

"Darling," Momma finally leans forward so I can see her and for a moment everyone else disappears except the two people I love most in the world, Momma and Da. "Grandma finds pleasure in her lawn," Momma's words dance out of her mouth. "She likes the large emerald expanse, that's the whole point." I glance over at Grandma almost hidden by an overly solicitous Uncle Eck. It never dawned on

9

me that she liked the front yard that way. "Please let the tree go back to the orchard," Momma continues, "And I really would hate to have to walk outside to tuck you in at night if you were buried in the front yard. It's much cozier to be indoors during the snows."

Well, I hadn't thought of that. "Yes, Momma," I say in a barely subdued tone. Then as she dips her head towards Grandma, I shuffle over to the Grand Dame of our household and lay a hand on her sleeve. Even though it's dusty, she doesn't draw away. "I am sorry, Grandma dear. I didn't know you liked your lawns that way. I was trying to help." Grandma waves her brother off and Rob, too. She looks into my eyes and sees my heart, sees I am sorry for disturbing her. And I see her heart, which is why I offer her a hug, which she declines as I am muck-covered; but she accepts my apology and she even smiles at me. For all her airs, Grandma likes me. And my heart holds a lake for Grandma, a large still lake just for her; just waiting for her to quench her thirst.

"Sit down, dear, and tell me what is wrong with a big empty lawn." Grandma indicates a space next to her. Instantly a chair appears, soon followed by a plate of tiny apple tartlets and a cuppa. My birthday tea is once again underway.

~

As is their nature, the bright memories fade and I work harder to recall the delicate and important parts of that afternoon. My last perfect afternoon. A day of dust and roots and water and apple tarts and people who love me.

Momma and Da, they loved me best. They loved me cozy warm.

~

Sunlight taps my cheeks. Buttery warm fragrance fills my nose. I am surrounded by family voices, which is calming in its familiarity. Am warm through and through. Sharp little six-year old teeth nibble tartlet crust - anticipation's the thing. Flakes drop to my lap and I swing my legs to see the fallen flakes dance.

"Sit proper," Grandma whispers.

"Proper?" I think. "What could be more proper for a six year old than this? *Amm* … perhaps leaning against Da would be more proper." And I glance over to see Momma and Da's knees squeezed close in an unconscious knee-kiss. Their shoes point towards me, include me. They always do. With every move their elbows bump, bump each other. When Momma turns away to answer a lawyer-question her knees slide away from Da's. I watch her foot slide on grass, pointing towards me but search, searching, until she nudges Da's foot - just a smooch - her foot stays close. Then she turns back and bows her head to sip tea; knees slide back to center, bump up against, find their home and settle until his attention is called away. His foot on grass, search, searching … I love this dance. They flow like brooks downstream always towards each other; always towards me. I don't think they are even aware of their flowing.

Using my tongue like a beak I finally scoop the tartlet's filling and roll the treasure across my taste buds. Mmm, apple's my favorite. With warm sun on my face I bite down on a plump cinnamony-apple chunk and juice like sweet water trickles across my tongue.

~

I contemplate sweet water. Momma was sweet water. And then there is big water - water as cabalistic power, just like Da. Daddy, he was the big ripple in our little pond. His power bubbled up from patriarchal pools and cascaded through genes, inclination, and the legal system as irrefutably as a river voice echoes in high-walled canyons. Da was power. He was only capable of big ripples.

Because Da was always the favorite, Grandpa couldn't trust chance to produce a suitable mate. He divinated about for Momma until he came upon her. He instantly recognized her as the one and removed a few obstacles so she could course her way to Daddy. Grandpa was right as he usually was on matters of his dynasty. His heir favored Momma and loved her above all. And Da was hers, too, the moment she tasted him. The tide in her unashamedly flowed out and

11

claimed her mate – maybe ladylike, certainly womanly to the core. She flooded into The Family and when the waters retreated, it was as if she had always been there. Grandpa crafted a water-tight marriage contract and the power ripples grew. The pond was healthier with Momma feeding it.

So single-minded was Grandpa in passing on the current of control to his firstborn son, when the patriarch died no one even felt a burble - except Grandma. She had a good deal more freedom after his death - although she never used it.

Da's power grew. In fact, the whole family grew stronger with taproots in sweet water - anchorage and assimilation.

When I think of my world in terms of roots, Momma and Da and apple trees come to mind. Different stock grafted onto a single trunk - one set of roots. Apple-Momma was the skin: tough, pretty, alluring. Apple-Da was the meat: juicy, heavy, tasty. And Apple-I ... I was their seed. Together they were potent. "Add me", they said, "and we formed an invitation no one could resist - a triumvirate to last the ages." And then they kissed me on my dirty face and shooed me out to work with the gardener, which I loved because he was my best friend and because I was a child of nature.

I was as wild and graceful and instinctive as a worm, as a goose in flight, as a squirrel reading the seasons, as a fox scenting the air. My place was on the ground with knees imprinting holes in the garden and nose and fingers rooting in the loamy wonder of the earth's bounty smelling her rhythms, feeling her mysteries. That was during daylight hours.

When it got dark, my place was sitting on my Momma's lap or on the arm of my Daddy's chair, leaning into him while he rubbed circles along my hairline with gentle ink-stained fingers. I loved being wrapped in the scent of Daddy-smell while learning family business to the rhythm of his fingers caressing my face. I was secure and seen and understood and loved. I enchanted them. My marrow was built of that stuff.

12

Just as surely, I knew there were tensions at the mansion, dark and severe resentments. I felt them in the cultivated areas outside, the places The Family gathered. Our wide lawns with topiary bushes running down to the English plot were visually stimulating and absolutely in order. There was a carefully orchestrated over-spilling of plants in the prettified places along the walking course. Sweet scented roses perfumed the air so heavily my stomach roiled and yet I could not stop myself from huge quaffs of it. These places reminded me of Grandma – perfect, perfectly delightful, and perfectly bound. There was no compassion in these places. The earth, my earth, was fertilized and nature's preferences had long since been rejected. Whatever root or seed the grandparents desired was forced into my earth's soil and, unable to fight her fertility, the gardens teemed with life. My earth was weeded and enshrined and I ached for her and spent my time elsewhere.

There were places for me on the mansion grounds; beautiful and wild places where I roamed free. These spots felt like Momma. I jumped across our bog and forded rocky streams and danced with my nose in the air to scent out wild berries and cautiously crept around the overgrown grotto with its collection of rare trees and little wild animals. No one went to these places except the gardener and me. We never combed out the tangles.

Inside the mansion the tensions were even worse than the outside cultivated areas. But the murky swirling emotions did not cast their net over me as I was safe within the inner circle. I felt them though.

Interactions between my parents and the aunts, uncles and cousin prickled my skin and lifted hairs all along my arms and legs and coated my mouth like thick cream – such was the maya I perceived. As I padded the floors of our place, my instincts reached out ahead of me and gathered information before I ever entered a room. Like a stalker of shadows I picked up on the acrimony beneath the smiles and groveling as well as the desperation behind the demands and the dense gall that flavored the very air we breathed in that house.

13

Daddy said I had the family gift. Momma said it was useful. And they smiled at me with delight even as the others looked at me out of the corners of their eyes and tried to build walls I could not see behind.

More than a third of my family died on my sixth birthday, including Momma and Daddy. Grandma was shaken to the core, I know; but the others only started wailing and gnashing and crying with bitter certitude once it was discovered that Da hadn't altered Grandpa's will and I was in charge of everything.

They came to detest me, my family. I suspect even Grandma did. And memories of being the apple's seed wisped along the edge of my soul like Mommy's puffed breath across my face or the smell of inside-Daddy's-shirt-pocket. Occasionally, I would catch a whiff but I could never be sure it wasn't my wishful imagination. It was not strong enough to build a life upon.

"Russell, what are you doing?"

"I'm pruning the yew tree, Smudge."

"Why?"

"Yur Grandmother said, 'Shape it or get rid of it.'"

"Ammm ..."

Chapter 2 – Ending Like the Seasons

"Leave the child alone," Grandma said the night Momma and Da died, "poor thing doesn't comprehend the magnitude of this disaster."

I didn't comprehend; couldn't grapple with the implications of crashed, perished, deceased, or left behind. Ugly words they were, forced out between lips taut with panic. Everyone in my world was panicked. No one had a clue what to do except Da and Momma and they were crashed, perished, and gone. They were gone.

Comprehend? No I couldn't comprehend. A terror of rain slashed down. There was no solid ground, just mire. Wind tore through branches and twisted trunks and up-wrenched roots. Trees toppled. This storm made no sense. And in the eye of this storm - oh, yes; this storm had an eye - and in the eye of this storm Death waited for me. Soon enough, I would understand too much.

Trying to make sense of this wreaked time after my parent's death, I talked to God constantly and I looked in closets and under beds and kept running outside to check the lawyer's conveyance. No one was allowed to leave the grounds; no matter what time of night or day, no one was allowed to leave without me checking first. I refused to believe my Momma and Da were gone. Because I was only six, I did not realize that I was looking for fidelity as diligently as I was looking for my parents. I was testing - offering a tabula rasa to The Family - well, to Grandma. Realistically, she was the only one who had the courage to even try to stand face-to-face with me, engulfed as I was in despair's swirling tempest.

She almost managed it. All night and well into the next day Grandma shielded me from censure. "Leave the child alone," Grandma scolded The Family. "There will be no discussions on that subject. I don't care what your expectations are."

And Grandma deflected the lawyer's pressure, too; "I know there are papers to sign, but not tonight. Let the child be."

For that first terrible day Grandma even defended me against her wickedly pompous cronies. "My Dear Friend, you have dirty wrinkles on your skirt," Grandma's closest friend pointed out with raised brows and a condescending air. "I suppose that odd grandchild of yours has been rooting around the gardens again."

Grandma stiffened in her chair, careful not to dislodge my grasping hands. Then with exceedingly gracious tones, Grandma frosted her friend, "Yes, both the gardens and I are of great comfort to my grandchild. Just as some of my friends have been of great comfort to me. Remarkable, isn't it, what consolatory effects refined people have in difficult social situations by simply adhering to genteel standards." Then while the visiting biddy rattled her cup in her saucer and struggled to control her facial expression, Grandma whispered at the top of my head, "Hold up your head, dear," and she lifted my chin with her bejeweled finger; "Don't let her hear you snuffle."

When night fell, Grandma cradled me with my back against her chest and my body between her knees like a shell around a seed and Grandma talked to me all night about things I could not quite grasp such as how she had spent her youth, her beauty, and her soul or how she too had been betrayed. However, when facing a fresh onslaught the next day, a fear broke her resolve. I'm not sure which fear it was, but it was stronger than her courage and it was stronger than our tie.

"Enough self indulgence," Grandma's tone sharpened as she stepped back into her familiar dignity-prestige-and-should-be set of rules. "It is time to stop clinging to my skirt. It's time to embrace Family Duty. Dry your eyes, Child." She hammered at me, "Buck up. Quit crying. We both need to get hold of ourselves. Behave yourself."

I suppose, in the end, my inconsolable grief was too constant a reminder that she chose safety again over love. To distract herself, she determined to mold me into something proper.

Although it was still raining the day fear broke Grandma's potential, I remember it clear as a cloudless noon. My childhood ended. Although I'm not sure I ever made the transition into adulthood, I was very different after that day.

I no longer felt green or exposed or feral enough to ignore the burdens of consequence. Horizons no longer expanded before my child's foot and for the first time I gave a thought to safety nets and whether I had one. I was no longer free.

Maybe freedom is the pollinator of childhood. Before that day my roots always extended. There was no drought. I was free to express. Like the stem's reduced tip, growth dominated me: budding, blooming and bearing fruit unstintingly for any bird or bat or bug that beat a path to me. Childhood held time enough to see promise unfold. Sensitive to ancient, sappy rhythms and invitations, I determined truth by their resonance inside my gut. The membrane is thin between God and a child, between instincts and knowing and imagination and doing. The essence of childhood is freedom wrapped in belonging.

In this place, death is explore-able. My turtle died and was buried and dug back up and checked on and reburied and re-dug up and rotted away to mold and stink and still I felt safe - so innocent.

But when I realized that parents could leave one day and perish and be put into a closed casket so no one could see them, that Grandmas could withdraw, that love could be taken away or be dangled like a prize to be won, or I, too, could die, then puerility ended. I could be alone. There was no safety net. My parents were not hurt in doctor's care - alive still or in a fog of forgetfulness or even with a new family that they liked better than me. They were gone. I was one of one. Inclusion was no longer guaranteed. No one wanted to know *me*. Only by keeping my desolation to myself could I hope for acceptability - only if I gave myself away.

All of this I understood on some level the instant Grandma pulled back from me. Even though the aunts wailed solace, the comfort vibrated insincere. And when Uncle Eck offered, "I will be your new Daddy now. Leave everything to me." the veneer over his greed was so thin he didn't even fool himself.

A wall came down between me and what was left of my world - a wall trapping me indoors with The Family - one more thing to grieve. Using my gift to monitor their whereabouts, I kept away from The Family, trying to decide what to accept, what to do. Only Rob was allowed near me even though he disliked me from the moment I was born and was mean to me every day.

Rob, whose Mom and Dad were with my parents on my sixth birthday and died in the same crash, was also surrounded by a miasma of grief. He had enormous fear of further abandonment having endured degrees of it all of his short life. His pain and denial echoed and supported mine so although he became increasingly truculent, we bore each other's company. As the hours passed, his dislike of me developed into something stickier and uglier. I think he blamed me, my birth, and my father for his parent's unrelenting ignoring.

Of course he blamed me. Rob's father taught him bitterness by example. Rob's daddy grew up focused on his secondary position, believed in his incidental importance. He was the brother, not the successor. Too often parental eyes skimmed over Rob's daddy while searching for my Da, which burdened both sons.

The tragedy is that the spare died alongside his older brother. If he had just stayed home that night, Rob's daddy could have gained all the power he ever dreamed. Instead, he insisted he and his wife join the party getting candles for my cake. And he died. They all crashed; were all gone.

Rob blamed my birthday for the loss of his parents and he blamed my existence for everything else. "I wish you had never been born," he told me as he grabbed my face and squeezed while staring me in the eyes so he could watch the pain light me up. "If you had never been born, then I would be heir."

He never spoke out loud about his real pain; if he was heir then maybe he would have been enough to hold his parent's attention or hold their continued presence at his side. Instead, he bruised me. I was bossed because he needed to control something and I was the only one paying attention. He banged me into walls and stood on my toes. I didn't tell him to stop, except once and that wasn't effective because, to tell the truth, the pain of his bruising was so much less than the pain of my loss, I welcomed the distraction.

The Family may not have seen the bullying. If they did, the sight did not move them into action. Yet I could not blame them; hiding was my goal, too.

I hid in counting; lost myself in sequential ordering; obsessively ticking off the number of times I rubbed my hands over my face trying to comfort myself like Da used to comfort me; the number of seconds Rob squeezed my cheeks before he let go; the number of bubbles in the crack between his front right teeth as he worked himself up into a rage.

19

I hid away from The Family and counted, "One duck, two duck, three duck, four - third call for dinner - one duck, two duck ..." I didn't count every second after my parents died, but I counted more often than not. I had just finished counting another set of twenty 'ducks', when Rob strangled me.

Until today, that first death was the clearest memory of my life – clearer than the memory of the strangulation that led to it, clearer than my parent's face, clearer than the memory of Rob's short, sharp scream when he heard his parents died with mine in the accident and would never come back. Until today, that first death was the most beautiful and exquisite experience I ever had.

*"Smudge! Drop that leaf. Go to ta pond and
wash yer hands; and, Smudge, keep yer fingers
away from yer mouth."*

"Russell, if the tree is bad, why keep it?"

"Not bad, Smudge, just dangerous."

"Why keep it?"

"Keeps coming back; wants ta grow here."

*"Oh." Long pause. "Race you to the pond,
Russell."*

Chapter 3 – The First Death

I died the first time when I was six years old. My cousin Rob
strangled me.

Three times he warned me to stop "my whispering". He hated
it when I moved my lips, which I did when I counted. I tried to avoid
counting when he was around, but not having been provided with step-
by-step instructions on how to deal with grief, I had to make do with
what brought me relief. Counting brought me distraction, which was
relief. It nettled Rob, though, and he expected me not to irritate him.
Even that young, Rob had a lot of expectations and a lifetime of
disappointments.

"I'm irritating him right now" I thought, even as I was counting his eyelash hairs and thus "whispering" while he choked me to death.

His face was right above mine, our noses almost touching. My whispering puffed against his upper lip. The rest of the room was blocked; Rob's face my only view. I saw it in minute detail, which is why I was counting his eyelashes at the roots. His pupils expanded. I saw this, too. My distorted face reflected back at me. Then, before I finished counting, his eyelashes went fuzzy and then his whole head blurred. Tears tickled my cheeks as they coursed a crooked path through the tiny feelers on my face and into my ears. "His tears or mine?" I puffed in whisper, but I didn't know and the question seemed far away. Finally, everything went black.

The black felt soft as good loamy soil and I was sorry to feel it pull away when first the light came. Filmy the light was and then brighter. By the time I was surrounded, I loved the white glow. I felt as if a tunnel was moving backwards over me absorbing me into its center.

My two friends were there. Until that exact moment I didn't know I had two friends. As soon as I felt them, I remembered them and remembered that we were friends long before I was born into life. When I was readying myself for a body, they vowed to cherish me and watch over me. Even though I forgot them, they never left me. Right then I knew they never would.

We were giddy, the three of us, glad I was fluid again. How remarkable it felt to taste sound and touch emotions and to be so very airy and silly. Joy bubbled up inside me and it didn't hurt because there was no reason to contain it. Filigrees of unconditional love unwound themselves through me – conforming to how I needed to experience love, tensile strength tougher than titanium, weight more delicate than a puff of air, and with as much giggle as a butterfly kiss. All other love I knew in life, even the best love, was like a cold mask in comparison.

I felt myself expand and with that, we started moving up the tunnel where something wonderful was waiting for me. The closer I got the more brilliant became the light and the more I became celebration.

And then I was there and Momma and Da were there and separation did not exist. I was infinite space. I was them. They told me to go back.

It was incomprehensible.

I resisted, of course. There was no way I was going back to plant myself in parched earth with anger-like-sun beating down on me. I did not want to re-seed me in a constraining bed of familial dysfunction and absorb the burdens lain fallow like some twisted compost. My feeder roots were too tender for the resentments that waited for me in life. The Family liked parched ground, had dammed themselves off from the flood of love's traitorous weakening - their description, not mine.

It was too hard to grow like that.

Life had nothing to offer me. I must absolutely remain here on the threshold of heaven. Here in death's springtime, glorious connection sang to my vigor, I burst forth tasting deeper than beauty or even hope.

In the end, of course, there is no resisting, so back I went. The trip was instantaneous – a blink of a thought. Upon resignation to the concept, I was floating high up in a corner of my bedroom, grief-filled and looking down at a tiny dead child sprawled in its own waste.

Rob was leaning over that child, staring eye-to-eye. Either he was grieving what he had done or was making sure that the child was well and truly gone before he removed his hands from around the neck. He placed a pillow over the dead-head and piled all my toy dinosaurs on top. Then he left that knobby-kneed-kid alone.

Bantam hands frozen into claws and thin stick-like arms protruded out from either side of the pillow hiding the youngster's face. I felt a drag towards it and realized the pathetic thing was me and thought, "I look so vulnerable." Compassion mixed with detachment, but I resisted my tenderheartedness and stayed where I was – floating up in the corner.

23

One hundred 'ducks' I counted off and then eighty more before someone found my husk. I felt or maybe I heard a gasp from the hallway; then a young maid fell into the room just as Rob yelled. He tackled her I think as she headed in. She got to her feet and grabbed the inside door jam as Rob hugged her leg. Her little hat jiggled as she tried to shake him off, just like a dog shakes pond-water off a hind leg. Bits of hair fell down as she swung her heavy black shoe at Rob's nose. He let go then and rolled against the far side of the hall curled up, rocking and moaning, "No, noo, nooo, nooooo …"

She knelt in my excrement to lift the pillow from my head and I saw her pause but not draw back from that gruesome face, the suffocated child. I wonder; was she scared when she saw my eye-popped visage; my mouth stretched wide open and my tongue hanging out – blue and long? Is that why she took the time to lay the pillow so neatly on the floor next to the bed, out of my mess, and to carefully line up my dinosaurs in alphabetical order? Mumbling to herself she described each: "spiky-sided pointy-nose is an 'H', flat-tail is an 'I' … the teethy one that's 'M' …" I counted each one she sorted; there were thirteen.

I never understood why she used-up that precious, careful time and yet refused to stop working over me, offering me her breath and the strength of her hands as she pumped my chest, not too hard to crush my small bones, but with enough force to coax my heart back into action even though it took sixteen minutes and she was exhausted and soaked with sweat and was told to stop by more than one person.

All I ever saw was the back of her head.

She was let go right after the incident along with every other member of the house staff. I wonder; was she prepared to survive on her own that young maid? Did she get lost in the big world, too?

Yew is dangerous. Stay away.

-Journal Entry, May 15, age 6

Chapter 4 – Thirty Years Later and with Deaths Number One & Two Behind Me

Starting the memories over at the beginning again is indulgent, I know. Shouldn't relive my last good day twice - shouldn't do it; need to stick to my disciplines, but this morning is May Fifteenth and I feel old today. It's been thirty years since my last good day and I'm dried out and cold.

~

"My proud little feet pound, pound ...," memories engulf me like kicked up dust.

~

I'm too dried out to face work without my memory-crutch. "Sweet death, oh yes, I remember you," I whisper. "Not an instant of death is diminished."

"What?"

I open my eyes with a start. Must have drifted. Might have whispered audibly. Four faces stare back at me: two horrified, one almost orgasmic, and the fourth face wears a smug look as if I am a child at a recital and I have just made my teacher proud.

25

"What … what?" I ask with raised brows. Oh please don't let me have said 'sweet death' out loud, I pray.

Smug Uncle Eck says, "You said, 'Sweet …'"

"No! No I didn't say anything like that." I interrupt and sit straight in my chair. I look at them as horrified as they look back at me. Uncle Eck turns to the man closest to him and opens his mouth to speak. He's just going to make it worse. I slam my palm down on the desk and all four jump. I can look imposing while sitting here in my beautiful office, in my power chair, in my perfectly tailored suit, groomed to within an inch of my life.

"So, now we all agree to the basics outlined in the contract," I bark with authority. They stare still; have no words. We have not actually addressed the contractual basics yet. I attempt a smile, which is a mistake. Two negotiators shrink back from my stretched lips and the third negotiator leans in, face darkening with concentration. But the third face is not concentrating on my words or even on my exposed teeth. My allure is the fact that I died two times and then I came back to life. Uncle Eck told the three negotiators all about it during the introductions.

They can't seem to get past it.

"The scar …" Uncle Eck gulps and melodramatically rubs his own throat. Three sets of eyes turn as if torn from my face to stare in horrible fascination at Uncle Eck's rubbing fingers. In slow motion they all glance back to my throat. Their eyes try to bore through my buttoned-up collar. Uncle Eck winks at me over their heads. I do not return his cue. The memory of my second death and the scar it left below my throat turns my insides even colder. Any warmth I managed to achieve from childish memories is now chilled away. I stiffen and two of the negotiators tremble; the excited one almost jumps over the desk at me.

What does my face look like? I wonder as I lean back. Why tremble because of me? Who are they, these pseudo negotiators, these peepers? Why stare at me? I didn't impose myself on them. They came to me. It's no use blaming Uncle Eck, he won't stop.

I do not understand why everyone finds it so frightening that I died twice and returned to life again. The returning-to-life-part of the story should alleviate fears, but it doesn't. Here they sit. In *my* office. Sweating. Veins popping. Ears redden by emotion. Negotiators? There isn't a gambler's face among the lot. They have signs painted across their faces: dread, titillation, and the last – he's the one who fears me. These are the most common looks directed at me. After all these years it still distresses me to be set apart. I ungrit my teeth and the smile falls off my cold, desiccated face.

I know my documented death and then continued existence threatens the dread-man, but I do not understand why. Is he dying? Maybe he has been perverse and delighted in it. Perhaps he rejects the idea of judgment while at the same time fear he's wrong. Or he dreads an empty abyss – no afterlife, no nothing. For twenty years I detailed deathLife to dreaders, have tried to say something to relieve the foreboding. Nothing makes that look go away. This dread-man despises me but his pall is self-made and there is nothing I can do to stop it; there never has been.

If I allowed it, the titillated one would forget about business altogether. Questions would begin the process, but it would not end there. No amount of honesty or openness or exposure dulls that knife's edge. I've met the excited face before - perfectly respectful in relationship to others, but desperate for something from me that stimulates rather than engages. This negotiator will do anything if I so much as nod; touch me or bed me or degrade dear-held-values; will try it anyway if I am simply neutral. Only an impenetrable façade damps that excitement enough to keep the curious within the bounds of polite society.

And polite society is my current maven. I have nothing for the titillated. I am the most unexciting person alive. I barely have enough energy to get up in the morning. Despite my extraordinary labels and the power bestowed by my job and my wealth, I live a caged and anxious life - doing whatever I need to do to stay close to normality.

The man who fears me is the worst of the three negotiators. His grey and sweaty face offends me, but not as much as the odor of his fear. He's probably afraid he'll catch death from me like a flu. Gladly will I quicken his exit.

I get down to business, speaking rapidly, staring at them each in turn; distracting the excited one with my cool responses while rubbing the scar through my shirt. It heightens the mystery. Yes, I use the prop to gain advantage. If I don't, Uncle Eck will. After handling the fabric over my scar I use the same fingers to push the contract across the desk, almost touching the dread-filled man. He twitches out of the way. Two want out of the room and force their distracted partner's hand on multiple points. All three sign the contract and agree to finance a venture in which The Family's foundation is heavily invested.

The deed is done. The Family coffers are richer and Uncle Eck will appear a hero as he is the one who brought me the three little sheep for shearing. Uncle Eck, the last to make his mark on the contract, signs with a flourish while I smile again; pleasantly this time or maybe it is inanely that I am smiling. I feel like gritting my teeth.

Immediately the three negotiators stand and hands are shook, but not by me. Two of the negotiators flee my presence. "Run away little lambs before the snapping jaws of death devour you," I think at their backs.

The third negotiator requires a firm arm to pressure an exit. Uncle Eck pauses at the door to wink at me again. It's no use telling him to stop bringing up the subject of my multiple deaths during negotiations. He's learned that it is effective and believes he is helping The Family Foundation and thus himself. Never mind what it costs me.

We don't need stories of my deaths to close deals. I have a genetically bred affinity for business, have been trained by the city's greatest business minds, plus the lawyers help a bit and my uncles - the straw bosses - deflect attention from me while I manipulate behind the scene to structure deals and grow the foundation into a monolithic yew-like entity with roots penetrating into everything. My little business feeder hairs weave their way into most business plots and my peers have yet to figure out that dried-out-me decides if a deal grows to fruition or is lopped off and used for fuel. We don't need 'horror' stories.

My assistant will witness their grating emotions as they pass through her office. Most days she sees these same expressions on people leaving my office. Apparently I have death scars, ones I cannot see. But other people see; they find me eerie. I am unnatural. I am an oddity and, to tell the truth, I am sick to ... well, death ... from having to deal with other people's emotional fallout.

The door snicks closed. I sit still as a glacier trying to prevent any more tattered bits of myself from calving off for the benefit of others.

I'm thirty six years old. Eyes close. I drift. May Fifteenth. Ah yes, I remember.

~

Death's black is soft, soft as good loamy soil. Feel sorry when it pulls away at the first fingers of white light ... giddy, so giddy, and glad to be fluid again and to be so very airy and silly.

~

It's indulgent ... I know ... shouldn't do it ... but it's May fifteenth and I'm so cold and I need it ...

~

... white light ... apple tart ... young maid's hat ... warm thermals... Russell...

~

I'm so darn cold from endless stretches of days after day earning my family's bread and trying to earn a sincere welcome.

"I'm thirty six years old." I keep saying that. It ought to mean something.

"Heartless," my assistant exclaims as she bursts into my office and starts setting it to rights. My eyes pop open.

"I finally figured it out," she shoots the words at me then pauses, waiting for me to urge her on although I seldom do. "Well?" she erupts.

Startled I arch my eyebrow, the only thing I'm willing to move just now.

She continues, "For years I have bounced between 'heartless' or 'idiots'."

Still I have no clue what she is yammering on about.

"Even though they act like idiots," she persists at my look of glacial incomprehension, "I have come to believe that your family is simply heartless. And you," she jabs her finger at me, "you, I have finally confirmed, are not heartless, merely an idiot."

My mouth drops open.

She takes a hard look at my face and then asks, "Are you surprised?"

Caught off guard by her, I am surprised into allowing my usual inscrutable face to give information I normally hold to myself. "How dare she say that?" I think, not in affront but astonished at her pluck. "How does she dare say such a thing about The Family? She has too much to lose."

She is an unusual young woman, my assistant. Grandma hires only a certain kind of person for the household and for anyone interacting with me. Always my assistants have been tepid males - timid.

Other than her gender, she appears to be, in many ways, the usual sort of assistant. She takes direction from Grandma and The Family without question. When she is finished with those tasks, she takes care of me: setting my appointments both social and business, herding me into and out of meetings, telling me to tuck in my shirts and to straighten my hair and to dig spinach out of my silly-tooth. She does research. She is seemingly innocuous and most people reveal too much to her. She helps me calmly, steadily, and efficiently. She does all that, which is normal and expected. She's been with me for three years and Grandma thinks she's doing a fine job so things are proceeding exceedingly well.

Occasionally, however, she says disrespectful things about us, The Family. It shocks me. And it amuses me as she always prunes the tree perfectly. It only happens when the two of us are alone. She speaks out on issues unrelated to business - voices her opinions quite empathically. She asks me piercing questions or laughs at things I say as if I am joking. And very occasionally, she arranges for me to attend lectures or events or presents me with fascinating reading material and works time into my schedule so I can devour it. This is quite out of line with any business need and is, therefore, taboo.

Since Grandma never questions me about these precious times away from duty, my assistant must make them appear regulation. I never ask how she arranges them and, of course, I never say anything to The Family.

And thus, this woman baffles me. Her ability to act on her own directive is so unusual within the experience of my life, it is freakish. She has never asked for a reward so I don't understand why she does these things for me. Since I no longer have intuitions I can't determine if she is doing the right thing. Grandma wouldn't think so.

My assistant must realize she would be fired if word of any one of these behaviors ever found their way to Grandma's ear. She needs the money otherwise Grandma would not have hired her. Grandma only allows people around me that are desperate to please - to please Grandma.

Regardless of the puzzles my assistant presents, I always participate in whatever she sets up and we never speak of it. When I see one of the events on my calendar, I maintain an aura of resigned tiredness and swear to myself to maintain decorum while on my adventure. At the same time I begin to pant and sweat and some rare part of me claws at its fine containment.

Like a well-fed spaniel on a spring day I am wound too tightly. When the kennel door is flung open and I am let free, the unfettered me lunges into excess. In these last three years I have barked a-frenzy while boozed to the tips of my ears. I've drugged myself, overeaten, run down dissident ideas and lost myself in lectures about far-off adventures. Thrice I had an idle hour. I spent them in lascivious imaginings. Most recently, I put some of those imaginings into action. After eighteen years of celibacy, while the condemning eyes of my family were turned elsewhere and I was presented with time and opportunity, and I found a willing partner, and I was overwhelmed with a torrential need to orgasm in all ways physical, which I indulged thoroughly. Since then, in my few spare moments, I have remembered that romp with a red face and ignoble pleasure.

I feel my face heating up just thinking about it. "Lock down those lips," I think to myself because bursting into intemperance humiliates me. Intemperance is dangerous - this I know for sure. Controlling this lip-trembling memory of debauchery takes effort today.

My assistant cocks her head in examination. She doesn't say anything, just studies me. Shame slides my eyes away from her. Hungers live inside me. I would rather no one knew that.

I fear the day I will not be able to crawl back into my dryCaged life and will, instead, drive myself to destruction.

She stands on one leg and scratches her ankle with the pointy toe of her left boot. Her head is cocked to one side. She looks like a beady-eyed bird - a bird staring at a seed. I am no longer a seed. There's nothing to me anymore.

Suddenly, the office door slams open. It hits the wall. Big noise. Bounces back. A grey head thrusts through the opening. Bang; the head stops the door from closing completely. We gape, my assistant and I, at Uncle Eck's head poking through that door crack. He winces and then, with a flourish, he thrusts open the barrier again and bends at the waist to invite someone into my office. We trade confused glances, my assistant and me.

Could Uncle Eck have brought me new lambs to fleece so soon? I glance down towards the calendar on my beautiful cherry wood desk. I cannot tolerate another set of staring eyes right now. Must escape, even for a few minutes. Distracted, I notice the swirling wood of the desk. In slow, detached motion I finger these growth lines, follow their patterns, appreciate the deep colors dancing behind the shine. I lose myself, calendar forgotten, assistant forgotten, Uncle Eck-Eck definitely banished. I would rather trace wood. Trace it in a trance. Trace the wood lines with a dirty little bird claw. *Tha-thump ... Tha-thump*

Someone is talking, but I'm not listening. I'm flying. *Tha-thump, Tha-thump* My name, spoken sharply, lifts my head, but not my full attention. I spy Grandma as if spellbound, finger-claw still tracing growth lines on my desk.

Grandma? Here? Standing in my office?

Confused, I look around. Yes, I am in my office. And Grandma is here, too, standing just inside the door in front of a bowing Uncle Eck. And now he steps close behind her, looming over her white head. He stands so close his shiny shoes bump up against her pumped heels.

Grandma sighs and minutely twitches her shoulders. It is all that is necessary. Her brother hops back. All this I notice behind a web of confusion. Grandma? Here?

Then Grandma's eyebrow raises – just the one, the left one. This is directed at me.

That ascending brow snaps my trance. In my haste to rise and brush a kiss to her cheek, I nearly knock my assistant off her pointy little shoe.

"Dear Eckhard, go sit down," Grandma commands her brother. "No, over there against the wall," she crisps the order. She waves the assistant out of the room and gestures me to sit behind my desk as she controls her decent into one of the negotiation chairs directly opposite me.

Nervously my fingers rub the desk surface. Grandma very rarely visits me at the office. What have I done? What has she found out? "Grandma," I begin but she shushes me, uncrosses her ankles in order to lean in towards me.

"It's time for you to marry," she announces, her voice calm.

I'm aware of the news screeching against my ears like a snowstorm among mountain peaks - screaming, ripping, and cold, so cold.

"The Whole Family is in agreement," she says then stops her voice and her eyes drill into me.

Uncle Eck gasps startled. He's horrified. Obviously the whole family hadn't known about this little agreement.

"I don't have time to go into the details now." Grandma starts up her voice again to lay down the plan. "It's become obvious Rob will never settle enough to give us an heir, and you're the rightful one anyway, so you must do it. Since you have no social skills, just leave everything to me. It will mean some changes for you, however, which is why I'm telling you about it now. You need to prepare yourself. Things are going to get a bit complicated because, Pet, we both know you have no skill at choosing proper alliances. Dare I say it? Look what happened last time you choose someone on your own." She stares at my buttoned up collar. Beneath it, my scar radiates out freezing fingers. Humiliated, I flinch against pain as cold as blue ice. Grandma keeps pouring out words like a blizzard against stone. "We can't very well have another stranger come into The Family and stir things up - absolutely unacceptable. Eventually there will be children, of course. That's the whole reason for this disruption. Children are important ... carrying on the line and all that ... well, trust me."

Her words are so aggressively glacial they burn me. I look studiously at my desk and wonder if I will freeze-dry into paper-boned fragments. Surprised, I notice my frozen fingers dance across the cherry wood surface, reach out and ring the bell that summons my assistant. I did not ask those chilly digits to dance or ring the bell.

Someone in the room makes a truly hideous sound, a kind of rasping wrenching choke. Embarrassed for this foolish person, I keep my head down and focus frozen eyes on the contract in front of me. My iced fingers continue to stab at the bell. The noise begins to irritate me. I wish my fingers would stop.

"Don't fret, darling, I'll see to everything," Grandma continues, her voice climbing in volume over the awful sobChokes. The door to my office opens and softly closes as my assistant enters and makes her way towards me. Water lands on the contract in front of me and I put my hand in it trying to warm the chill.

"Stop it." Grandma commands the fool making the noise. "What is this nonsense?"

Pity whispers along the edge of my mind, but I keep my head low. "Buck up, Poor Fool, not in front of Grandma," I think. "Throw back; quiet yourself. She doesn't want to know." The sob-chokes grate across my nerves, too; souring me into itchy restlessness. Another drop of water hits the contract. Who is making that God-awful noise? I raise my head, a quick, searching glance. Uncle stares at me. My assistant, now at my side, she also stares but with compassion. Grandma, a stone monolith draped in softest sweet-flowing white print, radiates a stone-cold chill at me. There is no one else in the room. And it dawns then, as another drop overflows my eye; it's me. I'm the fool making that sound. Head on a swivel, confirming, I throw back and count to thirty three for control. Oh, God.

"Stop those disgusting noises," the stone monolith commands.

I clamp down my throat and stop it immediately. And sit. We all sit. Just sit. Sit staring at me, at Grandma; sit.

Shoes tap-tap against the wooden floor. My feet are dancing now as if they will get up and run me away. I glance at my assistant. She is staring at me with her common expression – a penetrating, beady, piercing look. It is the look of someone taking the time to really see me, which makes me uncomfortable. I straighten up in my chair to the point of rigidity, legs stiff, balls of my feet pushed hard into the floor to halt their movement.

Uncle Eckhart makes a noise, I'm so glad it's not me again. In slow motion I glance over. There is something very wrong with his lips. His lips glue my eyes. Twisted his lips are. Could be a sneer. A wrong sneer. In my peripheral vision I see Grandma pivoting in her chair to follow the direction of my eyes.

Still in slow motion, Uncle Eck's lips relax into a grotesque half smile and he leans towards me, arm stretched to offer his clawed paw to me. What Grandma sees is the outstretched hand, the smile. In a whisper-soft voice he pierces me with, "So, you are going to start a family." The words look ugly as they leave his mouth but Grandma nods in approval, fooled by the mask - or at least approving the mask. She faces me again, satisfaction writ all over.

"So, you are going to start a family," he whispers again and a shudder wrenches my spine, exerting too much pressure. My surface ice cracks and in my gut a giant crevasse pulses in denial.

I stare at Uncle Eck and feel the blood leave my head. Am awash in physical sensations … strange sensations… feel stranded in these bodily processes. Normally, this vessel of mine and I are in accord: it does what I demand and does it quietly, with ignorable input, a servant to my strict control. On any given day, without much thought, I tune my body out and get on with the business at hand and it does what it is supposed to do to support my efforts. Now, however, my skin is clammy and cold at the same time. I'm shaking. My chest feels tight. My vessel's impingement is so severe it dominates my thinking.

I tear my eyes from Uncle Eck's mask and roll them up to the left searching for a reason behind the absolute appalledness that pulses through me. More family? My head whirls. My stomach heaves. Breath exits on a hiss. This sound is better, though, than those other ones that passed out of me.

"I am afraid." I realize and might have whispered it out loud. Truly, deeply afraid of my coldness. I have not one iota of anything to give to a child should one come into my life. All that is left of me is blue ice under crushing pressure. The thought of having to give anything to anyone else sends a keening wail of despair into this airless space of me. Spittle collects inside my cheeks, a new sensation, while yellow and black dots dance in front of my eyes. I have no idea what this portends. My assistant, however, grasps the situation immediately. She spins my chair and shoves my head between my legs over the trash can. I am holding myself so rigid she almost breaks me in two.

My body is a stranger. One duck, two duck … I slowly count to thirty three as I always do in times of turmoil. "Can't be airless," I finally murmur to the back of my knees and swallow mouth after mouthful of spit. "That would never do." The statement is ridiculous, even I realize that.

My assistant pats me on the shoulder. "You're going to throw up," she announces.

I heave, quite surprised at my body's rebellion. But she is correct. I do, for an embarrassingly dense time. And then, the roiling stops. I breathe deeply filling my lungs with foul air and realize I haven't breathed deeply for years as if expanded lungs would take up too much space and annoy someone important.

I had a life once. I remember that; remember wanting to explore, be, and do tremendous things. I remember intending to stretch my wings and fly until I'd used up every last drop of life. I remember flying. As a child I flew. I soared in imagination. At eighteen I flew. My stomach clenches again in rejection of that memory.

Far away I flew when I was eighteen. Heated passion lifted me right up to the sun and burnt me up and I fell to the ground. That's why I'm sitting here with my head between my legs and nothing important left of me except expanded lungs filled with foul air and ice, ice, blue ice. I flew and I burnt up and never got close to the sun again.

I take another deep vomit-smelling breath.

"So, you are going to start a family," I hear Uncle Eck whisper.

My gut heaves again. Astonishing what an internal ruckus one simple statement can cause. I clamp my lips but the movement refuses denial. "No more demands," a thought is born and it rides up and out of me on the retch.

My feet are dancing again. Although it tastes foul, my breath blows the cobwebs from the bottom of my lungs. And out of the very bottom of me a realization resounds, *I need.*

I need. I need a new life or, maybe, maybe I just finally want a life.

"I can't do it, Grandma." my voice urps up and out, riding on a dry heave, hitting the trashcan.

"Don't talk, dear;" she commands, "it's disgusting."

I have nothing to give, I think, because *I* need.

"Child," Grandma orders, "take a breath."

Now, now is the time to take action, some action, any action, just act. Now.

I sit up, bile thawing frozen throat and iced nose. I stammer towards her face, "There's not enough of me;" a bit desperately, "I can't be anything for even one … more … person."

"Hush. I can't understand you," Grandma's mouth as stiff as stone barely moves as she interrupts me. "Take a breath."

"Breathe?" I scoff, but only inside my skin. There is no oxygen to take a breath inside glacial ice.

"Sit still!" that stone mouth across the desk from me orders. "How can we carry on a decent conversation with you bouncing around in that chair?"

I press my feet into the floor again. Sit? I am trying to quiet the crevassing. "Everything has changed," I grunt, the effort of holding myself static tenses every muscle.

"Stop it, Pet! Nothing's changed. You're not making sense."

Silently I begin to count to thirty three but am too restless to finish. My hand traces the surface of my face and I realize the creaks and groans, scrapings and booms are only internal. But which emotion is cracking me? I can't tell. My back teeth ache with the need to sink into something – to take a bite out of someone – to take a bite out of life. Life, my God! I want to chew life, eat its heart; be it.

With a visible effort Grandma finally gentles her shoulders and voice and with a soft clucking noise she urges, "Calm down, Pet. Shhhh, you're being so dramatic. Aaaaand quiet. That's good. Take a breath. That's right. Tell me what's going on."

"I read a story, Grandma, a poem really."

"A poem? This is about a poem?"

"About a man ...

"Where did you get this poem?"

My assistant stiffens. I plow ahead unimpeded, "... who watches through the window of his soul as he beats his wife in anger. He is filled with self loathing as he strikes first with one hammy fist and then the other until she is bloody and dead. He stands over her body and fills with horror until it overruns him and he enters the night destroying everything he encounters. At that point he no longer sees through the window of his soul. There is no window. He no longer sees anything at all."

Pause, then, "What?" Grandma asks dumfounded.

"Exactly! I got it completely wrong. That's not what the poem was about at all. I just read that into it. It was really about a man who ... look the important thing is I read it over and over again the wrong way because, it began to thaw me when I read it wrong."

Silence.

"Don't you see, Grandma? I have been under the ice long enough. For you I have done the unimaginable. Don't ask for more." Then with quiet command I say, "Don't hide from me on this. We cannot go back."

I open myself. She stares. We connect. Grandma understands. And then, Oh God, and then she steps back from me - again. "Child, I can't believe you're making this scene, this disgusting scene, because of some incoherent poem that you read wrong. You know poetry, as any of the arts, should be treasured as-is without imposing yourself onto it. You are always trying to make it about you, Darling. It's not always about you."

And she keeps talking, talking - words instead of connection. My crevassed blue ice pulses denial and I despair.

It's strange. Despair feels more familiar than raw sensations. I know how to despair. It's comforting. Familiar lassitude sprinkles down over my void creating a filmy sheet of ice. By habit I appease. "No, Grandma. I know that, but what I'm trying to tell you is …"

"Don't interrupt, dear. You know I can't abide rudeness."

"Yes, ma'am," I do know that. I sigh, but the sigh is a mistake. The filmy sheet is gossamer and sighing breathes life into the thaw. I can't stop breathing. My God, I can't stop breathing! I fight my emotion and end up breathing very, very deeply and bite through my lip, too.

Grandma stares at my lip and her voice raises another slightly shrill notch. A thread of tension vibrates throughout the room. "Are you being smart with me?"

"No!" It's the truth. I hadn't even thought to be.

"What ever this is about, neither one of us has time to discuss it now." This is Grandma at her best: calm, commanding, concise. "Clear your calendar and come to high tea this afternoon. And then you can tell me all about this silly poem of yours." She stands up, a tiny mountain looming over my desk, "I have to go. I'll speak with you this afternoon." She tilts in trying to stare me down. My uncle in his chair stares wide at me. My assistant, off to the side, stares at me breath holding. I, too, am staring and silent, sitting on the arêtes of a new life. Deciding … deciding whether to stay recrystalized in my life's terminal moraine or to roll away, finally, and find a new place. I'm deciding.

Even shriller Grandma pierces my attention, "Dear, I really don't have time for this right now. Come have tea with me." And then with a bit of effort and a cajole she urges, "We'll take a walk in the garden, just you and I. I know you like that." Pause. "The narcissus are blooming - a marvelous, radiant flower. Say yes, then go clean yourself up for heavens sake."

Oh that dear cajoling mouth. Lips tilt. Hold promise. Tempt me. Even now, even knowing all that has gone before I want to believe there is warmth to be had. I watch her mouth. See delicate muscles play, her lips come together tighter in the middle, corners tilt up, pretty little crescent-moon-wrinkles brace the tilt. It's intimate, that smile for me. There could be a chance, I think too easily. Do I really need to roll away right now? It seems a sensible start to a new life – fellowship, sharing warm tea and a stirring walk in the garden and peace – and on May fifteenth of all days. This could be a new beginning, a better beginning with a different ending this time. It could be just what I need.

"Tea would be delightful, Grandma." I sound hesitant even to myself, but it is enough for her.

The crescent moons disappear. The smile slips off her face. Lips press into one tight line again. The blizzard-capped stone is back in control. Grandma's posture straightens. All breath is released and I, too, stand - stand as if propelled.

I round the desk and escort my Grandmother to my office door; my feet do not run me out of here. My hands do my bidding, too, as I open my door for my Grand Dame. And my mouth speaks the words I intend to say, "I look forward to spending time with just you, Grandma. We haven't done that in ages." I am back in control of myself - crevasses covered, a new coat of snow over the blue ice, no unwanted surprises.

Except one. At the thought of giving in, something tiny but wild shifts, something maybe even dangerous, and so I speak more heartily to damp it down. "I'll be there," my voice is the shrill voice now. There's time, I rationalize. I have my whole life ahead of me.

The stone monolith presents a cheek to me. I kiss it. She grinds her way through my door and down the hall filmy, flowy frock floating soft as a snowflake around her stiff straight spine.

I wave to the back of her head then turn to face my office. First I will get everyone out; then clean myself up, and then I will work on my new contract.

I act as if it is just another day - as if the tiny wild vibration is not gaining momentum inside of me.

*The ego is a powerful yew sending down deep
roots even within a rotting paradigm.*

-Journal Entry, May 15, age 18

Chapter 5 – Dying For the Third Time

Today I die for the third time. But I do not know it yet. Death is once again hidden in the eye of a storm.

That tiny-wild-shifting-born-of-my-relenting was the leading edge of this internal tempest. But it is not tiny now. It has grown, is relentless, will not be pacified. It is a full-fledged tempest.

As I march on gravel the length of the mansion's driveway, I shiver. When I advance to marble - hallway - quiver. Cross grass - the yard - tremble. Stride on path - garden - tremor. Possibilities of a positive outcome seem less likely than they did in my office. But regardless, I press on. The storm, my vibrations, will not be ignored - I tried.

All morning I focused on everything but the wild shifting - got nothing done - but distraction didn't work.

For once I couldn't escape into old memories or counting. Deadening me with work didn't do the job either.

Finally I focused on worries, pouring anxieties into my skull until my head was full and frenzied - a fret-filled fog. Getting anxious usually distracts me.

But not today.

Not May fifteenth, not this May fifteenth.

At some point during the day I lost control of the wild shifting and of my anxiety, too, and now I am in vibration overload.

Here, at the mansion, in the garden, striding my way to high tea every part of me is shifting, swirling, anxiously pounding. I stride with hands held up in front of my face thrumming with delicate tremors. I pinch my chin hoping to stop both my fingers and face from wobbling.

My hair, my hair keeps tapping against my forehead. Fretful. I'm fret-filled. Wipe sweat from upper lip. Thrust shaking-digits down the front of my coat to dry them.

My lips tremble so I press them together hard. The white of my eye twitches. What do I press against that?

Runaway thoughts. No control. Grandma will not approve of me vibrating. Must master a thought, any thought. Keep one vibrating part steady, that's what I need to do. Shaky breath hisses.

<Deflates. I'm late.> I rhyme. That's as good as counting for distraction.

<I'm late for high tea> That phrase keeps resounding through my brain ... <Late, late, late>

Hush, brain! I'm not sure how late happened. How could I be late; I left the office in plenty of time.

<Late for the fete must increase my gait. Self hate. Berate. Birth rate. >

46

"Muzzle it now!" I tell myself out loud. Twitch, twitch goes my eye. "Turn here," I order myself.

<Go straight. Negate. Misstate. Irate. I'm late. I'm bait. Procreate.>

Stop it! Then I try a cooing voice to calm myself. "Don't worry so much."

<All's great. Dictate. Obligate. Desecrate. Create.>

"FINGER PLATE!" I yell, then look around to see if anyone is around. The words make no sense but I shout it to drown out the anxiety. "Yes! Finger plate."

<I concentrate.>

High tea and a walk with Grandma may heal all things. I must concentrate. Today is about possibilities.

<Update, concentrate>

"Tea - high tea - with Grandma," I think, proud that I've controlled a thought. I sigh with satisfaction.

<That's great>

<Relate, debate, conjugate>

High tea today … with Grandma … I am excited.

<Ecstatic state. Figure eight. Translate>

<Abate>

<Wait! Freight, concentrate>

This will never do. My mind's humming too fast.

<Heart rate>

I'm anxious. But ...

<I'm late>

... we are going to have tea, Grandma and me.

<Self hate. Procreate. Birth rate>

"RAIN" I shout inside my head to change focus once again "Hey, look at the clouds. The weather is perfect; what a lovely afternoon for tea." I'm trying to distract myself, "The wind is picking up."

<Hair keeps tap, tapping against my forehead>

"Ah, look at those diagonal fingers of rain slashing across the sky to the east. Beautiful,"

<Vibrate>

I love inclement weather and sniff the air with nose to the sky. Then I suck wind, trying to taste it. Grandma doesn't enjoy blustery days.

<Fret, Pet>

Hopefully our garden party will not be cancelled - and our stroll. I hope we can still stroll.

<Too late, obligate, commiserate>

Well, the garden looks well-groomed. I concentrate on that. So green, the lawn; it's rich and thick and both sides of the walk are spangled with every hue of flower. It is always spring on this part of the mansion grounds.

<Although it takes two full-time gardeners and a rigid planting schedule to make it so>

Once a pansy wilts around the edges, it is ruthlessly yanked up and a pretty one takes its place. Nurtured back into budding flower in the privacy of the nursery, tended by the gentle hands of invisible people, it is set out again and again and again.

<Valued only when its image is flawless>

I glance out over the manicured lawn and gardens. How constrained this earth is. The thought pulls the corners of my mouth down.

<Desecrate. Same trait. Relate.>

A terrible thought judders across my brain. Oh no.

I am Grandma's wilted pansy. Having failed to uproot and replant me in the office this morning, it would be unGrandma-like in the extreme to deal with me alone. No. She will have called The Whole Family together. There is to be no intimate walk in the garden. This is re-planting season.

I stop short. All vibrations stop. Suddenly I am calm and sick. It's re-planting season.

And since no one in The Family is known for their nurturing abilities and no one has a clue how to relate to me, they will, most likely, try yanking on my stem and shaking the dirt from my root ball – threatening me or guilting me. No one will be inclined to take me to the greenhouse and tend to me. If I don't unwilt myself pretty darn quickly, they will probably drive a stake into the ground and lash me to it. Hell, they might even glue paper flowers on me.

My lips, shaped like an "O" right now, press tight together. But I am not trying to stop them from shaking, oh no. I am as quiet as a rejected rootBall sinking in the lake… Silent… Soundlessly sinking… Still.

Impossible to unwilt myself this time. And I cannot nurture myself back into a flawless image - not quickly, not slowly; it is beyond me. I may hate myself. I'm not sure. I don't know myself well enough to say with authority, but it feels that way now.

"I have no value to them." The thought hits with a thud. Hope slips out of me with not an ounce of self-pity or martyrdom distorting the truth. I cannot fix this. I sink even as a lick of anger warms a small, small corner of my gut. I will not be a pansy any more.

<*But I owe …*>

It's a lie.

<*At least I owe her an explanation*>

It's a lie. Turn, leave, now.

<*Oh, God; I've left before and landed in disaster*>

Go to the grotto at least.

<*And then what?*>

And then … what … that is the question. What *matters* to me? What matters to *me*? I haven't visited the grotto in too many years.

<*May not belong to the grotto anymore*>

I'm anxious again, but only slightly. Even as my feet move across a miniature bridge suspended over a river-rock folly I look across the lawns for the way to the wild grotto. If I would just slow down, I could choose well.

<*Confused, diffused*>

What matters to me?

<*I am trying to decide*>

I should go to the grotto - now. But before I finish deciding, I find I have walked my way to her. She's regal in her chair under a rippling garden tent and directly in line of sight. Grandma catches sight of me and then frowns at me. My mind buzzes worry like a bee around a stamen even as my hands fidget to smooth my hair. I hate the fact that I am thirty six years old, running a bit late for high tea, and am anxious about what my Grand Dame thinks of me.

Grandma glares at my feet.

<*Wrong shoes?*>

I look down. They are perfect. Oh, yes, I'm moving too fast like an undisciplined child. I slow, I glide powerful as a shaking cat. And then, as a pack - no, as a pride - the rest of The Family turns to look at me, I smile inanely with gritted teeth (for the third time today).

Automatically, I look for Rob. It is always better for me if I know where he is. He is off to the side talking to Uncle Eck but as soon as he sees me he moves towards Grandma. I will reach her first, which is good for me, which he will hate, which will be bad for me in the long run. I arrive, despite my rebellion, at Grandma's side - as always. Taking my eyes off Rob I start the ritual lean-over to buzz Grandma's cheek; hear a deep thud, stagger back while meeting Grandma's startled eyes.

"Something wrong with your rouge," I say as I notice red splatters across her cheeks.

Then I hear the Angel of Death's wings flap like rolling thunder directly above me. Based on the length of the sound, the wings must span fourteen feet at least. (Flap, Flap) I have no desire to look at the thing. I am interested, however, in surveying the family to see who the Angel might be here for. I glance around, moving only my eyes.

The trouble is, I can't seem to lift my eyelids. Trepidation wrinkles down my spine as I take stock of the situation: unable to open my eyes, Angel of Death hovering directly above me, my back is somehow pressed flat against the grass. It's a thoroughly disquieting summation.

Then, it starts. My chest hurts. It hurts with a burning, explosive, far-reaching pain. It hurts my skin and at the same time, it hurts in a whole tunnel down inside my chest. Every part of me hurts, even my hair. Damn it. I recognize this. This is the dying part. (Flap, Flap) Not fun.

I try to summon recent recollections, but my thoughts are clouded, mix up in time. My chest hurts. Why? Why do I hurt? My heart was ripped out and burnt up, but that was eighteen years ago during a disastrous escape and was a metaphorical rather than physical injury. As for more recent events, I am foggy. I remember walking through the gardens. I remember coming to Grandma. Something dips erratically along the edges of my mind like a bee. I remember … my ears are droning ... I almost remember something important … something I took for granted.

(Flap, Flap) The Angel hovers and, I realize, it waits for me to die. Despite my great pain, I don't seem to be in any hurry to get on with it; more's the pity. All around me, beneath the angel, The Family screeches and murmurs. This adds a sense of solemnity to the experience. My name is oft repeated. I hate that I have an audience.

Attempting to lift my hand fails but excites quite a response from the crowd. My Angel settles in - his wing beats slow. Quite a lovely sound those beats are, even though they intimidate.

I try again to lift my eyelids. It hurts. Having now decided Angel is here for me, curiosity stirs. I want to look at it. I have never seen an angel on this side of death before. With great effort I force my eyes open and am greeted by the sight, not of my angel, but of many grey-out-of-focus-blobs-for-faces. People are bending over me to get a better look.

Opening my eyes opens my ears, too, and I hear no one attempting to rescue me. Not one soul is trying to ease my passing. No one is tragically lamenting. A wave of pain ricochets around my brain. I close my eyes quite decidedly. I am not so curious to see this angel that I would gaze at harsh faces. But my ears do not close. I still hear all that is lacking.

Too much spit fills my mouth. I recognize this sensation now. I am going to throw up. And to put the crowning glory on my painful dying, I hear Rob's voice cut through the murmuring.

"Not going to make it. Not going to make it," Rob says, his tone more gleeful than horrified. I am about to tell him his attitude is unseemly, but Grandma beats me to it.

Voice stridulous, Rob fights back. "I'm not the one drawing unbecoming attention to myself," he says. "… but I'm always the wrong one …"

"That is enough!" Grandma's stern tone thunders. Theatrics all around me. Concern has little to do with me.

"Stay dead," Rob encourages just above my nose. He must be bending down to whisper to me. No one is stopping him. I'm glad my eyes are closed. I don't want my last sight to be his eyes again.

Lord, I hurt.

Where is the compassionate face silently urging me to pull in one more breath? I puff my question, silently moving my lips. Where are the gentle fingers to brush back my hair? Is there no sorrow to wail me through my passing? Is Rob's the last voice I am to hear? Ears strain but no one pleads with me to resist slipping away. I ache, I ache.

I have never slid into oblivion peacefully.

This is the worst part of dying, when even laying flat on my back I feel like I'm on a slithery slope and there is nothing to hang on to. It's not fear of the destination that keeps me clinging to life; it's the awful feeling of loosening control - spinning fastSlow, not-doneness. Life cannot be surrendered until there is ... until there is a full feeling of stretched-thinness.

The world tilts and a delicate streamfall of tears course down my cheekbones into my ears, warbling the sound outside me. I fight to keep my balance but despite my great efforts, I cannot gain a purchase. (Flap, Flap) I hear the Angel perfectly. Finally death summons. Disentanglement reached, my attention shifts to those delicious wing beats. I tumble down into darkness and for the third time, I die.

PART TWO – *"SEASONS OF THE HEART"*

Yew spreads its scrappy limbs to gather all of the sun.
- Journal Entry, May 15, age 18

Chapter 6 – Crossing the Verge

My first conscious thought in death is happy anticipation. Liberty releases. Joy burns deep in my core. I love, love, love this transformation and gladly release my mortal snakeskin. Like I said before, death is really quite wonderful.

Any time now, I will see the white light, a bit slow in coming today. Ah, my two friends will wrap themselves all through me as I indulge in one last gaze upon my dead body, floating high above it and embraced in peace. There will be no pain while watching The Family's reaction. Despite myself I still hope to see some vestige of anguish or regret on a face – any face; a sense of despair or grief or even guilt would be nice.

I am also curious to see how I was killed. And who was it that murdered me. And maybe - okay, I'll admit it - I also hope "they" did a proficient job this time so I don't have to go back into that dry cold snakeskin. I am done with living and am ready for the final white light.

With a smile on my face I ... wait a moment ... unease flickers ... what face? I have a face? I open my eyes - which come to think of it, I have never had to do before. There is no white light, no light at all. I see nothing. It's dark.

Thoughts pour through me now. I'm not floating; am not airy. There is no tunnel, no two friends. I still have my snakeskin and am inside it. And The Family, be they grieving or not, in death or in life, are not here. No one is here.

Rock is here, however; rock is all around me - above my head, touching it actually, and hemming me in like a closed sarcophagus. I push my elbows out from my sides – no more than three inches of movement is available. Alright, I'm uncomfortable with this situation.

Because of my second death, I am reluctant to be in small, closed-in spaces. This space is very close. I suck a quick breath. Although I can see nothing, my eyes roll around like two snail shells in a canning jar. Happy anticipation is well and truly gone. Confidence erodes. This is not correct.

I long to rub my forehead; need comfort, but can't move my hands to my face – too constrained. So rattled. Why am I here? Have I been buried alive? Buried without a casket? I can't wrap my brain around the fact that I'm not in the death that I know so well.

Bowing my shoulders to lean forward gives access to the rock wall. I rub my forehead on rock although it is unresponsive, insensate comfort. That's when I notice air rushing up from below; which explains why the oxygen in my sarcophagus is not stale.

I tap forward with a foot and find the hole ahead of me. Not a rough stone casket, then. I'm in a cave. Further foot exploration reveals that the hole is very narrow – about as wide as my shoulders. More investigation with shoulders, forearms, wrists, knees, and head lays bare the fact that there are no other openings to be found in my pure rock, ultra small space. However I got here, it must have been through this hole beneath me.

56

Obviously, something went wrong in this last death.

<Where is my help?>

Probably, just on the other side of that hole the white light waits.

<Someone should fix this problem>

I rub my forehead again against unyielding rock. "I should wait," I tell myself. "Or should I climb down? It's a pressing-in fit. I must get to a familiar death." this is said with more than a modicum of anxiety. A familiar death is what I require.

My feet are dancing again - pounding really. I hope this is not a new habit. They pound all around my hole as if they want me to get going. I clench my fist and push my elbows against the wall to keep my body in place. There is a rumbling sound, very faint. And then the ground begins to crumble beneath me. I grab hold of the wall, but cannot hold myself up with my elbows alone. My feet dance against the wall looking for a toehold. Only when I start to slide do I finally give in to my feet's demands. I coordinate fingers and toes and begin my decent.

Much later than I anticipated I am still worming my way down the tunnel.

I have squirmed through places I could not get back into should I need to reverse my direction. Shuddering repeatedly at the thought of being stuck and panting, I can't seem to draw a whole breath although the wind in the tunnel blows constantly. I remind myself I have no place to go back to, so proceeding along is the only option.

Sick and slick with sweat despite the breeze, I feel for my next foothold. If I had a tail it would be tucked between my legs. Back hunched I reach for my next handhold, neck down, shoulders rolled forward. I cannot see where I'm going, but my eyes are stretched wide.

(*Flap, flap*) The sound of the angel's wings, softer now, keeps me company or perhaps it is my shirt, come free of my waistband and flapping in the breeze against my waist. All around me rock.

~

When I was a child I sat in a boat at the headwater of two rivers careening together. One river made its fast way down a steep slope, singing through deep gorges, bouncing around boulders and over rocky bottoms. It was lively and deep green with jaunty white wave caps and spoke with a joyous voice. The other river, old and heavily ladened with dirt, had crossed flatter, used-up lands. It spoke of outrage in measured tones. All it said was edged with melancholy; its voice resonant and deep. It lumbered its brown way into the confluence. And I sat in the boat and watched them mate – so unlikely and so passionately. Their songs morphed into one voice – rich, powerful, agile, with clarity enough to force a moan and sigh and flush even from a child. And that new river took us for a very dangerous ride.

~

In this tunnel, just so, I have two rivers meeting at the headwater in me. Snarled fears co-mingle with a lifetime of bound biological needs - lending one voice to the other – an odd kind of mating. I cannot shut them off. For me this decent has been a dangerous ride. "I am not up to this task," I repeat like a prayer; and yet, I fumble for the next lower outcropping, swept along, unable to control anything after all.

"I've never wanted to be on my own,' I sub vocalize. "I've paid to not be on my own. I don't deserve this." My mouth is tightly open and I pant through it.

<Worried>

I am worried about falling - about losing my strength - about going the wrong way.

<Worried>

I am worried I'm wrong and this is not the way out.

<Or even worse, there is no mistake that I am here.>

I was quite competent at my other deaths.

My calves seize, every muscle sore and ossified. I am stiff. Stiff boned. Stiff necked.

"Okay, maybe," I admit to myself hanging on by my fingertips as my feet scrabble for a toehold, "I have lived a bit proud, carried with me a slight moral superiority from my victimness. Perhaps I have become smug and need only shed my shabby self-righteousness to find the white light." My voice bounces off rock two inches from my nose. Deepening the tone I boom out a prayer.

"Oh, God-Proficient Teacher," I cantillate, "forgive them, they knew not what they were doing." I try to feel pious but fall short because I'm aware of my plagiarism. I can't help thinking, "It worked for Jesus ..." which I realize is a bit sassy, but I cannot control the thought. I also feel a tinge of belligerence at being forced to perform for my reward. I know I am loved, damn it, where is everyone?

<Am I forgiving them correctly?>

My eyes are gritty and I blink repeatably.

<It's not fair>

Seized-up fingers dig for a new purchase to support my shifting weight. Toes scrabble for a lower ledge but step into air. Freefall. Climb-weakened arms cannot save me. I plunge ungracefully.

My face smashes into the wall on the way down. I flap miserably with just one moment of regret before I fall into a swift-running river – powerful beyond belief and bone-chillingly frigid. It steals my wind.

As I had no idea water was beneath me, I am not in prime landing position. The force of hitting water pulls my legs into a grotesque parody of a pirouette, ripping my straight leg back and driving my other, bent knee into my shoulder – at the same time tearing groin muscle and tilting me forward so my face slaps the water like a belly flop. Down I plunge, down, down, end-over-end, arms waving to slow momentum.

It is too dark to see the surface…

<Which way is up>

… so I blow bubbles and follow them up.

<Not much air left>

Pulling with both arms and legs despite the teeth-gritting pain in my groin I fight the water. I pull to the count of five-ducks, counting my stress down a notch.

<Eyes are popping>

I cannot allow myself to breathe underwater.

<But I need to; I need to breathe>

Seven duck … I count inside my head … eight duck … I smash my lips together … nine duck … lips fold under, bottom lip burns between teeth … ten duck … I hold my air in.

When I break the surface I cannot hear my own desperately in-drawn breath above the roar surrounding me.

<When did that roaring start?>

I think irritably, still out-of-sorts by the whole experience.

<It would have been useful to have heard it before I hit the water> This, even before gratitude. Then, all I can think of is getting

set to rights – hair out of my face, air into lungs, water out of eyes, shoes - heavy - off.

Cold. Teeth chattering.

<I cannot last long in this icy water>

Desperation tunes my ears for sounds of land or better yet, the sound of a voice calling my name. I suck a deep breath.

<Someone who loves me should call for me; my death-friends should be looking for me>

"I'm here!" I yell and strain my ears to find their voices above the roar but hear nothing. Indecisively I pull first in one direction then the other, head up, listening.

I would love to have someone with me during this death. I so desperately want to not be alone.

I pause, treading water, fighting the current, and notice the roar getting louder.

<Ooo, Not good>

One duck, two duck. Up whip my legs. Three, *ahhh*, three duck. Water grabs at my back pulling me down. Legs swivel to the right. I kick, kick from the hips trying to straighten. Butt muscles staining. Summersault. I hit something. Then I'm rolled.

<Getting dizzy>

Upside down I paddle. Am helpless; spun first one way then the other - twenty-two duck, twenty-three duck. Much like a pathetic little leaf bobbing along I am dropped again - into mist this time. Twenty-eight duck.

The envelope of water tumbles away from me but I have no sensation of falling. Instead, I feel suspended in a thick mist of droplets and water's roar. For six long seconds I hang in delicately kissing motes and awesomely furious sound. Then I hit another pool of water, this one at the base of the waterfall and this time in an actual belly flop, bone-jarring in its impact, knocking the desire to count out of me. If I wasn't already dead, this would have killed me. Driven unresistingly to the bedrock bottom and held by a turbulent fist of pounding water, I lay stunned, spread-eagled, face-down, in utter darkness, compressed.

Although I have done death before, the memories of it are fading from my mind. All I know of death is this death, this pain, this fractionated, devoid of hope, aloneness. I lay through the abuse, enduring it – flattened up the middle.

<Where's my help>

No one could be expected to endure this. *<Escape>* Shut down, withdraw, be gone forever. *<Good riddance>* I leak out. *<Gone>*

And gone, gone, gone …

~

It has been so forever. I must have rotted away by now - must have melted into a thousand different directions. I am nothingness. No dark exists here, no peace, no me exists, no time; I am void.

The void is. Has always been. Will be, always. Just is; or rather, just is not. Forever.

~

Until … until somewhere in the great insane ease, a whisper drifts; so plaintive it causes a tightening, which creates a pulse. A quiver is born, which causes friction, which creates heat, which condenses water, which traps air and thickens into something that is me. The whispered sorrow flutters against me and this is when I gently cup my soul - such a frail, thin spirit. With compassion comes resignation. Resignation solidifies into consciousness and I am, again.

"Well, gone-forever, it seems, is far shorter than I had hoped it would be," I bubble the words under the falls, recognizing I am back from catatonia and still held in place by pounding water.

My nostrils expand, are distended, wide open – trying to make room to breathe - the water all around me fills my lungs. "Stop," I bellow. I've had enough but the water continues to pound my body, hold me down, and grab at my hair like pinching hands.

<I have been grabbed before. I have been held down and pounded before. I hate squeezing hands.>

There, I admit it. I embrace the thought.

<I am tired of having my hair plucked and pulled tight and controlled>

I heave a scream of rage from the back of my throat behind my tongue so deep I gag on it but no sound emerges. I am too angry for sound. Forever, right now, I hereby reject hands bruising me, pushing me into walls, and choking me. Water pounds my head but the pounding serves more to rile me than defeat me and a desire to advance out of this situation is ignited within.

I don't remember feeling this surging determination before but it feels … seemly . . . and intimate like bedding myself with thick socks on a cold night. I decide to start. Because start I must.

I thrust out my elbows and arms to push myself up from the bottom. I attempt to spread my knees and throw back my head and kick my feet. All that moves, however, are my toes. They spread slightly as I strain. I push so hard with toes and fingernails my temple veins are in danger of popping free from my head. Even with every muscle straining to the limit, I cannot push myself up from this bottommost floor. And yet, I am not deterred.

Two rocks fall from above. One bonks me on the head causing my ears to ring with pain and distracts me from my efforts. The other hits my hand and bounces off. Reflectively, I make a fist.

While it has proven impossible to forcefully raise my hand up, it's easy to make a fist. And this body re-configuration changes the turbulence pattern around me. Suddenly, like wind flowing around the dip of a bird's wing, the water shifts, shooting under my hand and with no effort on my part at all, the water thrusts my hand and arm above my head where they are wrenched wildly back and forth in an enthusiastic parody of a queen's wave. Realizing that re-configuration rather than brute force is my salvation, I flex and tense muscles, minutely shifting the planes of my body in relation to the elements around me. Never have I been so in tune with my body. Never have I paid as much attention to my environment.

At one point my upper body rises from the bedrock and waves like a flag while my pelvis and legs remain pinned to the rock. It is ridiculous. During this undulation, I twist my right foot slightly and as sudden as that I am off on a wild roller-coaster ride of water.

I am banged around and twisted and rolled and flung with limbs dancing their own silly separate rhythm completely out of my control; but inside I am quiet. In this pregnant pause, this deep silent still place, I feel a minuscule, gentle fluttering at the center of my being like butterflies are trapped in my belly only infinitely smaller. This new sensation is completely compelling. It is different than the wild shifting. Although I don't know what it means, I know that something significant has occurred and that I will never be the same again.

Yew drops small bits of coded immortality to seed future plans.

-Journal Entry, May 15, age 18

Chapter 7 – Eye Island

I smell blood.

"Ah," I think, "I am aware again - must begin gathering clues and taking stock of where I am and what I know."

What I know first is where I am not. I am not at Grandma's tea party and I am not in the white light and I am not buffeted by roaring water. I am, in fact, lying face down on rock with space around me. I'm cold to the core except my front is warm. My front is warm because I'm lying in a fresh pool of blood. There is no doubt the blood is my own. It is the same blood I smelled upon awakening.

<There is a lot of it>

I also know that I am still blinded by darkness. My eyelids are spread wide – so wide the orbs feel like they'll pop out – even so, I can see nothing. It's darker with my eyes open than with my eyes shut.

<Sigh>

My hearing is fine though.

I am a bit confused by the sound of the river near my feet, gently flowing, lapping at the rock I lay on. It sounds so foundationally different from the river I last remember being in. The change is not just roar and fury muted to gentle lapping, no. The voice is different. More ominous somehow than the raging fury I was in before. This river's mellifluous serenade causes caterpillar feet to tickle up and down my spine.

<Not in a good way>

It smells different, too.

<Odd that>

Water drips into the river from the walls and ceiling - a delicate chorus of drip drop drip. They echo. So I must be in a large cave.

Rolling over informs me my chest hurts horribly. I feel blood flowing from a hole in my sternum down my belly and under my arms beneath my shirt. It pools behind my back. Although not spurting, the wound is bleeding at a profuse rate. A chest wound this severe could not have been caused by being banged around in the river. I think this wound may be the cause of me dying. I vaguely remember looking into Grandma's startled eyes as a blow to the chest knocked me to the ground.

Old habits die hard and even as I contemplate the disturbing fact that someone may have murdered me, I move with a creak to straighten my clothes more presentably about me. Just the thought of Grandma and I am anxious to arrange myself.

<My hair is a sodden mess; my comb is gone; my shoes are gone> Of course,

<And>

I rub my feet together.

<My socks are in shreds>

66

So now I know I am in a cave, on a rock, clothed.

<But uncoiffured and holey and bloody and sore all over>

Gingerly I sit up.

<Ooh, stiff joints>

The blood tickles as it trickles lower, soaking the area between my legs and the soft nerve-ladened intimate thighs. Reaching into my chest hole I stretch the muscles around my lungs and push apart my ribs to feel my heart. Although it feels odd, it doesn't hurt. As I thought, my heart is not beating. The muscle lay lax in my hand. When I squeeze, nothing happens, which raises the question, "Why then, am I still bleeding?"

I sit with my feet splayed and cock my head. Then with mouth firmly clamped shut I plug my nose, effectively stopping my breath. Slowly I sing 'Rhythmus'. Even after ten rounds of "Ad perennis vitae fontem, mens sitit nunc arida, Claustra carnis praesto frangi . . ." without a breath, I'm no more or less gasping than I was before. I don't need air - it's as if I am connected to an invisible umbilicus.

Psychologically, though, the thought of existing without breathing is like a noseless face. When confronted by a face with no nose, the mind's eye keeps trying to place a nose back on the face. Just so, my mind's ear strains to hear my breath. So I start breathing again and am soothed by the sound.

<No answers; there are no answers>

I guess I am supposed to move. Go find the white light.

It hurts to bend my knees. It aches to straighten hips. I stumble and fall. Grandma would tut disapprovingly and tell me to stop acting the fool and get on with it, which makes me chuckle as well as groan with each creaky articulation. Starting with the outermost extremities, fingers and toes and face muscles, I jiggle and shake and blink and tighten and relax and bend and bend back again. For the first time, I appreciate being alone as my "unkinking" process is not dignified.

Once in an upright position, I hop and twist and stretch. I stink – quite terrible actually – and move my nose away from my arm in front of my face. Dancing a foolish clumsy jig I make my way over to the river's edge and I shake out my jacket like a bull-teaser. That makes me chuckle, too.

~

I remember the day Grandma sat in the shadows at my desk, which is why I failed to notice her. I am sneaking into my room at the mansion. Hunkered over and moving quickly I slink to my fireplace and strip off my outer gear, leaving them in a sopping pile on the hearth. Donning a robe and stepping on towels with each foot, I dance my way back over my wet tracks, mopping up all traces of my disobedience. No one will discover I've been to the pond again - in it, actually; which is forbidden. I dance out into the hall with a towel under each foot. Down the steps - mop, wipe, twirl - and through the kitchen - dip, bow - pond puddles mopped up.

At fifteen years old I mostly do as I'm told except for the pond. In all other cases it's worth performing to expectation. I want to be good; but cannot resist the pond.

I plop the towels on a kitchen chair and push the chair under the table. Anyone could have left these towels. They cannot be tied to me. I bound back to my room, three stairs at a time, robe flapping as I leap down the hall and into my room. I stop short in front of my fireplace. There is a puddle, but no sopping clothes. I scratch my head then sniff pond on my fingers. That's when I feel her behind me.

I stiffen and turn to meet her eyes. The sodden clothes are in a pile in front of her on my desk.

"I've bought you new clothes, Dear." That's all she says. But the way she sits with her hand hovering above the wet clothes shouts out her intention to take away my adventuring gear.

"No." I still say 'no' on occasion at fifteen. "No, those clothes are Da's. You can't have them."

"What? Are they precious to you? Is that what you are trying to tell me? This is how you treat precious?" Her voice trails off. "My son's clothes ..." It amazes me how her tone can be both condemning and filled with pain. In her next breath all I hear is disapproval, "I have asked you repeatedly to avoid the pond, but you seem incapable of following even one of my requests."

This is too much for me, I who perform like a dancing bear in hopes of a kind look. I bristle, but before I can get a word out she continues.

"But that is not the subject here. And don't you dare interrupt. Your wardrobe is highly inappropriate. Everyone agrees. I have replaced every stitch. These," she looks mournful as she glances at my sodden treasures, "must be removed. I don't want to lose them, but you cannot behave yourself, so ..." She looks back at me with gimlet eyes. "So selfish." Then she braces her back, every inch of her the Grand Dame. "It wouldn't be too much to ask you to wear the new blue for dinner. Your aunt helped me choose it and she is especially looking forward to seeing you in it. You'll look so handsome. Wear the blue. It's all laid out."

She took Da's clothes when she left and I let her, fully intending to dig them out of the trash as soon as she released them. But she out-strategized me. My clothes were destroyed not tossed out. In my room that night I played matador with the blue outfit and accidentally snuffed out a candle. Snuffed it out quite a few times. Ended up burning a large hole back and center. When I wore it for dinner that night, the assembly was treated to the sight of my underwear.

At age fifteen I can count on one hand the times I told Grandma "no". I only said it when I couldn't back-up any further. I never wore any of those clothes without first playing matador with them. They were replaced one by one until not a single outfit remained.

~

I whip my jacket back and forth, teasing an invisible bull - or maybe an invisible candle. A feeling almost as strange as those continual butterfly movements in my stomach come over me. I'm proud of myself. Not happy because others are proud of me. No, this is different. I *have* done a few things in my life that I respect - me, no validation required.

Even though I eventually got too busy for the pond and I stopped noticing what I wore and I ate whatever was served to me and slept in my same old room without decrying the decoration changes that went on without my consent or approval; even with all that bending, I am proud of my matador days and respect the fact that I had a line I would not compromise.

And I have done a few things in this third death that I respect, too - me, no validation required. I have persisted. I'm proud of my gumption; forgot I possessed any. For the first time since I was a dirt-child and a matador, it feels satisfactory to be me.

I shake out my jacket again and smile. I choose to wash because I don't like my smell. I choose. I'll wash with my jacket even though jackets are not appropriate wash cloths. I choose to bend at the waist to wash even though it is more dignified to bend at the knees. I choose.

When I bend at the waist to dip my jacket in the river I notice my reflection. Well, really it is a silhouette of my reflection, but the important point is that this means it is no longer utterly dark. Behind me a light source wavers.

70

I freeze and my new-found pride slips behind me, hiding behind my legs as if it were a naughty child. Funny how the opaqueness, at first such a disadvantage, so scary, became an ally. Funny how my pride, at first such an advantage, left a hole when it slipped away.

I cannot turn around to look at the light.

<Afraid of what I will see>

Instead I stare, transfixed, as my watery reflection becomes more solid. There are dark holes where my eyes indent and a shadowy hole lower down tells me my mouth is hanging open. I snap it closed. Now I can see the outline of my nose and a dual glistening that are my eyes. Then I see my hair.

<So unkempt>

I comb my fingers through it. The dark has pulled away enough for me to see movement over my rumpled clothes – blood flowing down my body and into the river at my feet. I watch it join the water and feel, once again, that strange reluctance to let the river taste of me – even my blood. I step back a half-step and rearrange my clothing.

I'm panting again, quick shallow breaths making me lightheaded. What I want above all else is to rub my forehead and sooth myself. There is so much to fear in this death. But what I fear the most is what I hear behind me - shuffling footsteps scraping the rock as they draw closer. Nervously, I plug my jacket into my chest hole. I'm fussing, I know. The jacket sticks out starkly against my white shirt, but it makes me feel more dignified that an attempt was made. Thus girded, I turn to face whatever is making its way towards me.

My intention upon turning to face this new scary thing was to perform well and face it with dignity, which has been sorely lacking in my third death thus far. Instead I gasp and start at what I see and stumble sideways. Like a baby, I close my eyes for a moment and pretend, just to myself, that I haven't already seen her.

Wheezing and so very slowly shuffling towards me is an old, old woman – a dust ball of a woman, a true hag. She is bent and tiny - can't be five feet tall. She is wizened down to skin lying on bone, and upon closer look, there isn't all that much skin. What skin she has is black and leathery, which makes it easier to see the white boney skeleton poking through the tears in her rind - bones so bright they gleam. She has hairy moles in all of the wrong places. In the correct places her hair is white and fine and thinned to wispy declarations of stubborn steadfastness. She is completely naked and the light that fills our space comes from her eyes. Torch eyes would be handy in this dark place, but are spooky as hell to look at.

She cackles at me, which does not make matters any better. Then she raises a boney hand with twisted finger to point at me. When the finger bends, I realized she wants me to come to her. I hesitate as she seems to be hideous and dangerous. And yet, I cannot resist her. "What do you want?" my too-high voice queries. Then belatedly, "Who are you?"

"*Aeeei, what wet home fang mot dove shit lim,*" the ghastly old girl answers. "*Tow wafo datum honey?*" Her voice is not a pretty sound, grating on my ear like a rusty key it also sets up reverberations inside me. I can feel her words and yet have no idea what she is saying. Half-consciously I pushed at my chest as if to rid myself of the feel of her voice. "Who are you?" I demand again.

She rolls her eyes at me as if I am a dunce and speaks very slowly and condescendingly. "*Aeeei, what wet home fang mot dove shit lim,*" she answers. "*Tow wafo datum honey?*" I wince at the sound of her rusty-key-voice screeching even slower in the lock and still have not a clue.

Weary-eared, I back away from her, "Get away from me."

She looks down at my heels an inch from the water and grates a bit more gently, but no less rusty, "*Granaams.*" And she raises her eyebrows and her chin and looks at me as if to say, "Did you get it this time? Maybe this will be easier for you to understand."

And it works; because I think "She really doesn't look all that intimidating, just really, really old and naked and kind-of decaying-like." "Grana Ams?" I ask. Then, "Oh, Grama Ans;" more confidently now, "your name is Grama Ans."

She beckoned me again with that twisted bone of a finger and I inch forward, words spilling from my mouth, explaining my confusion, my dying, asking where everyone is and making not a lick of sense – a word casserole, everything mushed up together, no thought distinct enough to claim attention and when I get close she takes my hand and I almost cry with relief so desperate am I for a gentle touch.

She backs us even further from the water's edge and looks up at me, head tilted to one side and softly whispers, *"Tow wafo datum honey?"*

Looking into those flaming eyes I blurt out, "I'm lost," which causes her to laugh. She laughs so hard I am afraid she'll shake her bones free of her thin leathery skin. I am not nearly as amused as she.

Her cadaverous breasts jiggle and sway with each heaving gahauff. She leans into me and laughs in my face, breath hot. I snatch back my hand and watch her in affront as she bends over and puts her boney claw-like hands on her equally boney knees. She is barely able to hold herself upright so racked with mirth is she. Her laughter bounces off the rocks all around us and teeters her body back and forth and then, eventually, as the laughter continues, she begins weaving like a tiny drunken prostitute and ends up on her boney butt - the fusty, intractable, malodorous old dust rag.

I am so furious with her I want to rough her up. Never before have I had a desire like that. It shocks me more than she does, and then, in my head, like an endless loop, I keep repeating, "The Family would never accept her. No way!" With every repetition of the refrain, I get angrier. She is as unredeemable - as I am. You'd think I'd be compassionate or feel a bond but she just infuriates me. This old hag of a crone of a disaster would rile Grandma. Grandma would find this woman more unsatisfactory than anyone I have ever met. I breathe so

73

hard I actually spray spittle. Am thunderously enraged - and well and truly disturbed by my thoughts of violence.

To distract myself, I look away from her assessing the situation. My lips press inward mashing against my teeth. We are on a small eye-shaped rock island surrounded by the new nasty river. Beyond the nasty river, sheer rock walls slope up into darkness. The roof is far above us. I can discern no way out except the river inflow and outflow caves. Perhaps Grama Ans knows of a way out of here.

"Suppose I was thinking rationally," I try and calm myself. "What would I do?"

"Well," I answer distracted, "I would try to settle Grama Ans down and get her to show me the way out. I need her to be focused." I glance over at the old biddy laughing still and rolling around on the ground waving her legs in the air howling like a wild thing. She really is an objectionable piece of work. I feel great resistance at having to win the intolerable one's approval but remembering the deaths I am familiar with and desiring to get back to that place, I resolve to endure her shockingly repellent ways just long enough to get out of here. Then she begins farting as she laughs, like quick-fire-repeating exclamations to a joke.

"That's enough," I say out loud, deciding she is utterly demented and I am best served away from her. I am arrogant and oh-so-superior as I turn back towards the water, deciding to swim into the outlet cave; but my skin crawls at the thought.

She stops laughing, then, as quickly as she started and the silence startles me. I look around and see her reach out her hand to me so I can help her up. "No," I shake my head. She frowns a tremendous, frightful grimace that quickens my breathing and my steps toward her. She grips my arm quite strongly and I know I will be released only when she is ready, not when I am.

Surprisingly nimble she pulls herself up, leans into me and sniffs at my holey chest. "*Ah dearie obey raw hell venue yeah,*" she

74

states. That close, I can smell her, too. She smells of wet earth - of mud and good loamy soil. I have not smelled that earthy smell for thirty years. Hell, she smells a lot better than I do at the moment with my steel-blood and damp-river fragrance. And then she intones, "*I beg chant took no trod rive, tense woe.*"

I frown back at her a tremendous and frightful grimace or at least that is the intent. She smiles at me, though, so perhaps I haven't quite pulled it off. "Let go of me," I demand without the graceful manners I have been taught. I don't know what's gotten into me to speak to her like that. I need information, even if she is demented. But the negotiating skills I am so famous for are out of my reach just now. Every time she touches me I seem to revert back to the precocious wild child I was when my parents were alive and I knew I had no wrong in me.

She smiles and pats me on the arm and plucks a hair from her pubic area. Her pubic area! With an audible boink! Before I can react to this new disgust, the crone begins to wave it and to my surprise it grows longer and longer with each whip-like motion. When it is very, very long she wraps it three times around her wrist and mutters something to it. It lifts her straight up to the ceiling and through the rock. With her departure I am plunged back into darkness, but only for a few seconds. That quickly, she returns with my mother's locket. Momma was buried with that locket. She offers the prize to me for examination. As I turn it over and over in my hand I realize the significance of this magic hair. With it, I can get out of this death place.

Once again I look upon the crone with slightly more favor than dismay. Maybe she is not unbearably demented after all. Granted, she is ghastly but for a bit of magic hair I can willingly overlook her bad habits. I point to myself and then point to the hair and point back to myself. It's fruitless. She does not get the message that I would like the hair. Instead, she seems entranced by the fact that my flowing blood has soaked my jacketPlug and now pooled at my feet staining them reddish black.

She looks back at my face with real pleasure and points to my feet and nods. Then, she does the one thing I could never imagine anyone ever doing in front of me. She pops out one of her eyes and offers it to me. Dumbstruck, I simply stare.

I am at such a loss I have no resource to address her actions. The eye in her hand is wet and grisly. It turns cataracty white and moves around like a blind man moves his eyes when processing sounds in a new environment. Before I fully comprehend what is offered, she shakes my arm in a strong whip-like motion to get my attention and tries to hand the eyeball to me. I yank my arm and raise it so violently that I jerk her off her feet and she dangles from me, never letting go. Cackling with delight she kicks her feet and swings. My opinion of her rebounds, she is no longer favorable. Once again she is a demented-freak-better-off-anywhere-except-near-me. I want nothing to do with her. I try to shake her off. But she will not let go. Over and over the crone points to my eye and then offers hers and shakes her hair wrapped wrist again and again. Now, finally, I understand what she wants. For the magic hair still wrapped around her wrist, she wants to trade one of my eyes for one of hers.

"No," I whisper appalled. "No! No! No!" My voice sinks on each exclamation. "Let go of me," I say on a breath of sound and I slowly lower her to the ground holding my other hand out in a stop position between us. Roughly, the Crone pulls me close and reaches up so she can work on popping my eye out. I twist my head back and forth pushing away from her as we stumble around the rock. She yells over and over again the same insane, loud pronouncement, "*Liar why git you; an eye hops clue.*" I assume she is yelling, "Give me your eye. I want your eye." Or something similar to it.

A rock twists under my foot and I fall to my knee bringing her down with me. She drops her eyeball. We both freeze. I look at it and she stares blindly at me. Then moving faster than she, I shake her off of my arm, flick the orb away from us, and stand while grabbing her wrist and unwrapping the hair. Then I drop her arm, which she immediately uses to paw the ground groping for her loose eyeball. With a flourish I wrap the hair around my wrist and smile down at her in triumph. The hair tugs on my arm as if trying to get away.

The crone scrunches up her face. In the dimming light she looks delicate and defenseless, the eye in her head now milky, too, and obviously blind. Triumph turns bitter. Unlike Rob I was never able to delight in cruelty, never able to justify, even to myself, being a bully. I stumble towards her, hand outstretched to help, my heart overruling my head. In the end, neither heart nor head prevails.

Blind now, she cannot see my hand. She closes the eye in her head and the room pitches into blackness. At that signal, the hair takes off, lifting me so my toes barely touch down every third step or so.

Regret wars with relief as we circle the island then rise a bit higher and I am tip-toeing on the rocky sidewalls. I hear the old woman cackle below us. She yells, too, filling the space, *"Awe silly, sigh hate nicked insights I must aid."* Her raucous laughter and anal explosions ricochet off the walls. She is a lame-old-duck; I don't like her. But I don't like myself either.

Ashamed of my meanness and embarrassed by so much, my cheeks heat up. I'm abashed that I looked to the hag for comfort when she is so obviously obscene. I tuck my chin to hide my face even in the dark. And I'm mortified that I still fantasize The Family will grieve when I die although they never sorrowed before. And, well, there are other embarrassments big and small and I think of each as I run to keep up with the hair.

We keep circling, circling. I can't tell if we are getting closer to the roof, but it's taking too long and it appears that we're not going anywhere; just circling with my arm stretched uncomfortably above my head and the hair digging into my wrist. Toes bounce. Can't see. Unable to control anything I whisper into the dark, "God, why don't you help me?" The hair tightens around my wrist and lifts me away from the rock.

It carries me quite a while before gently lowering me to my toes so I can leap again. We run straight now; must be in a tunnel. We never made it up to the roof where the old woman went to get my mother's locket. So I am, actuality, no closer to the death-I-want than I was before I met her.

The hair lifts and gently sways me to the right and a mossy rock whizzes past my cheek but I am not bumped into it. I'll admit that leap-running on tiptoes in the dark while dependant on a wild pubic hair is daunting. But truth be told, as nerve-wracking as it is to run headlong into rocky midnight, the dark also acts as a comforting shield. Swung by my wrist I sway to the right again, feel breeze, miss another rock. I lend my trust to the hair and loosen control for a moment. We work hard, that hair and I. We go full out.

I've heard of "runner's bliss" although I never felt it before. Straining muscles feel good; and no blood pounds in my temples or beats in my teeth. My breath is what I make it, no lung swell-and-tear-and-wheeze for me. Despite the fact that I am dead, I am inordinately present to both my body and thoughts. I never knew that hard physical exertion prunes away the ability to hide from oneself but it does.

I remember the first time I felt this way. I'd buried it for years; but now, bouncing hard with a wild pubic hair in a dark and rocky place I cannot hide anymore.

Russell swears that cemetery yews instruct
their roots, "Go now dear feeder hairs and
penetrate the mouths of the dead. Twine right
to the center of the skull."

"To give them voice?" I asked him.

"Or to steal their secrets?" He suggests in a melodramatic
voice.

"Well," I press, "which is it?"

My friend won't say.

-Journal Entry, May 15, age 18

Chapter 8 – [re]Sounding Run

The Family never did work well together even for a common good, but they did a fine job of it the day I first died. By the time I made it back inside my body and up to consciousness, all staff members were packing or being escorted one at a time off the premises so there would be no discussion among themselves. The authorities were never called.

Rob was twelve years old.

Silence was a shield drawn solidly around what was left of our little group. We were a hotbed of emotion girdled by an impenetrable escutcheon. The Family, already in crisis from losing so many members, needed the chosen leader to take the mantle of control and guide them through the changes as Da would have done. I was the chosen one and, actually, I had the best idea of what was needed, but I was young and I had just been killed, which weakened my position dramatically.

And I scared them. I always had.

My death and then, even worse, return from death caused tumult and from the chaos, temper tantrums long suppressed erupted. Adult eyes protruded and spittle flecks broke free from rough lips and epithets pushed against unguarded faces while we children stood in separate corners and wrapped arms around ourselves and stared fearfully at each other across the room. I saw one aunt hit my uncle and understood how Rob could bring himself to kill me.

"Stop the ferment," Da had instructed me while I was still dead and bathed in white light and compassion.

"How?" I wondered.

"When you go back ..."

"No!"

"When you go back, be the harvest. Change how we all interact."

I knew it would be difficult. In the white light, I could see the past and future and felt my heart breaking. "I will not go back," I was the declaration.

"When you go back," I felt Momma say gently as if I was both her voice and her beautiful firm will, "Tell us to take off the masks. Tell us to present ourselves."

And I understood what she meant in the white light, so I never asked 'how do I tell them?' It was so obvious. But when I was in my body again and standing in front of Grandma's puzzled face after I had just said, "Take off the mask; we need to present ourselves," and she stared at me like I was crazy, then I began to lose my death-clarity just a bit, just a teeny bit. So I leaned in towards her with my scrawny hands on the arms of her chair and tried again. I said, "Grandma, take off your false face;" and I told my aunt to "make yourself as a green shoot;" and to Uncle Eck I said, "Uncle Eck-Eck, you need to see, not just look. Try to understand what you see. These are the two hardest steps of living."

That's when Uncle Eck told me I was a fool, even for a child. "Try being poor, kid. Try being hungry and without resources. Then tell me that 'hardship is seeing'."

I couldn't get the words right. In my heart I still retained the messages, knew what I was supposed to get across, but the connection was not there - the connection to Momma, to my friends, to knowing, to Da. I ached for the white-light-connection. I needed it.

"Grandma," I said, pushing my face in towards her as she sat in her chair; we were almost nose-to-nose and I could smell her face powder, "we need to support each other, like the tree supports the shoot." At that, something flashed behind her eyes. I felt a white-light-type-of-connection for one precious moment before she brushed my arms off her chair and stood up, causing me to stumble backwards. She didn't even say anything. She just closed her face down like it was made of stone. That's the first time I saw her turn to stone. As she walked past me, I touched the point of her elbow with my fingertip. I touched her as gently as I spoke my words, "I'll support you, Grama. You be the shoot. I'll be the tree. I can be the tree for you, Gramie."

And she whirled on me with a snarl and said, "Grand-ma. My name is Grandma. Don't ever call me Grama or Gramie or Gran or anything else ever again. It's both childish and disrespectful."

Now, I was confused by her anger but I was even more upset by her words because neither anger nor words seemed to have anything to do with what we were talking about. I said so. That's when she bit out, "Look at the hate in your eyes!"

81

Me? Sweet Hoary Toad! I couldn't be less hate-filled if I tried. I was just returned from Heaven! But I was taken aback and so paused for self-examination. It took a second or two. By the time I was finished, she was gone. Grandma was gone in every way possible.

Not even one person listened; they didn't want to know. Rob was especially scared of what I had to say and next to Grandma, he was the one I most needed to reach. Rob ran from me whenever we were alone in a room. I tried sneaking up behind him and firing off information, but he wouldn't listen even when I mentioned his parents – especially when I mentioned his parents.

"Rob, you hurt me because you hurt."

"Get away from me."

I tried again, "When I died, I saw your parents."

Hands over his ears he chanted, "I can't hear you, na na na na na na na."

"They were there," I raised my voice and followed him. "When I died, they were there, Rob."

"I'm not listening ba baba ba baba-baba."

"They love you, Rob;" I shouted, "They are all love for you."

His face paled and he ran from the room with his hands over his ears but I was right on his heels. I wanted so much to explain death and bring relief to his pain but when I cornered him and said, "I was inside their hearts so I know that they are with you right now. They loved me, love you. Can't you feel them?" he grabbed my arms and kicked me. He shook me like a dog with a rat.

My head flopped back and forth, not a smidgen of resistance in me. I knew where this could lead but the violence didn't faze me. I realized, even in the white light when I was merged with his parents and when I knew everything all at once, I realized that he might consider me merging with his parents as the ultimate rejection. Children know these things. So it was easy to stay engaged with him even while he was shaking me like a rat. Children are either made of fear or made of compassion; and death was fresh on me so even if I was making mistakes in translation, my heart knew what I needed to deliver. I flopped there, waiting for his anger to abate so I could try again. I didn't fear pain and although I hated dying, I certainly didn't fear death. This last part is what finally got through to him, I think - the fact that I no longer feared him. For years he kept his abuse to himself.

~

The hair speeds up. We are going so fast now that if I hit something ... well, I am already dead, so I don't know what would happen. So I leap; all I can do is leap.

~

Inside The Family's girdle of protection a definite power vacuum developed. Legally I was in charge so the goal became control-of-me. All was babbling confusion and jockeying for position. The uncles circled like dogs, salivating and fighting each other through loud betrayals and legal maneuvers, diving to take out the legs, going for the throat. During this hair-flying, snarling time, the women of the pack made quiet, clever short-term strategic alliances. Power shifted. The uncles lost to an enemy they didn't even know was in contention and for this oversight they were de-fanged. It became women's work, the keeping of me in line - and the keeping of Rob.

Grandma finally came into her own, ruling with arched eyebrows and other twisted grimaces. There is no voice more intimidating than the silent one. Looks flog the soul more surely than a word or whip. The lesser women, The Aunts, settled down to follow Grandma's lead. And I came to understand that power never minimizes a person's flaws. It accentuates them. Subtle female manipulations cause as much damage as strong-armed action. I think history validates my theory.

83

The brawling was suppressed. That, at least, was beneficial. It saddened me, though, to see the emotions underlying the sturm-und-drang slink off to the shadows because shadowed tensions invite gall to ooze into every interaction. And gall did ooze. Dark and severe resentments hunkered down for a long reign in the mansion. Harshness begot harshness; malice and suffering increased, too, built upon the spine of a foul secret. The Family agreed to wrap the-killing-of-me in cotton wool - esoterica ménage - which meant neither Rob nor I were ever supposed to speak of it, even to the ones who should have loved us.

"It never happened, Child," The Aunts repeated often especially at the dinner table. And when I questioned the bruises on my neck, The Aunts claimed, "It would be best if you could forgive and forget . . . Others are suffering, too ... It was an accident . . . Surely Rob is sorry . . . We're making sure you're safe from now on ..." and Uncle Eck's wife said, "Not while I'm eating, kid; the idea makes me sick."

None of The Family's meaningless articulations ever addressed the issue at hand. It wasn't until I crawled into the cupboard upstairs in the playroom that I figured out that words alone were not going to break through generations of resentments.

They wanted to ignore the traumas.

"Not while I'm eating, Child ... forgive and forget ... look at the hate in your eyes ... makes me sick."

I couldn't blame them. But as I lay in the cupboard breathing chalk dust I devised another method of shaking up their psychological apathy. I gave The Family visuals instead of words.

Head down and shoulders bent I haunted the halls continuing to slowly curl over until my hands dangled near the floor at my feet. I drooled, mouth open and slack. Everyone bossed me to stand straight and shut my mouth. When the lawyers visited and I was summoned, I entered the room hunched over, shuffling, zombie-like. Upon receipt of a greeting I sunk to my knees and groaned and slowly collapse to the floor as if pressed down by an oppressive weight. I crawled to the table and listened on the floor at their feet and moaned my answers to their questions. The lawyers thought I was whacked. Rob said the problem was brain damage. There were no words to stop me, no looks, no amount of time alone or food withdrawal, no punishment. No one could get me to stop this pantomime because nothing was getting fixed and no one was listening to me.

I had suffered a heavenly rebuff to be a catalyst; no earthly power was going to stop me from delivering my message. So, I crawled and I moaned my burdens in every room in the house.

"I blame you for this," Uncle Eck-Eck's wife harped at him when she entered her bedroom to take a nap. The three of us were on the floor: me flat-on-the-floor groaning, Uncle Eck on his knees wafting a candy-bribe under my nose so I would 'stand upright and act normal', and Rob on the balls of his feet, crouched down, grabbing at the candy. Uncle Eck's other hand was pressed flat against Rob's chest to keep him back from us. "This is entirely your fault, Sir," The Aunt declared at her husband.

I rolled over onto my back and reached twisted hands towards her, "No blaming," I moaned. "Stay green. Trust enough to hear what we have to say, then it will be safe to accept each other."

The Aunt snorted - a very inelegant noise. "Do something useful, Idiot," she commanded her husband as she nudged her foot under his rump and tilted him forward.

All he did is yelp as he fell and dropped the candy. Rob scooped up the treat and ran. But no one chased him.

I groaned at her meanness. "Commitment, acceptance, these are the paths to love. If you do not see the child you will not love the child, you will only love the image of the child." It seemed so clear to me. I remembered what I felt in death.

85

"Get the kid off my floor." She was almost kicking her husband now, nudging him aggressively with her shoe. "Get the kid up;" prod "Get the kid out of my room;" nudge "It's your fault, you old coot. Get the kid out of here; you idiot;" poke, poke.

I reached for her legs to stop her feet, "Husbands and wives will not survive the task of commitment unless they remain calm. Seek first to understand." Uncle Eck rolled behind me for protection. "Look at how we error. We are all at fault."

"This is not my fault!" cried The Aunt at the same time Uncle Eck shouted, "This is not my fault!" and got to his feet.

"Take off the masks," I begged.

The Aunt was mad. Uncle Eck resisted me. Rob was long gone.

"Stop! Don't jump to emotion - that's the mask." I wailed. "Take time. I'm doing this for you."

The Aunt said, "Utter nonsense."

Uncle Eck sidled towards the connecting door away from me, away from his wife who was shooting daggers at me and didn't notice his surrender-of-this-battlefield. "Listen ..." I beseeched The Aunt.

I think deep down The Family wanted to be good people and do the right thing. The problem was that "good" and "the right thing" were now defined by Grandma's time-honored rule-set, the rule-set she had imposed upon herself her entire life. She delighted in its established perfection. Truth and right were based on what the majority decided together under Grandma's direct leadership. That's how Rob and I were schooled once our parents died. But having been schooled by God, in death, made me a relentless youngster.

"Stop;" The Aunt said when I spoke of unfurling love and deathLife, "You don't know what you're talking about. You had a hallucination."

"It was no dream, Aunt." I wouldn't let the subject drop.

"We have rules to live by. You need to get up off the floor and start behaving as fits your station."

I explained that majority decree was ridiculous. It had nothing to do with anything of value. Vulnerability and compassion were Heaven's decrees - resoundingly. How to live, how to die, how to love – it's not the stuff of genius; it's pretty straight forward and easy to contemplate. But The Aunt, in fact The Whole Family, lacked both discrimination and perspective and, worst of all, they projected onto me the craving for power that was eating at them. As such, my weight-of-the-world-pantomimes and childish death edicts were suspect.

It took a week before Grandma finally said, "What was the reason for it then? If you were killed, if you died, what was the reason? There has to be a reason. What did you do to deserve it?" And it began to be my fault or at least the fault was shared equally between Rob and me. Then she said, "If it is all so wonderful, why come back?" And that question successfully closed my petals up tight because I didn't quite understand the-having-to-come-back-part myself.

I was such a little soul with too much of a job. The epistle was not getting across. If it was so important, why couldn't I stay in the deathLove while God-the-Great-Negotiator did the job of schooling The Family? And if it was not that important, then why did I have to disconnect from the greatest joy ever? I was confused by rejection all around me; hurt and also shamed. There seemed to be something wrong with me. Something so wrong, heaven wouldn't allow me to stay. Something so wrong, Grandma couldn't love me. And Rob wouldn't get past the idea of me.

Too puny ... too hard ... confused ... I quit pushing and became part of the uneasy silence that hung over our mansion like a thick enchantment. I lost my feeling-connection to God although I remembered it. In the end, I put more effort into achieving approval than being the catalyst The Family so desperately needed. I was just six years old.

87

~

A sob lights my throat as I bounce in the dark going who-knows-where. That old confusion, the old wound of having to return to the living pit of discard and betrayal and away from heavenly completion causes pain worse than anything I felt in life. My parent's accident, them leaving me, that was hard to accept. But the second time, during death time ... how could Momma and Da send me back? I was a baby and I needed them! My two friends, why did they allow it? They love me. God? How, how, how could any of them do that to me?

Even though I have just walked through memories like a cold clear stream, once again my heart is muddied by so-huge-a-rejection. Sorrow floods over me carrying enlightenment downstream and out of sight.

"And now what?" I attack the dark with bitterness. "I'm dead again and I don't even get what I got before when I died? It's not fair. It's never been fair. I need the white light. I want help," I demand.

The hair tightens on my wrist and carries me for quite a ways. No need to put my foot down. This frees me to concentrate on my pain.

"Where is my help?" I despair louder this time.

The hair lets me down with a thump and I bound to keep up with it. We bump three times.

"Hey," I shake my wrist. "Stop it." My stomach acid churns and those small gentle fluttering butterflies in my stomach roil and bang against my diaphragm with greater intensity. I run on, deadening my right-now-misery with old-pain.

~

In the mansion dark with a predilection towards enmity we learned, Rob and me, that The Family's paradigm was more important than The Family's children. Because "The Incident" was never talked about, understood, healed or forgiven, a pernicious silence seeped into us. We became changed children as we began to understand how alone we were going to be for the rest of our lives.

That's when Rob began eating his resentment, absorbing it like food. It became his basic causal motivation. There was no resentment left in the situation for me to grab onto, which was fine as I was not attracted to resentment anyway. Instead I became less conspicuous, tried to fit in. I dropped the pantomime of heavy burdens, straightened up, closed my mouth, paid attention, did the right thing. Though I instinctively knew resistance was important, I allowed myself to become socialized - looking outward to The Family for stability. Once they held my attention, The Family gave me rules to live by. The rules themselves were not important - rules don't damage children. It is the lie behind the rules that damages.

"Get up on that horse, now!" Uncle Eck demanded. "I'm going to teach you to ride." Just then the wind blew a brace of leaves across the stable yard and the horse shied against his lead ropes almost pulling me under his sharp hooves.

"Isn't this the same horse that broke Rob's arm?" I hesitated. Rob was still laid up in bed, sick with infection from a broken arm no one admitted he had until it was almost too late.

"It's a perfectly good horse. Rob was careless. Don't argue, Child." Uncle chided me. "Just get up on the beast."

"But," I began.

"Up. Horse. Now."

Just then Grandma strode into the yard, pulling on her gloves. She frowned to see me still standing instead of astride. So anxious was I to please, when I noticed I had failed to meet her expectation my flesh crawled with dismay. I needed to do whatever I could to fix the wrong.

"Grandma," I began to explain.

89

She held up her hand and the words froze in my mouth. She took the time to contemplate the horse. But the wind had died down. No leaves blew. The horse was as mild as a cow. "Are we riding today?" She asked, one brow raised, "Or are we having a debate?"

"Doesn't like the horse," Uncle Eck misled her.

"Nonsense," Grandma repudiated her brother's claim as she motioned for a stable hand to throw her into the saddle. Once seated she turned towards me and asked with chilling politeness, "Are you rejecting a present? Do you think that is appropriate behavior?"

"No, it's just ..." I picked at my arm until it bled.

"Uncle Eck is an excellent judge of horse flesh. Generally good mannered people graciously thank their family for considerations. I expect better manners from you whether you ride the horse or not. Personally, I cannot help but consider it a failure to refuse to learn the rules of good horsemanship." She rode off without a backwards glance. Almost anything could be expected of me if it had the weight of a 'rule' behind it.

The rules oft repeated became my guiding principles. Repetition acts a cruel prod. Although The Family never succeeded in building a wall I could not see behind, I was terrifically successful at putting blinders upon myself. The Family relaxed after that; they breathed a sigh of relief, stretched and maneuvered. I did just the opposite. I tensed up, panted instead of breathed, pulled myself in-tight and tried to walk as lightly upon the earth as I could. Putting blinders on my instincts was too high price to pay for inclusion, but I didn't know that. And by the time I suspected the truth, it was too late. Blinding myself had become habitual.

Surprisingly, most surprising of all, I never did fit in. Although I paid for it and it was my deepest desire, my reward was never delivered.

Rob fit into The Family fold, however. Black sheep Rob - devilish, dangerous Rob - disarming and charming Rob was tucked in close. He was spied-on and suppressed. He seethed at being kept in the center of the fold, never allowed far from control. He acted the rogue; while I was the saint. Neither one of us ever understood his inclusion or my culling. Confusion thoroughly connected us.

~

A whispery, sibilant, plaintive cry drags me from my memories. Was it me that made the broken sound?

It could be me, distracted and whimpering out loud. I hear nothing now. Could be nothing - a hallucination or distortion maybe. I strain my ears, but the sound is gone.

The fluttering in my stomach strengthens to distinct movement like something has fallen and is bouncing around inside me. Even though I have been out of touch with my body's workings for years, I know this is not normal. I suppose dead organs can drop. Or perhaps the memories have raised a need in me; bouncing around inside my gut a numinous hunger grows. Lord knows, I hunger. Lord knows.

Immortality is a stifling concept.

-Journal Entry, May 15, age 24

Chapter 9 – Hungry Serenity

Running in the dark grows hunger like sunlight grows weeds.

My hunger grows into an ecstatic ache, which surprises me. I didn't know hunger could feel good; never felt hunger so physical before. Never felt a hunger sing to me. My hunger serenades so plaintively, it breaks my heart. My hunger sings of devotion. I undulate my head in a figure eight. It's the only way I can bear the song.

Hurts to hear it.

Achingly sweet is this starvingSong. It comes from my gut area. As if a poor dark hungerBird stands on my gut with tight little talons, leaning his breast against the sharp tip of my rib to trill beautiful agony into my heart. Poems will be built from this aching, have been conceived already, are built now.

"Burst sweet heart;" my hungerBird sings, "swell and burst." But that sounds dangerous to me - and yet, and yet … I *need*, *I* need; need overfills me. Contemplation seems the smart path; hunger has been a dangerous guide in the past. Devotions can mislead. If I was sure, I might risk following my hunger.

<Don't ever hunger>

It's been a long time since I hungered. The song grows, overstuffs me; my organs feel squinched up tight.

Squinched organs ache. My runner's bliss is long gone and I burn all over. Wrist and shoulder feel stretched and toes need a break. When I focus on my hurts, the song is overshadowed. This is probably the safe thing to do - focus on my hurts, subdue the song. I need to find the way out of this death soon.

Ahead, quite far ahead, a faint light wavers the dark. A light at the end of the tunnel. Literally. Dear God, I have found my way to the white light.

Politely I tap on the hair, "I'd like to stop up there in the white light, please."

It gives no indication of having heard me or of stopping and that irritates me. This hair, this pubic hair is ignoring me…

<It has never taken my needs into consideration>

… is uncouth. I have almost forgotten how I obtained the hair. Almost.

I reach up and tug at the hair coiled around my wrist. We bounce, landing hard on raw toes but there is no discernable other reaction. Still the hair drags me forward at top speed. Now I'm mad.

Swinging my feet, twisting and spinning and trying to make myself heavier cause the hair to pull back and whip me around. It tries to set me right, but I will not be righted. I will slow us down. I will not miss this light. Hand and feet reach out and grasp every available outcropping. We bounce low to the ground; I drag my feet. Rebounding high, I drag against walls. Suspended hand grabs the hair and whips it back and forth. I don't rub it against the walls but I want to. I want to hurt it and slice my way free but I don't because I cannot quite bring myself to damage the old broad's confederate. I am such a pansy.

Instead I hurt myself. Abrade hands and arms against rock, drag feet, stub toes. I will halt this demented sprint.

And I do slow us down as we approach the softly lit entryway bludgeoning up and down in a kind of destructive resonance. It hurts, of course. Just outside the entrance we barely move forward, but we barrel around like a spastic bush caught in a dust devil. Both of us are out-of-control, struggling against each other, slamming, taking a beating. Then I hook a foot inside the rocky opening and wrench us inward, into a cave of light.

The glare hurts my eyes. It is light, but not my white light.

Damned hair picks up speed. Does not plan on stopping. I really shouldn't care. It's not my white light anyway, but I find a new stubbornness rear up my backbone. Seems I have awakened stubbornness. I have bid us stop in the light so we darn well will rest here. Right now.

But the hair thinks it is in control.

Whoosh, fast, brush past a tree.

We dash past a forest; well … into a forest.

My eyes are not used to the light. Can't see too well with lids just cracked open.

Whipped, left. I just miss a tree.

Feet fly to the right. Stretched out. Turned tight.

Still right; fast right, steep right. Whoosh. Left again.

My feet airborne -

Flapping - barreling past green.

Face stung by twigs. That's it!

Down, kite!

This flight is finished.

I have had enough.

Up goes my free hand, fingers snaffling the hair. Using momentum from the next turn, hanging midair, I pull myself up, hands to my chin; then throw myself down in a terrible spin. Hair, moving too fast, is caught completely off guard. When my feet hit the ground and the hair tugs me back, I take a huge hop. That's when I attack. We shoot straight up. Out of control. Right through the branches. My thoughts on one goal. I will tangle us in these branches.

Ha. That stopped us.

The hair twists and turns, but is wholly tangled. *"Never had to deal with this kind of lacing before, I imagine."* I say it out loud <*snottily*> Most unbecoming I'm becoming. However, I am pleased with my strategy. I *almost* got exactly what I wanted.

The hair falls slack and my arm lowers to my side, muscles prickling in gratitude. My toes curl around a branch, taking up the weight, but they slip and slide, the branches not quite sturdy enough to support my weight. I feel heavy. Crack, that's all I hear before my arm jerks back over my head and I feel a sickening rip between shoulder socket and shoulder muscle. Suspended, helpless <*furious*> my left toenail is barely able to swish the ground.

I swing my legs and shake my arm to no avail. That smug hair is not moving.

<*I hate the thing*> <*The light is too bright; I hate the light, the not-my-white-light*>

Splenetic and waspish, I am.

<*Want to hurt something*>

I have a genial nature. I am quite famous for it. It's one of my better qualities. But not lately. Not in this third death. I have no access to geniality. Instead, I bellow and shake my whole body taunt with fury.

<I must look like a caught fish>

Crack, crack, crack, crack, that's all the warning before I thump to the ground. Still yelling I land on my feet with locked knees and it hurts. That damn hair falls on my head and then coils daintily around my neck and shoulders.

My hand curls naturally to cup my belly – heavy now that my weight has settled onto my feet. The hair lays limp - utterly still. I shrug it off my shoulders in spastic rejection.

<I don't want the damn hair touching me>

The ground feels as if it is heaving. I remember feeling this once before, at the end of the day-I-rode-the-two-wild-rivers. The child-me climbed out of the boat and found the solid ground unsteady. I laughed that day and teetered and tottered and fell and rose again and again, performing for my parents. Today I don't feel like laughing. I feel wobbly in my mind and the illusion of ground heave irritates me. Ungainly and awkward, I re-plant my feet wide, pettishly feeling for and finding the hair to grind my heel on it. It undulates once then lies still. Guilt rises for a moment at my shocking new meanness, but that irritates me, too - compunction and fractiousness - crankyGuilt.

<I don't like the flavor of myself right now>

Arrgh.

Head bowed, eyes closed against the light's glare, I raise both hands to my forehead. Thumbs plant under my jawbone and I rub comfort into my spirit. This is a full hand rubbing, not just finger tips. This is nose massaging, cheek smooshing, eye stretching, temple smoothing, de-stressing jaw line, comfort-giving massage. My querulousness seeps into the ground and I can breathe again, more deeply than before, although I still feel full up, everything squinched together. When I remove my heel from the hair it caresses my leg once then lies limp. I feel terrible.

Cracking open my eyes I see that I can see. At least I can see. "That's a delight," I tell myself trying not to focus on what I'm really feeling.

<It's not my white light>

Although the light is harsh on my dark-adjusted eyes, in actuality, the glow is soft and delicate, coming up from the ground, which is odd but not fearsome like torch-eyes. The room is filled with trees - upside down trees - trees growing from the roof, upside down, leafy arms spread towards the luminance coming from the ground beneath my feet. The forest duff glows softly. Illumination casts shadows up. I look up at the ceiling, not so very far away. At this juncture, roots intermingle. Tree roots dangle mid-air from the ceiling. These roots are from trees growing the other way, the right way, above ground and roots extending into this cave. Oh Sweet Reward!

This is the closest I've been to the surface. If I can just climb one of these upside down trees I might be able to dig my way out of this third, awful death. I could escape into life.

<Life is not as good as finding the white light, but even life would be better than this place>

The tree I just fell out of is big. The top of its canopy almost reaches the top of my ears.

<Oh, if I had not been such a knucklehead!>

I could have climbed it when I landed in it.

<If I had just paid attention>

Now the substantial branches look too far away.

I am not deterred. I'm just berating myself.

<*Fool, fool, fool*>

Slowly, with hands pressed to the underside of my belly, I walk around the upside down tree looking, looking for a thick branch I can climb. Although experienced at scrambled up many objects, clambering up an upside-down tree requires a whole new strategy. The limbs within reach are all twigs, not large enough to support my weight. I grab a bunch of branches and try to pull myself up. They break; my hands slide off and I am left with two fistfuls of new growth smelling of turpentine.

The leaves are unique, dark on one side and light on the other. I recognize the leaves. We have a small stand of black poplars in the grotto back at the mansion. When I was a child I would climb the deeply ridged trunks and rest my back against their large woody bosses. The tips of the twigs are sticky and are covered with a fine down. I used to gather the sticky down, the colored catkins, and make small people. Then I would line them up along the branch nearest my head and spin stories for them and pretend they loved me.

I close my eyes and snuff their fragrance, but just for a moment. Then I get back to work figuring my way out of here.

Maybe I can jump high enough to grab a thicker branch. I continue round and round the tree, looking for my opportunity. There is an appropriate branch quite high up.

<*Too high*>

Rocking back on my heels I accidentally step on the hair. Once more it undulates against my ankle.

The hair! Of course; I can use the hair to fly me up to the branch, or better yet, up to the roof. I glance down at my wrist-with-hair-wrapped-around-it but am distracted by my body.

<It's rotund. The belly is hanging down or out or ... it's huge. I look like I have a whiskey keg strapped to my ribs>

My big belly bulges out and strains shirt buttons.

<When did this happen? Whose round belly is this? Who do these fat fingers and swollen feet belong to?>

The skin on my feet is greenish blue and blistered; the toe skin is missing, rubbed off, I assume from my jog.

I can see my body for the first time since I died and am frightened by the looks of it.

<This is not my body. My body is lithe, I have a flat stomach. My belly button pokes inny, this one pokes out. I have long slender fingers and narrow feet. My toes are long. My big toe is so long it almost doubles my foot length. At least that's what Rob says. Now my big toe all but disappears in bloat. My feet are so swollen the skin is ashy and patterned like a reptile's. I cannot see my ankle bones. Nothing makes sense.>

I sink to the ground; a whoosh of gas escapes my bleeding chest hole and the pungent ammonia-like odor wafts up from under my shirt. Once I remove the shirt, I notice an almost black soapy, waxy, cheese-like substance on the shirt. The wax is also along the sides of my waist. Any section not covered in wax is greenish blue and blistered, just like my feet. I do believe I'm rotting and this mound of swollen stomach is probably gas collected through decomposition.

I poke the grotesque stomach mound and flatulence escapes from my chest wound. Cause and effect. I push it firmer this time to empty the gas; want my flat stomach back. Only a small urp of gas erupts, but a ripple moves across my belly. With head tilted in skeptical concentration I poke hard again. Something inside my belly kicks back, surges out of the way.

<I have something alive inside of me!>

In my hurry to rise, I trip over the flaccid hair.

<Damn hair>

I'm scared back into anger. Minuscule pulses and ephemeral humps lift my mounded skin.

<Grotesque>

Sweet Holy Madre! I'm panting too fast. My head is spinning and those yellow and black dots are in front of my eyes again. I feel fuzzy.

~

There was a dead squirrel I once found in the grotto by smell. It moved this same way, ripples under its obviously dead bloated skin. So I pushed its belly with my foot and the squirrel's skin tore like tissue and a mass - a-squirming-jelly-mass - of baby white slugHorrors oozed out on a wave of stench and fluid. I spent three minutes hopping around the grotto, count 'em, three minutes, hopping and brushing the sauce and buggies off my long big toe.

Then I went back and watched the dead-white buggies, nose plugged, in repulsed fascination.

~

It is not with fascination, however, that I watch the ripples under my own obviously dead belly. Maggots? Are slugHorrors devouring me in this death? "Oh … Oh … Oh … oh, get me out of this misery," I finally squeak a sound out, "Oh …" I hold my arms away from my body so as not to excite another movement from the things inside. But I need comfort so eventually I rub my forehead and whimper under my breath and walk around in circles. "Can't be, can't be. No, no. Oooo."

The skin on my paunch itches where stretched. Tentatively, I scratch and the things push away from my fingers again. *<Oh!>*

<Tattered, so tattered>

I'm still bleeding from my chest wound and I am torn and scraped and scared and gashed and bruised from various forces smashing me in this death. My clothes are rent and begrimed and I smell of rot and river and blood and dirt and sweat, vomit, and fear – a distinctive and unfragrant fruit salad of smells. The concept of maggots, their little mouth hooks pulling at my innards and raising my temperature and jellifying my tissues is too much - is overwhelming. I cannot take anymore. Swamped by weariness beyond belief, I cannot hold my eyes open long enough to lie down. I lose consciousness even as I am lowering myself to the ground.

~

For a long time I have lived in a moist, squishy place dripping with red-black blood. My nose bleeds. My gums bleed. Everything in this place bleeds except for a green pustule growing on my belly. It glows emerald in the redness. Occasionally, the top layer of skin over the pustule slides back to expose a watery green eye. When open, the pus-eye follows my every move. I have become used to it and even come to depend upon it for company. My eye and I.

This day the eyelid is closed and I cannot make it open. I am singing to the eye and tapping on my stomach like a drum to encourage it. Instead, the eye squints down tight. I feel a deep pain welling up inside me as green liquid is squeezed out from where the tear duct should be. It looks like pus but, as it is from my eye, I treasure it.

I gather up the pus on my fingers and form it into the shape of a tiny baby me. I am delighted with my creation. I toss the pus-baby-me into the air and catch it. It opens it eyes and laughs with me. My God! This tiny green me is precious. I am no longer alone. What a good me this is. Surely The Family will approve of this me. I hold it like a trophy. The little green baby looks solemnly at me and thrusts out its hands and cradles my head against its tiny chest. It loves me. For the first time in an endless time I feel as if I can loosen the controls and sleep. I am tired. Even in my dream I am bone-tired. I lay down and the green baby croons to me and I fall asleep.

But too soon, I am jarred awake by rough handling and the sound of my pus-baby crying. The Family is gathered around to view the baby and, just as I hoped, they love it. "It is perfect", they say. "But what have you done to the precious baby? It's dying."

I glance down. The baby looks perfectly healthy to me.

"How can you feed the baby?" The Family demands. "You have no milk. We will take it and teach it what is right and how to be." And they grab the baby, pulling at it in order to take it away. Fearing the loss of my precious pus-baby, I hang on tight. They pull. I tug back and we all hear its little bones break. Still I will not let it go. The baby cries and grabs onto me.

"It wants me," I speak resoundingly, "me, me, me, me. Go away."

The Family disappears.

I am concerned and try to loosen its hands in order to examine it but the baby won't let go of me. Its ribs are broken and sticking out of its body. "I don't know what to do! It's awful." My little one stops crying. It looks past me, over my shoulder, and so I turn around and see the old woman from the cave. Her ribs, too, are sticking out from her skin. She pats us both and coos and is delighted by us. "I have nothing to feed this baby," I lament.

The old woman laughs at me and pushes my green baby to my chest and my little one starts to suckle. It bites and pulls trying to get at milk not there. It hurts. I watch as my chest caves in. That's when I realize that I am also hungry. I need food. I am the one that needs food. I must have it now.

Terrified that I will be consumed, I try to pry it loose, but the baby has sucked the bones from my arms and I can no longer detach it. The old woman whispers in my ear, "Stay, dye mar, I hinder ruin to roost, I hinder ruin to roost." Even in my dream I can only understand the first word of what she says.

When I next look down I see that the pus-baby is sucking my ribs then my hips from my body. I can no longer get up to run away from it and still it hungers.

I don't like this green pus-y thing. It has made an embarrassment of me. With my bones gone, I am ugly, no, I am fearsome looking and of no use to anyone. I determine to throw the thing away. That's when it looks up at me with sad eyes and knows the time has come for it to die.

~

I wake up.

No waking in stages for me. I open my eyes and, I anchor myself like a tree. Am still; searching dreamland.

I am full slow; looking for truth. New seeds, old fears enlace. Mind quivers, but heart acts the sleuth. Signs churn, liberate grace.

Well, could liberate grace.

If I let grace be liberated.

Sad. I am saddened by my dream when appalled is what I should be. I press my skull down into warm leaves - placid, sad, so blue.

Quietly I breathe in *seeeeee* and then, pause, out again *ahaaaaaaaaa*. Here I am. I just am. Am very still. *mmm*

It's important, this breathing, this calm. I'm not sure why but I feel it - something epochal bequeathed to me by my dream. Laying here I am a measured pace; utterly implacable and somehow embraced. Although silent, this solace is undeniable.

My dream - my mystery - is mine. <A*ll mine*> Just out of reach, it is impenetrable to reason. However hard I try, I feel like I'm following a dog sniffing a tree. I know there's a message there, but I cannot access the information. All I smell is stink. I take a deep breath.

seeeeeeeeeee

Yes, quieting helps. Deeply interior my dream reconnects me to … hope? *mmmm* … maybe, hope of … hope of some kind. I have forgotten its name but I crave another noseful or two of hope.

Huff, huff Eyes wander around the black poplar grove. My busy brain wants to supply input.

<*Black poplar leaves are rich in an aspirin-like substance; chewing them lessens pain*>

But my brain's input is not very useful right now. I work to keep my body soft and warm and melty. Seems like I should try and keep my brain nice and soft, too.

Maybe it's esteem I crave. *Ahaaaaaaaaa* The things inside of me are quiet, too.

Maybe I crave to make the right choice.

<What is the right choice?>

Feels like I should choose something.

<Choose; go; get on with it>

What choice - I can't quite sniff it.

<Better not choose wrong, though>

As my brain speeds up the things inside of me stir, too; settling low in my pelvis. *<Gotta pee>* It is easier to breathe with the things-inside-of-me down low, which is a relief. Although my back aches and I feel increasingly heavy, my gnawing hunger is diminished. I smile.

Rolling onto hands and knees I grasp a fallen tree limb.

<Haul that belly up>

Something comes apart inside me. It doesn't hurt but it feels like layers of my chest are pulling apart and like my stomach lining is … I don't know … stretching.

Momma once arranged a taffy pull at the mansion. We stood on separate ends, the kitchen help and I. We pulled and stretched the candy and it kept thinning out. That's what this feels like. I look down to see if my belly looks as odd as it feels.

<It doesn't hurt; don't be a baby>

I feel increasingly unpaired, which upsets my serenity.

<Focus on the white light>

Almost nicely I flip my wrist to wake the pubic hair. "Hey Hair," I say to it overly polite, "could you wake up and fly me up to the ceiling, please."

The hair remains limp, but I feel a small pop in my pelvic area, kind of similar to biting down on a cold thick-skinned grape.

<What ...>

A trickle from-down-low pees out of my chest-hole. "This is a new development," I think as I slip out of my remaining clothes. It smells ... odd ... this glittery new pee. I've wet myself all down my front.

<Don't like this>

Somehow it's worse than the never-ending blood. I wring out my shirt and walk choppily towards the center of the forest.

<Seeping is unseemly>

Halfway through the forest, cramps seize. I press both fists into my lower back, which helps, but as soon as I take my hands away, the spasms return. I admit I'm getting a tad bit irritable now.

Maybe if I lay down, I think. So I do and push my back against the ground, which is warm and that helps a bit. But I'm restless, so around I lumber onto my knees and I scrape my palms back and forth against the duff to distract myself.

Although the pain originates in my back, it radiates all the way around to the front, down low all over. I squeeze myself into as tight a ball as I can manage considering this mound of mine.

<I'm a dusty seed>

I stretch my toes and bite my teeth.

<Nasty>

Am at a loss.

The pain comes in waves with each new round beginning before the previous one is finished. I grind my face into the duff and the things inside my stomach spar. I pant rhythmically to get me through the rolling pain. As soon as I feel the first edge of relief, I stand.

<Run>

So I do.

<Get out of here; don't think>

Maybe I can run right out of my body.

The next spasm hits so fast and hard I slam into a downed tree limb. I grab hold, squat down, and bite into the limb screaming. I literally scream the poop out of me. But the pain is so bad, I am beyond embarrassment.

With each spasm I claw and bite that limb. Between spasms, I rest my forehead against the tortured bark and kiss the bite marks and pant into them. In a world of hurt, that limb is something to clutch with every limb I have. <Squeeze> I squeeze my eyes shut <I've got to> I need to push - feel like pushing.

Blood and water gush out of my chest as I push, I push I push <And then> I feel movement from my pelvis into my chest.

<I can do it>

Push it out.

<If Grandma was here she'd be screaming, "Don't let it out; Keep it down; for heaven's sake">

But I have demands. My body's demands are too great to ignore. It seems like it will feel good to push.

Amid a gush of blood, I push a wet, steaming body out of my chest wound. It sounds like a bar of soap slipping out of my chest - very fast; then everything slams shut. My eyes are still closed but I feel the-thing-I-pushed-out dangling between my legs. It bites my inner knee. My eyes pop open. I look.

Oh, God! I have given birth to a monster.

Immortality is a stifling concept.

I realize the irony of making such a statement at age twenty four, but it's the logical construct of considered contemplation. Amassing an immortal bulk of experience makes it hard to have an opinion having seen all sides of any point at one time or another. Every disaster could be viewed as an opportunity and every joy as fleeting. Thus, with passion truncated and hope unnecessary, an immortal life is simply irritating.

-Journal Entry, May 15, age 24

Chapter 10 – I Am the One Rejecting

Rejection, I am your name. Never have my hands moved so fast; acting a shield and creating an opposite reaction so my back thrusts backwards. These shield-hands of mine are even faster than my toes twirling in tight little circles or my heels peddling grooves in the duff - *aiiee*. Adrenaline flushes my chest hot red and that flush shoots up my neck and burns my ears like signal fires just in case there is an aspect of me that is not yet aware that I am trying to get away. But every aspect is aware. My lips slip on my teeth in their hurry to get as far away from the birthling as they can - my eyelids stretch taut as they try to climb up my forehead - the skin all around my mouth moves out from center - and my fingers, already thrust out, spread as wide as the

skin can tolerate. All of me is scrambling backwards away from the …
what I birthed.

The thing hangs by its by its white umbilicus still connected inside my chest hole. I don't know this thing, but it knows me. There is intelligence in those eyes. "No" I shake my head.

It reaches for me with tiny arms and legs. I brush at the cord coming from my chest in a sweeping motion - away, away from me. I step back and it bares its teeth and starts chewing on its umbilicus, the only thing it can reach. Dear Revolting Fear, it has teeth!

But I knew that; it has already bitten me.

The thing is covered in blood. It's red, wrinkled and gorges on its cord. With teeth-grab and head-shake it pulls the cord from of my chest. Inside me still, the cord slithers. My body answers with another contraction. I go back into labor, not as long as before, but it hurts. It hurts enough that I hate the reject even more. Gritting my teeth I tug on the cord and the placenta slithers out. I drop it to the ground away from me and the ugly birthling with it.

Terrified. I am terrified that I have birthed this toothed thing. Because there is no doubt that what I just went through was a twisted sort of birthing process. I would rather have had maggots. Maybe this is a giant deformed slugHorror.

It worries me that I was host to this thing - me; I hosted it. There is no getting away from the idea. If this is what I birth … if I am the master of this creation then no wonder God never lets me stay at heaven's threshold. This whole scene, this third demented death, is worse than anything I have lived through. "I don't want you," I yell at the creature and another contraction hits and fells me.

I land face first next to the small-toothed beast and it bites me again. "Ahhhh" I yell, racked in pain. The contractions come fast and hard, no gradual lead up to the main event this time. I know what to do

dangerous one looks militant as he leans toward us; all parts of his body are forward: the eyes stare directly at me, his ears stick out and press forward. The corners of the lips push forward. Then, without warning, he runs at us again, slamming into the pile of brutish bodies at my feet. He bowls me over but is off and running again on his stilt-like legs with no pause.

Gagging. This different, dangerous beast is gagging. Now I look sharper and can see that his stomach is distended as if he, too, is pregnant. I'm confused because just before he rammed us he was skinny. He turns to eye me and that's when I see a small hand disappear down his throat. The dangerous monster has grabbed one of the birthlings at my feet and eaten it, has gorged on one of his brethren.

In an instant I think, "I wish he would eat them all!" and at the same time I exclaim, "He just, he, he ate his brother!" There is a squeak at my feet and I look down into the horrified eyes of the first birthling. My aversion expressed exactly in those eyes.

We are all shocked immobile until the dangerous one runs away. Once he is out of sight, I take a deep breath and, as if on cue, two more hideous things are born – red, faces screwed up caterwauling, twisted wrinkled things fashioned to live in the dark – scary as hell.

I, mimicking the predacious one, bounce onto my toes and run away from the others.

*The English yew has the capacity for
immortality.*

-Journal Entry, May 15, age 24

Chapter 11 – Womb Of Nights

It's getting dark. The trees, spaced widely apart, produce less duff; which means less light. Plus night is falling - the duff gently pulls light back underground. Ahead, is the forest's edge and beyond that three tunnel openings.

The one on the left is most attractive because it is most intimidating. That's where I head, still at a dead run. The rock wall is solid at the base but as I scramble up, a fair amount of gritty flakes and loose rock comes off in my hands. It's more slippery than it looks and more strenuous, too, but I don't slow down. My arms are on fire. I want to get as far off the ground as I can.

The final bit of climbing it tough. The cave rim is lipped with the overhang longer than the length of my arm.

I start with feet on high holds under the lip and move my hands through the crux of the overhang. "Keep going," I mutter as each move gets harder and my arm strength fades away. "Keep your feet attached to the rock. There, that's it." I grunt and clasp the slightest ridge with my thighs. "Push. There, a higher handhold ... reach, dammit. Don't stop." I don't want to swing out away from the wall as I am having a hard enough time using my hands effectively.

117

Once I scramble over the rocky lip, I roll into the cave and spin to hunker down just to the right of the entrance. I brush my hands over my body to make sure nothing is attached to me. It's a nervous gesture. Nothing has bitten me for a long time. I'm pretty sure I've left them behind. Reflexively I run my hands over my body again and shudder. I will do that quite a few times during the night.

Feeling the hair still wrapped around my wrist, I give it a tentative tug. It flows easily across my palms. Gulping, I twitch and jerk it towards me, pulling it hand over hand into the tunnel. Smoothly it undulates, not seeming to be burdened with extra weight. If I feel the slighted resistance, that damned hair and I are through.

I think I have outrun them, the interlopers. I have to believe that they, like this whole farce of a third death, are mistakes. I hiccup my air and coil the hair ropelike around elbow and hand.

At five wraps it is stretched longer than when the old woman gave it to me. I wrap it nine more times before I am calm enough to steady my breathing. Twelve more wraps and I am calm enough to peek out of my hidey-hole. It's caveNight. I see nothing. They could be there. Anything could be out there and I wouldn't see. I wrap the hair thirteen more times before I sit down again, back against the rock wall and try to relax. At wrap number three thousand one hundred and two the hair end flops inside the cave next to me. None of those dismal wretches are attached. I hope they will bite each other far away from me.

Coiled hair is my pillow as I lay on my side facing the entrance. I strain my ears and run my hands down my body again. My belly is slack – no more butterflies, maggots, or monsters. I can't believe I am back to being flattened again – right up the middle. I burrow down. I'm hiding. Hiding from the brutes, but hiding from this death, too. I rub my hand over my chest hole, swollen and torn wider, sore to the touch. It's still bleeding. Will I ever run out of blood?

I probe at the chest wound again.

<So tender; it'll probably get infected>

It must be my fault; I must be doing death wrong.

<Wrong and stranded, alone in my body>

I am more than abandoned.

<Feel separate from everything>

One mind, two arms, a scared little voice, nearly invisible - I am pathetic . . .

. . . and shaken to the core. I could not be more scared; but, I am more scared. All I know is moving away from me. "Chin down," I mumble to myself as I stretch the skin between nose and lip and let the grief flow like a column from cheek bones to chest center - bleak, weak, devolved, dissolved. I am a deep-rooted sickness.

<Can't sleep> Even if I could, I can't. Birthed ugliness may be out there somewhere creeping their slimy way to me. The only connection I have to anything in this death is the-connection-I-utterly-reject.

I lay fetal-positioned in the dark with eyes wide open. Rubbing my forehead offers no comfort, but I do it anyway. I listen to my blood drip down the lip, down the stone face and plop into a developing blood pool at the base of my shelter. And I weep.

For the first time since my parents died, tears overflow the bands of my eyes. I cry softly so as not to attract monster attention – or the attention of anything else. Not even God. I mourn for myself; not trying to earn anything, negotiate anything, or extract anything. I just sorrow. Such a gentle expression of the force behind them; but they don't end, the tears. They stream and flow and wash my face away until only separation exists. Then they mix with the blood flowing from my chest and cause a flood. Or, at least that's what I would like to believe.

~

At age nineteen I feel as hollow as a horsetail plant. Plants don't have hearts - don't need them. Seems like mine is gone, too. Much safer that way, to live without a heart.

Been without a heart for about a year now - no heart, no words. Haven't even been outside since they brought me back to the mansion. The mansion, my home from whence I escaped into disaster and died for the second time.

Eighteen is too young to die. Nineteen is too young to be without a heart.

Hiding has been all I could manage until today. Today Grandma decided hiding time is over. She pried me from my dark room. Guilted me back into the skin I used to wear; back into the expectations and obligations that are mine, just mine, always mine to bear. So here I am alone in the great hall all dressed up for social rounds. I'm surprised anyone would believe in the illusion I present.

My eyes roam. Am not really seeing, not really feeling. The echoing hall is empty; feels friendly. No escorts. No handlers. They are not ready yet I suppose. A thought passes through me, "Wait outside; no one watches." It's strange to have an urge. I've been urgeless for over a year.

The light outside is bright.

Air smells good. It's fresh. Feels like imminent rain. Inside-my-nose turns cold as I fill my lungs through it. Eyes to the sky I walk a few steps into the emerald expanse of grass that looks like it stretches forever. Grey puddles dot the landscape - same color as my insides - same color as the sky. Slosh. Same color as the water all over my shoes. Grandma is not going to be happy.

Physicality impinges: cold feet, cold nose, fresh air, bright light. Don't move, I think. Maybe I am real; maybe I'm alive; maybe I will allow myself to feel again. Maybe not.

Ripples smooth themselves out and the puddle's brown-grey glassy surface reestablishes itself. The only thing separating my upside down image from my physical self is a thin bead of black distorted light all along the horizon of my shoe. Such an insubstantial boundary between reality and fiction; I could almost pretend it doesn't exist. What's holding me here? Just a thread, just a thread.

In the puddle, in front of my shoe a big green apple sits. Jutting my chin slightly moves my reflected face right over the apple. That green apple now sits smack-dab in the middle of my reflected head. "Did you roll all the way here from the orchard to get away from the other apples?" I wonder inside my head. I haven't said an out-loud-word for over a year. "How could you have come all this way just to end up in a puddle? It seems, I don't know, anticlimactic somehow."

I don't move, not even an inch. I like the idea of having an apple for a face.

"Apple head," I mouth. "Apple, apple, apple head, heard you had fled and wound up dead, but instead of staying dead you went and said ..."

"I've been waiting for you," a voice outside my head interrupts my silent song. This voice is as deep as an avalanche. "Russell sent me."

I don't feel like attending to this person. Would rather stay inside my own little world. I close my eyes so no other image can replace the one I capture against my eyelids - apple, apple, apple head. My face is an apple head.

"Come," the gardener's assistant rumbles. "Walk this way."

Since I've become hollow, I find it nearly impossible to resist orders. It's not surprising then that I follow the sound of his heavy feet in wet grass even as I resist opening my eyes. After all, the gardener's assistant did not demand that I open eyes.

I know where we walk because I hear our footsteps echo between the close-together-walls of the greenhouse and the shed. If I reached out my hand I could feel the rough shed siding, but I don't.

Other voices chime greetings to me, tell me it's been too long. They tell me they are happy to see me finally outside in the light.

I dip my chin. It could be taken as acknowledgement if they want to take it that way. Or they could assume I am hiding my apple face from their searching eyes. They have all heard what happened to me, what I did a year ago.

"Go through these doors," the avalanche-voiced assistant guides me. I hear a creak as he opens a door. Chin tucked, eyes closed, I step inside the greenhouse where the air is moist and muggy and tropical. As the door shuts (I hear it shut) the noise outside becomes muted.

Feet shuffling I feel the floor in front of me so I don't trip on anything, but it's too crowded. My hand knocks a pot off a shelf, which falls with a crash. I can't help it, I open my eyes.

Apple head is replaced by the vision of an old man. He's on his knees holding a wilted pansy by the stem. I know those hands - my old friend's hands. He's examining the poor wee flower, plucking at it with a tender smile on his face. When I shuffle into the room, his smile widens. He is happy to see me. Despite myself, that feels good.

"I'm mak'ng my way out to the grotto t'day." He tells me as if we were carrying on a conversation we started thirteen minutes ago instead of thirteen years. "Heard we gotta fox living there. Sorta hopin' you'd come along."

I smell the dirt he's working in. It smells fine. My fingers ache to go digging but I'm clean - well except for my shoes I'm clean - and must stay that way.

"Keep me company" he invites and although I greatly appreciate his sentiments, I am shocked. In fact, I'm so flooded with shocked feelings, I can't fixate on which to address first. I'm shocked that I am flooded with feelings. I'm shocked that after thirteen years he's asking me to spend time with him again, like before, like during the good days of my life - before we were forbidden. I'm shocked that the grounds have a fox. Surely the aunt who wears almost only skins would have ordered every available fox killed. And I'm shocked by the idea that I'm actually considering going to the grotto - the wild grotto - an untamed place. I'm shocked that I'm outside in the light after almost a year inside the house and that I'm in the greenhouse. I'm shocked Grandma isn't right here beside me throwing a fit and demanding me back into the mansion. I suppose I'm even shocked that I'm not worried about the fact that I have ruined my shoes.

The master gardener holds out a flower. Of their own accord, my hands cup the delicate root ball. I look closely at the plant. "I think it's a goner," I say relieved to have an excuse to reject it.

He takes the pathetic thing back in hand but otherwise doesn't react to my first out-loud-words in a year. "Hep. It'll take fix'n right enuff. But it'll pull through. Hurry up, Smudge. We gotta get these planted before we head out to find the fox den."

"Oh, no; I can't." I'm still shocked. "I mean ... I'm too busy. Now's not a good time."

My best friend smiles gently at me. "Now is the best time," he says, "when it's important." He means I am important and I flush with pleasure. "Is this pot yellow?" He asks me. At my nod he hums, "It'll be perfect."

With a purple flower? Once again I wonder how he ever got to be the master gardener when he is color blind. I don't say it out loud, though. Reluctantly I pull my fingers from soil. Somehow my fingers managed to burrow into a nearby pot when I wasn't paying attention.

"I've got to get back now," I inform him. My fingers are filthy. Russell grunts and hands me the purple flower in its new yellow pot. I wipe my hands on my backside before taking it and grimace when I realize what I've done. "Thank you," I murmur.

He grunts again as I shuffle out the door, eyes open and glued to the pot in my hand. I'm fascinated by the contrasting colors. The door shuts behind me.

"You gonna come out here and work with the old man or are you just passing through?" the gardener's assistant asks me once I'm out in the light again.

I jump. Didn't know he was waiting for me. "Well," I start to answer him with my eyes glued to my prize.

Then my friend's voice floats through the closed door. "Think about it before you answer, Smudge."

That stops me in my tracks. I trust Russell. I realize I have always trusted him. I trust him now more than anyone I've spent time with since I came back to the mansion, since I was brought back from my disastrous adventure and second death. I pause to think things through as instructed.

Avalanche-voiced assistant rocks back on his heels (I hear his shoes squeak but I don't move my gaze from my flower). He levels his stare at me (I feel his question). "Well, now," I contemplate, "what exactly am I supposed to think about? I've put on nice clothes. I can't just take off and get all grimy." I open my mouth to speak and the old dear voice rings out through the door again.

"Are you just thinking, Smudge, or are you reflecting on your decision?"

I close my mouth with a snap. "Upon reflection," I think, "if I stay and work in The Family Foundation I could hide. That makes a lot of sense. But in the long run it isn't really what I want to do or to be."

"Yes." The old gardener chimes in from behind the door.

I pause at that encouragement. Then re-reflect and whisper, "It isn't what I want to do?"

"Now you've got the idea, Smudge," his voice through the door.

Now I am a tad confused. Figuring out the correct answer to this question is hard work for me. I'm not used to paying attention to my own inner landscape; am covering new ground here. Bottom-line then: when I think about staying around the mansion and working in The Family Foundation I feel wilted and apathetic; okay, now I know. When I think about leaving the greenhouse and never seeing the fox, I feel terrified. I don't want to work in the foundation.

Hey, I finally figured out what I would like to do!

On the other hand, it seems a little selfish to abandon family duty again. Neither I nor The Family have fully recovered from the last time I set out on my own, last year. No! I can't put The Family through that again. Besides, foxes are wild and I am not good at wild. Dear Lord, everyone knows I am not good at wild. All is silent and still. I stick a finger in my yellow pot. The soil is warm.

"Keep working on it, Smudge, you'll get there," the master gardener encourages.

Whatever I decide seems to be okay with my friend and it would not be fine with Grandma. I might be happier in the grotto, but I would be safer in the mansion. I push through rationalizations and justifications and excuses, but when I get to the bottom of the pile there is only one little idea. "What I want is most important." I pull my finger from the pot.

Although I have a lot of negative attachments to the idea that 'what I want is most important for me', the idea stands like a crocus in the snow. Brave little idea. But I am uneasy. Don't know what to do with the idea since I don't actually trust myself enough to put me first. I can decide later. That's what I'll do. I'll decide later.

I tell the assistant gardener, "I better be on my way; I have a lot to do today." I hang on to my plant, though.

The old dear voice rings out through the door one last time, "You can always visit me here or at the fox den."

And the gardener's assistant says, "Okay." That's all. His shoes squeak as he rolls back onto the flats of his soles and he leads me back to where we first met. I keep my eyes on the yellow pot.

When we get to the puddle I step right in. Very gently avalanche-voice says, "You can always visit him ..." His voice trails off.

"Thank you," I say sincerely, "No foxes for me." I dart a quick look at him, just in time to catch his nod. As he turns to go he boots the apple out of the puddle, out of sight.

It starts to rain.

Grandma calls my name.

I watch him walk away and to his back I say, "It's good to know they're there, the foxes and the old man."

~

In my cave, bleeding, sore, raw and eyes puffed and swollen from crying I admit I chose wrong that day. I knew it at the time. My great friend died shortly after and I never went to his funeral. I worked instead. I don't even know where he is buried.

And yet, despite all that, I still feel sustained by the memory. For the first time I wonder if I was ever a yew tree in the family stand or if I was a seed dropped wrongly. "Not a yew," I taste the words in my mouth. "Not yew," I muse. And a newly-found emotion-searching-tool notices how I feel inside. It feels straighter to not be yew.

For the first time since I died I am not wailing the question, "How will I ever make it on my own?" This time when I think the question, it is a starting point - just the beginnings of a map that may lead to a place where I can claim all the sun and nutrients I need.

It's an important idea, I think. I want this idea - not like before. After my second death, if an idea itched my brain I caught it without looking at it and sent it off to be hogtied and branded and butchered and wrapped up for someone else to buy and eat. I was an idea vegetarian. No indulging in meaty ideas for me. No time to. But now, sitting blind in the dark, I see that vegetarianism has never worked for me.

Not a yew. Not yew - I want to own this concept.

<Yes, learn what God, The Big Heavenly Stonyface, wants>

Then I can finally earn my way into heaven.

When age or inclement weather rot the yew's
innards, its central trunk sends down a new
organ within the moldering core to take up the
tasks of assimilation, aeration, and anchorage.
Thus, decay informs rebirth. The yew becomes
a hollow pregnant tree; a tree contained within
and surrounding itself; simultaneously
neoteric, vernal and ageless.

-Journal Entry, May 15, age 24

Chapter 12 – Surviving To Petition Again

Dawn's light and I peek out of my hiding place before I climb down. Tentatively we stretch, the light and I: light stretches the dusky veils of night in weird fits and starts while I mostly stretch my jaw. Eventually my arms join-in reaching over my head with palms flat and pushed towards the many-rooted ceiling. Sight is still more veiled than revealed as I relieve myself so aim is validated by the sound of urine hitting the blood creek outside my shelter, one foot on each side.

"As nighttime's mists regress," I sing-think, "it's probably time to dress." I'm feeling ... well, hmm ... I feel straighter this dawn. Drained and tired, but also I feel straighter, almost lined up. "Dress in clothes, breathe through nose. Arm in sleeve, but first hair goes." I drop the coiled hair in through my sleeve, wrist following right behind it. Hitting the ground seems to wake the hair up and it slowly lifts into the air and stretches taut. "Good morning, hair." I stretch my arms, too. "I see you are back to your proper length," I comment.

129

Off it meanders, billowing its non-attached end above the blood creek. Hurriedly I don the rest of my clothes. My slack belly hangs over my belt. Looks tacky, I think, but it's comfortable so I follow where the hair leads underneath a near-by generously-canopied tree. With a foot on either side of the urine-blood stream I follow the hair moving my arm this way and just so and we manage to stay in accord and untangled within the woven branches, perambulating through the leaves. We pause once for me to gather a handful of pain-relief-leaves and stuff them in my mouth.

During the brief pause, I notice two dark spots in the branches near me, directly above the blood creek. It's difficult to see in the pre-dawn so I step closer, gape and freeze. There, in the very beginnings of light, I see two birthling's outlines sitting, jumbled up, not moving – among the branches at waist level, near me. Are they dead?

I stand in the not-quite-dark, fingers fumbling covertly with the hair trying to recoil it, which it will not allow and its resistance shakes the branches, which I do not want. Failing that, I try to untangle myself. It's a convoluted process as the hair resists my efforts to get free of it. Finally, I manage to unwind my end of the hair from my wrist bone – literally, all the skin has worn off and I'm bare to bone. The hair wiggles itself free from my fingers and slithers down and winds itself around my ankle. Next time I fly, it will be upside down.

The other end of the stubborn hair is still wending its way through the tree towards the things-I-do-not-want-disturbed. Despite the small fuss, no monster twitches. As if they're waiting. As if they're staring at me.

I have to know - want to run; but have to know if they are staring, or dead, or going to grab at me and bite. I must understand this … *ammm* … situation. I crouch and sidle under the canopy. With one hand above my head dampening tree rustle and the other hand flat on the ground for support, I work my way towards the shadowed shapes. Thighs ache, squat walk. Down I crouch low to the ground. Almost slithering am I as I ease closer. No wiggle on their part. Closer - they're still. Am underneath the lumps, breath held; nothing grabs me. No one seems to be breathing. These are very tense moments. Not an eye do I see. Nothing is staring at me. Am past them, now. Still there is no movement. Am safe. Big sigh. I freeze. No, nothing. Am safe.

I swivel on heels to keep my face towards the little shapes and I ease back. Ease away. In case they sleep, I ease backwards quietly. But the hair jiggles the branches and tugs at my ankle. I must untangle myself from this damned shaft of protein.

"Hair," I twitch it twice. "Ssst. Let's go. Last chance. Ssst, ssst." I tug a little harder - almost a pull. "Fine," I whisper; "You want 'em, they're yours. Not me." I squat-walk backwards out from underneath the canopy, keeping the hair as taut as I can to slow it down. Determined bugger.

With my face as close to my ankle as possible, I battle the hair. Try to unwind it and lift the thing away from my flesh. It rewraps itself into impossible knots. I am as soundly caught as I was when I began. I grit my teeth in a ferocious growl of frustration and straighten and turn.

Facing me is a soldier. He has a sword pointed at my throat. "I'm going to kill you, beast," he claims as calm as rock and clear as crystal song.

Some of these tough little trees have outlasted religions.

-Journal Entry, May 15, age 24

Chapter 13 – Second Crown

My brain is dense. I can barely wade through the idea that I am not alone. Confused I glance down at my feet like they can peddle reason up to my brain. I note that I'm standing in blood and my feet are stained blood-red; and I note that I like the look even though it should be disgusting and I know that none of this makes any sense and that I'm in danger, but I can't bring my thoughts to order.

"There is a person standing in front of me." My sluggish brain runs through the important information again. "He is a soldier. He said he going to kill me. He thinks I am a monster." I struggle to speak. "I'm not what you think," I finally squeeze some words past my thick tongue and I rearrange my face from ferocious growl to a look of harmless sincerity. "I just look like, well, hell." I take a step back pressing against the tree twigs. "I'm a person, too."

His sword still covers me. He doesn't look convinced.

"I was wounded," I explain, pointing to my still-bleeding chest hole. "I may be dead or at least partially dead, which is why I look and smell so bad." Here I try a one-sided smile. He doesn't say a word but my mouth cannot seem to stop now that I've gotten it started. "I'm trying to get to the white light." This at least catches his attention.

Behind me, inside the canopy, all is silent. Now I know that the creatures are alive. They are so utterly quiescent, their presence weighs like a wet cloak against my back. I have never felt such focused stillness; waves of it beat against me. Although I have no desire to protect them, I am certainly not going to bring them to the swordsman's attention. He'd kill me for sure if he saw me dragging around monsters-on-a-string.

"How do you know about the white light?" He asks, a nice timber to his voice.

So, I keep talking about what seems to distract him, "I've been there before." And then, as that seems to impress him I add, "I've got family there."

He lowers the sword until it is only threatening my flabby belly. "Family?" He seems to taste the word. His sword drops another few inches. "You've met family in this place?"

"In the white light," I say watching the sword-point carefully.

"Do they love you?" He asks me and his sword inches up a spare notch.

I nod, "Of course they do. We're a very close family."

Up his sword arcs. All I can do is tuck my chin to my chest and close my eyes until the blow lands. But no blow lands. I simultaneously hear "Huhm" (a snide grunt from Soldier) and a singing metallic kiss (steel into sheath) and a burst of twigs rustling (the birthlings moving through the canopy towards me). I pretend-cough to cover the tree-commotion even though coughing is the worst sound-cover-up technique in existence. It never fools anyone.

Maybe this time it worked, I think; because when I steal a glance at Soldier, he seems to be contemplating his scabbard.

Emboldened, I move my arm to the small of my back and make a shushing motion inside the tree canopy. Soldier must not notice these beasts behind me. A tiny hand grabs onto mine. I cannot shake it off.

In profile, the soldier is a fine-looking young man; far too young to be a warrior but not babyish. He has a long jaw and prominent cheeks that blend smoothly into his nose. Nice pressed uniform - very clean, distinguished - he dresses well. Decorations dot his chest although he seems too young to have earned them. He's tall with long, stilt-like legs and wears an impressive authoritative air for one so thin. His belt buckle is made of gold. His fingers are manicured. And his shoes are of the highest quality. This is no frontline soldier. Finally he looks up from his scabbard. Did I mention he has only one eye?

"These people who love you, describe them to me," he demands.

I don't like his tone but he is well-dressed and seems a worthy youngster so I answer. "Mother, father, friends ... They're in the white light." I smile the answer, attempting to keep him engaged while subtly twisting and tugging on my hand to free it.

"The white light," he nods his head and murmurs as if he's heard of it before.

Now it is my attention that is captured. "Do you know where the white light can be found?" said quickly. I'm excited. "I'd be happy to introduce you to my family. Do you want to go to the white light together?" I'm trying to impress him; hoping he will show me the way; hoping he will decide to stay with me and I won't have to be alone in this death anymore.

"Are you inviting me?" He asks, too intently, all parts of his body leaning forward. His stare drills into me. "You want me?" He almost whines. He may be a tad bit desperate. I notice his teeth. He has more teeth than I have. And he doesn't seem to like me staring at his mouth so he closes it with a snap, his jaw line now sculpted from stone.

Ammm, that stone-jaw reminds me of someone … His hand twitches on the handle of his sword and I realize I am not out of danger yet. The canopy behind me moves and I pretend-cough again and shift my weight and babble about my family in the white light, but I don't answer his questions. He is presentable, yet unnerving.

The whole time I'm coughing and babbling, I'm trying to disengage the tiny clinger. Instead, a tiny foot with prehensile toes latches on to me. Now both hands are caught. Two small bodies press up against my back. Waves of need, need, need beat at me. Since this situation will not tolerate noise, I brush thumbs against a tiny arm and an almost imperceptible sigh of relief blows against my hand. Although bothersome to have the creatures clinging to me right now, it is better than them coming out into the open. I cup a fat little leg to keep it still.

Soldier watches me closely; takes in every slight motion. He's noticed I have not answered his questions and I get the feeling he's irritated. He may know there's something in the tree behind me. The muscles in his face twitch, then he smiles and I'm relieved. He's actually quite charismatic. I choose to label him friendly instead of dangerous and smile back.

"I'm familiar with the place where the light can be called," he says. "And I know how to call it." I forget all about the sword. I forget about little fat legs and knotted pubic hairs and being killed. I forget about everything except his words. This is the information I need. If my heart was turned on, it would be racing.

"Tell me!" I whisper leaning forward; well, I try to lean forward. The little brats won't let me go. They pull me back. His eye narrows and to distract him I cough again. He moves sideways, placing each foot down as if feeling the ground before settling his weight. It is a disconcerting movement - hitting a balanced stance with each step - graceful and panther-like. His narrowed eye tracks me like a bird of prey tracks its prey - head still; only the eye moves.

I smile nervously and shift my position to cut off his line of sight into the canopy. At the same time my stomach gives up a tremendous growl.

He looks down at my hanging gut for a long moment. For the first time during this encounter I am minutely uncomfortable in my body. As my feelings of discomfort rise, so do the little offenders tighten their grips on me.

"I can help you." He grins a slightly feral smile, noticing my discomfort. "And I believe you can help me." Then with a flourish he pulls a mango from behind his back and tosses it gently into the air over and over again. My mouth instantly fills with digestive juices. He holds out the mango while I try to get my hands free. His smile widens into a knowing grin. I'd just as soon he stopped smiling. I like him more when he's dour.

"I know exactly what you need to do to for us both," he says holding out the mango. I cannot grab the damn thing. So he shrugs, pulls it away and bites into that silky yellow skin almost without thinking. "I need one thing from you." His front scraper teeth strip away a large piece of peel, which he spits to the ground.

"Tell me." I drool and struggle gently to free my hands.

"Time is of the essence," he counsels. "Everyone here has a time table. Each person is different, though, so you never know how long you have."

"Wait," I interrupt him. "There are others here? What do you mean 'others'? What others? Why are they here? And come to think of it, exactly where are we?"

"Wish you had time to meet them - good people." Soldier says. "But there's too much to do in a short time. I've learned everything you need to know. Since your family is waiting in the white light, let's get going. Trust me."

I hesitate. It's probably not a good idea to tell Soldier my loving family already rejected me twice - sent me back. And what will he do when we get to the light and he understands we can't stay because of me. Then again, he might be acceptable. Maybe they only send me back. Maybe I do death wrong. Maybe I need more information. Maybe Soldier or these other people can tell me how to stay in heaven's cocoon once I get there. "Where are these people?" I ask. "Could you introduce me?"

"You don't need them," He clips out, irritation coloring every syllable. "I said, 'trust me'." Then Soldier calms his voice. "Focus," He commands and points at me with his mango-hand. "If you don't make it to the white light within your set number of days, you will never get out of here. You'll be too dead to leave and yet you will never die. There's an old woman ..." Sharp little teeth bite the fruit and he leans over so the juice runs down his chin and onto the ground rather than onto his clothes.

Hunger gnaws at me - for the white light, for company, for that damn mango. The waste of even one drop of that ripeness hurts on many levels. Finally I rip a hand free and wipe my own mouth in an unconscious gesture. If only I could capture some juice ... "I've seen her, the old woman," I jabber. "The one with torch eyes, I've talked with her."

"You talked with her?" He straightens up. "What did she say to you?" He glares at me and like an idiot I long for the feral smile again. He looks ready to kill me again.

"I, I, I couldn't understand a word she said." And watch his face slide into approval. Then in response to his previous statement I worry, "I may have already been here too many days. I'm not sure how long it's been. I haven't been counting." And that stops me. For a moment I contemplated my startling statement. I haven't been counting the days. Other than the number of times I coiled the hair, I haven't been counting anything – not for a long time. This is important but I don't have time to figure it out because Soldier leans over and slices his teeth into juicy flesh again. We both moan, him with pleasure, me with longing.

I raise my chin and don't even realize I'm licking my lips. He smirks with eyes focused on the canopy behind me. Between bites he talks. "We'll have to hurry, then, won't we?" *Bite, dribble, lick.* "Let's start with what I want. I need you to get something for me." *Bite, lick, dribble.* "The old hag, the wild one that doesn't make any sense, she lives around here and she has something that belongs to me. Something very important." He rips into the mango, eye now looking past the canopy, off into the distance. Juice dribbles down his chin. I lick my lips. There is a pause as I digest what he said.

The old woman has something of importance to him. "Your eye?" I finally gasp out. "I'm sorry."

He looks at me with a snarl and pitches the half-eaten mango among the trees so far away I can't hear it land.

"I only ask," I stammer, "because she tried to take one of mine." The tiny grips tighten on my still-caught-hand.

He glares at me and then, after too long a pause, he pulls himself together. I think he's a bit unstable, this formative soldier, on edge or maybe suffering from a stress disorder. Definitely he's dangerous. "Yes, she has my eye." he rasps.

I blink my own eyes with a silent prayer of thanks. I was cursing the wild hair earlier this morning, but now am grateful to it once again for getting me out of there when my eye was at stake. My stomach growls again and he grins.

"Oh," he says charmingly with a shrug. "There's a bowl of fruit in the white light. I can show you where." Then seriously he continues, "But first, it's true. That old biddy has my eye and I do intend to retrieve it. But there is something else I want more than my eye. She has a locket that belongs to me."

"Your mother's locket?" I gasp. "She has my mother's locket, too."

He stares into me. It's unnerving. "*Your* mother's locket," he spits the words at me. I've offended him and I'm not sure how. Then he gets himself under control and continues with his previous thought, "My eye is important, but of the two, the locket is more important to me."

I am impressed with his sentimentality. Although I love my mother, if I have to choose, I will take my eye over a locket. I wonder if he is dead, too, or has given birth in this forest. His stomach isn't stretched out. He doesn't have any noticeable wounds on him. He's definitely not bleeding like I am; and he's not rotten. But he has met the old woman and she took his eye and she has his mother's locket like she has mine. "What are you doing here in this third death of mine?" I want to ask him, but decide it's safer not to.

"Once I have the locket and my eye, which you will get for me," he nods his chin towards me; "I can help you get to the white light place and together we can call it. Do this one thing for me and all your problems will be solved."

Suddenly, I don't care about whether he is dangerous or not. Oh, how badly I want his words to be true. I am tired of being in the dark, I think. And I'm so confused. I want this death to be predictable and orderly. I'm desperate for a commander to tell me how to achieve my goal. I believe him. I believe he knows more than me. I want the protection of his sword rather than the point of it. Plus, my heart is lonely. Although he is young and touchy, he seems like he could be a suitable companion in this tough passage.

And I would be an honorable companion, I declare silently. I can work hard, especially if it earns me the right to go to the death I love. I'll do the dirty work, he can stay clean. I'll perform the tough work, he can command. As long as I get to the place that will get me out of this rocky mixed-up mess.

"We have to do it right away," he adds urgently as I am thinking things through. "There is no time to waste or it will be too late for you. I'll tell you where the old biddy is. Here's my sword." He unsheathes it and holds the handle out to me, fingers gripping the flat portion of blade. He's strong. The sword is heavy and under his cuffs I see his forearm muscles play to keep the sword balanced. "Kill her quickly." He commands. "Get my locket and don't forget the eye."

I look from sword handle to face in confusion. My hand is already moving to grip the sword, so used am I to obeying orders. I frown. "Kill her? I won't have to kill her." I envision wrestling the locket from her old bent hands. It feels wrong to do even that much.

He snarls at my hesitation and commands me, "We have a ways to go. Hurry." He wiggles the handle towards me. When I still hesitate, he says, "I know where food is. I know exactly how to get what you want."

It sounds good, but I don't take the sword. Instead, I eye him consideringly. He looks prepared. He has a plan. Everything is laid out for me to follow. Following is something I feel confident doing. I will go with him I decide. But I will not kill the tiny old woman. I am not so desperate as that. I will draw this line. "I'll get the locket," I tell him. "You can count on me. And I won't forget about your eye. But I won't kill her. Absolutely not."

"You must," he reasons. "We need her skin to call the light."

*And although the trees appear innocuously
pretty, they are deadly trees.*

-Journal Entry, May 15, age 24

Chapter 14 – Blind as Faith, At Last

How long I stood staring at the soldier I haven't a clue. I know neither of us moved until my eyes went dry and I blinked. I hiccup in a breath and refocus my eyes on his sword as I flutter my head side to side, tiny vibrations.

"Tst, tsst, tsst. Don't say no," he jiggles the handle towards me again.

I cannot kill the old woman, I state silently. But does that mean I will not be able to call the white light? Beneath the calm of shock I must be quite agitated because the monsters begin to jostle each other, and therefore me. It feels like they are fighting for the right to climb up my arm.

The soldier narrows his eye and his smile looks pointy for a moment. I've seen that look somewhere else before …

Suddenly sharp little milk teeth deliberately pierce through the webbing between my middle and index fingers. I vault into the air and let out a blood curdling yelp. I must have performed a three foot vertical leap.

143

The little biter falls out of the canopy next to me, dangling by the wild pubic hair wrapped around his tiny fat leg. I sense movement and out of my periphery vision; see the young soldier flipping his sword end-over until the handle is snugged into his capable hand. My blood-curdling shriek is echoed by the upside down idiot-baby staring at the soldier and by the soldier staring at both of us. The second baby is screaming, too, as it climbs my back.

Soldier lunges towards me and before I can gather my wits to react there is an explosion between the blade and me. The little savages squeal and tumble out of the tree and away from me. The hair loops around my neck, as well as my ankle, and pulls me back and off-balance. I'm blinded and assume the soldier is too, because I feel his sword thwat through the buttons of my shirt. He missed the monsters and hit me by mistake. I stumble back into the canopy, tangled in the tree, tangled in the hair, half sitting, half falling backwards, awkward and off balance and unable to right myself because the monsters begin crawling up into my lap, yapping and snapping at each other and pulling on me as they vie with each other to be held. They are trembling, truly scared and though they are uncouth and shrill, I can not reject them completely. I am scared, too, and their toasty little hideous bodies warm me. My hands are full.

"Stop!" I command the soldier at high volume; breathing hard. Through the blinding light and smoke I hear Soldier's blustering threats and his sword swishes. But his voice is further away so I no longer fear for my unprotected legs.

I smell loamy soil and realize the old woman is near before I hear her or see her. When Grama Ans roars at the soldier, "*Post, Caroused Thievery! Who dents in!*" I expect the wee yammering monsters in my lap to cringe and shake at her bellowing, but although the old woman's tone is harsh and rusty, the creatures in my lap seem to relax. I, however, tense up. I'm glad she never spoke to me that way.

Soldier hollers back at the crone, his voice mean-spirited and ugly. "You stupid old cow, you, you nasty swinging utter, you have no right to interfere in this. Haven't you done enough damage? You crossed the line, bitch. I'm going to cut you into fluttering pieces."

She responds with, "*Gaunt man framer of lies he renews thee. Oh how so scatted agape a bend* you *chimere fetish,*" which inflames him even more. I didn't think that was possible. I guess he thought she would be scared by his threat.

He shouts a warning to me, "Don't do anything that cockroach says or you'll never get out of here. She is responsible for everything happening to you. She's trying to control you. Do you want to spend eternity here, gnawing on your tongue in agony?" And so it continues, a venomous stream of unending vitriol. Right then, when I am unable to see his well-pressed image, he reminds me a lot of Rob.

Movement creates a breeze which clears the smoke enough that I can make out a few details of the scene before me. Grama Ans paces side to side in front of me. The soldier's eye patch stark black against his bloodless face is an easy marker. He backs away from Grama Ans. With each step his stance is wide and his weight balanced equally on the balls of each foot. His sword is held aloft, over his back and shoulder. It's a very dramatic pose.

"Give me that eye," he growls to the old woman then glances at me to check that I am watching him. "It's mine," he snarls. And in Grama Ans' hand there is indeed an eye staring up at her leathery old face – same color as his eye, the shape is hard to tell out of the head.

He talks roughly to his petite opponent. "There's no dignity in you. Where's your sense? Put some clothes on, old hag. No one wants to see your ugly old wrinkled buttocks … " Although the scene unfolding in front of me is compelling, I am taken back in time for just a moment.

When he said, "Put some clothes on, old hag." I also hear, "… and where are your shoes, child? Really, Russell, I can't believe you allowed this. I'm going to have to insist that you keep away from my

145

grandchild since neither one of you can behave. If you value your job...
You hear me on this!"

When Soldier rasps out, "... No one wants to see your ugly old
wrinkled buttocks, Raisin ... " I also hear, "... Get out of the pond. Put
your shoes on, child. Now! No one wants to look at your ugly wrinkled
toes. There is a proper way to behave and this is not it."

Lost in memories, Soldier's voice merges with memories of
condemnation rasped at me - years of it. "Behave better, Pet." "You
must earn this." "no," "nooo," "No!" "You're wrong." "Not like that!"
My chest feels heavy and sunken-in just like it used to feel.

In life I collapsed under the constant pressure of demeaning
looks and harsh words so my curiosity stirs when I finally notice
Grama Ans is sparking back at him. She is completely unaffected by
Soldier's brutal denouncements. She responds calmly, saying to the
dirtyMouth, "*Unsaved bifurcated flouting. Hating deaf ego help in root
try you yes.*" She motions for me to get out of the tree and stand behind
her.

Seeing her motion, Soldier orders, "Get over to me. I'll protect
you from her. Move your butt, you fool." He doesn't put down his
sword and his voice is Rob-harsh. "And those, those, things - get rid of
those disgusting things. They're her demons. They'll drag you down.
She'll use them to invade you. They'll undermine your progress and
then when you finally strike back, she'll plead, 'Please, believe me; I'm
on your side,' but she is a pathetic, sniveling, sneaky cockroach. Get
away from her."

The things in my lap squeak and bury their heads against my
stomach.

I'm highly undecided what to do. My stomach hurts. I look
down to see my hanging gut flayed open. His sword must have sliced
me open instead of the upside down critter. Maybe it was an accident or
maybe he's not as trustworthy as I assigned. I feel a tug and a sharp
pain. One of the brutes is trying to crawl inside me and is chewing on

… I don't know what … an intestine? I haul myself out of the tree dumping the little beasts in a heap at my feet.

The hair pushes behind my back to help me upright and to regain my balance. Oh, nice. Where the hell was this helpful hair when I was getting gutted by a sword?

I feel off-center and irritable again as I brush the monsters away from me with my feet. That doesn't stop them, though. The lure of body parts spilling from my splayed stomach is much too attractive for them to behave themselves even in this tenuous situation. I use both hands to keep my guts inside. The bloody beasts nip at my ankles and lap at the blood that always pools around my feet, but I am paying most attention to the scene in front of me. Was the soldier trying to protect me or hurt me? Did the old woman just save me or cause this accident? I am wary now and alert to the combatant's positions.

"Give me what's mine!" The soldier screams at Grama Ans all sense of decorum gone.

Torch eyes ablaze, Grama Ans lobs the eye in her hand to the ground in front of him and it explodes in another fire bomb of light and smoke. He screams with rage then yells, "You miserable, underhanded, two-faced, offal-eating insect. Look at you. You're different than us. She is, you know." This last sentence was directed to me. "She is genetically different from us. I have now conclusively demonstrated that she'll do what ever is necessary to penetrate us if we let her. She'll take every good thing that either one of us ever developed. She's a dead rat. She wants the white light for herself."

The old woman paces in front of him, creating a protective wall so he cannot get to me. I don't think he is trying to anyway so it may be a moot point. She engages him forcefully but without anger while he rants on and on. Occasionally she stalks towards him and he backs away in his graceful, cat-like, fighting movement - always away from Grama Ans.

147

Among that hornet's nest of sounds from Soldier's mouth he orders me to get out of here, to run away. Of course I can't because the monsters are still attached to me, all tangled up in the hair, and my guts would all fall out if I tried; but he doesn't know that because he takes off running himself, threatening the old dame as he goes. Did he think she would follow him and I would be safe? Maybe he believed I was right behind him. Or maybe he was only concerned for his own hide. In any case, Grama Ans hobbles after him a short distance then lets him go with a wave of her hand and makes her slow wheezing way back to me.

"A wormy dna trailed him until he lordly hew," she tells me. *"A wicked brewers parenthood not kinship unto a dense* you. *Tub,* you *thaw knot,* don't you?" It's mostly nonsense to me, as always. To tell the truth, now that the soldier is gone, I'm paying full attention to managing my guts and fighting the little imps, trying to keep my balance and trying not to look at the body parts in my arms. I'm also figuring out how I feel about what just happened. There are no resources to spare for her verbal nonsense.

The crone taps on my arm a few times, but still I ignore her. I am trying to figure out how I feel about seeing Grama Ans again. She stops talking and just stands next to me. I feel her gaze on me but am not ready to face her. I battle with the beasties for long minutes, making no progress nor losing any ground. Actually, I'm marking time until I figure out what I'm going to do. Grama Ans huffs once, reaches up, grabs my ear, pulls it down, and bites it. That gets my attention.

"Loup yaw yow attention *nil, coy lauras?"* She asks me.

I look her over. Actually, she doesn't look as bad as I remembered her or maybe I've degraded so much in comparison she looks a lot less offensive to me. Once again, she smells better than I do. "Attention?" I ask her, having recognized that word, at least. "Yes, you have my attention."

There I stand nearly naked to her scrutiny. My clothes, sliced down the middle, are falling off me. My stomach is laid open. I'm bruised, bleeding, tangled up with monsters who are misbehaving, of course. I make a pretty pathetic picture right now. Heat rises from my chest to my cheeks. But although I stand before her, vulnerable to the core, she looks at me with delight as she has done since we first met. It disarms me. I could get addicted to that lack of condemnation on her face.

"Good." She states quite clearly. Then she focuses on the little beasts … or the hair.

"You *deter beaten* okay?" She asks with a frown of concern down towards my feet.

The little babies whimper persistent cries of distress while the hair undulates in waves all along its length.

"Be careful, they bite," I caution her, one hand motioning her away. Now that I'm not found wanting, I find I want a little more attention for myself. "Settle down," I command the baby-beasts roughly. She looks at me, me, me. Ah, that's better. "Quit biting me. I don't like it." During this last bit my head is pointed at the birthlings but I'm hoping she realizes the words apply equally to her.

"*Bet melt he,*" she berates me. "They have *unblessed gene props - goon lot. That woeful brainpan friction doer* you *keep goat extinct* them *a heartless ok time sits on a known fate emit.*"

I glance at her, recognizing the tone if not most of the words. I wonder what my face expressed because her stern aspect melts away and she regards me gently once again. Then she smoothes my arm and stoops to gather bits of sliced up clothes. I am so grateful for the reprieve I follow her, not even complaining about the ankle bites I receive on the way as I drag the tangled fiends and hair with my every other step.

We make our way over to an urn sitting on the ground in the dim light. I never saw that urn before. Did she carry it with her? It's almost as big as she. Grama Ans keeps her eye-light turned from it so

149

the design is hard to discern. She motions for me to settle on the ground. She sits, too, her back propped against the urn. Both monsters gather around her, look up at her.

I feel comfortable on the ground, have always loved it. I miss sitting rooted to the earth. She appears as comfortable as I feel. Not many people enjoy the dirt. She delights me right now but with our history, who knows how long that will last?

Plunk! She holds up a new pubic hair stretched tight between her two hands. My eyes are on that hair so I don't notice where she gets the needle; but a needle she has, stuck between her lips. Lights from her eyes focus on my body; everything else rapidly falls into darkness. Much to my surprise, the little horrors are quiet around her as she asks the new hair to go through the eye of the needle and it does, then lays limp. She scoots closer to me and pinches my gaping skin closed. She intends to sew me closed. The beasts chew on her leg bones and rub themselves against her leathery skin and stare at her adoringly. But they don't fight with each other or go for my guts. I could use some of the calming know-how that she's got, I think.

I end up holding my stomach closed while she stitches. Then, when the angle is wrong for her, we trade jobs, working well together like we've done the same task for generations – each of us doing what the other one needs at just the right time. It's satisfying. I pull the thread tight so my belly is puckered and rippled but in-tight instead of sagging down towards my knees. She ties me off.

We have not said a thing to each other, yet I'm as comfortable as bare feet on a warm day.

Just so, we continue to sit in silence. Only her fingers move. She teases the original wild pubic hair wrapped around my ankle. About the time I realize Grama Ans is trying to unwind the hair from me, the hair realizes what she's doing and goes into spasms. It's quite a show, Grama Ans untangling the hair from the baby-beasts and me. The hair is recalcitrant, of course, and she has to fight it each step of the way. She's deadpanned but I know she is playing a game. And she's funny.

Grama Ans implores the hair to behave itself. She demands it straighten so it curls. She begs it to let go so it tightens. Everything she asks of it, hair does the opposite. She lunges on the hair and rides it like a bronco. She loops it around her neck and it playfully chokes her. She tells it off and laughs and weaves it into knots. They seem evenly matched.

The hair is wended through the firstborn creature. It traverses in the mouth and out the nose. She has to hold the creature on the ground with her feet and pull on the hair while both of them resist her. It must have tickled as it traversed the sensitive areas because the little beast giggles and gags and makes twisted faces. They are, all of them, hilarious.

I am relaxed when I finally catch my breath. The little stinkers, however, are hepped up from the play and wrestle with each other bumping into us.

She stands up, pulls something out of the urn, spins, and plops back down, gently depositing someone between us. It's my last born monster. "Where'd you get that?" I ask her.

"*When I rot hero seethe*?" She asks me pointing to the two wrestling bodies and then gesturing to the one limp one plopped beside her. "Warped polyhedron, you *behold us sieved-ends*. Did your *deprave doer unroot, True Stagnated Coward*? *He aped nascent?*"

She called me a Warped polyhedron. "Is that supposed to make sense?" She frowns her terrible frown, but I have no response to her questions and shrug.

"You *sorrower fan. Miracle* your fragments," she insists but I'm watching the beasts play. Grama Ans stands up and moves away from us. Instantly the creatures start misbehaving. Now I ignore them all.

151

She shakes her head in exasperation and reaches into the urn. She removes a small leather bag with three ornate keys tied around the outside. The keys are magnificent, jeweled, breath-catching. I don't get a chance to see them clearly because when Grama Ans catches me eyeing her keys she turns her shoulder towards me blocking them from view. I lower my eyes ashamed. The last time I wanted something of hers, I roughed her up and took it. I even considered doing it to her again to get the soldier's locket. But now, face-to-shunning-shoulder with her, I don't want her thinking I'm that kind of person.

She hands the keys to the monsters and I feel a mush of emotions: shame, guilt, envy, frustration, self-pity and gratitude. The gratitude rises after I realize fighting-over-the-keys will keep the ugly things occupied while she pays attention to me. She ties the bag to the short hairs at the nape of her neck and lets her hair drop over it. I'll bet the soldier's locket is in there, my Momma's locket, too. Maybe I can talk her out of them.

She snaps her teeth to get my attention and she gets it immediately. I find I am developing an aversion to snapping teeth. Grama Ans gestures me out of the remains of my tattered clothes. She motions for the original pubic hair to thread itself through the needle, and sensing, I guess, that play time is over, the hair complies. Grama Ans sews my clothing into a large bag – a bag with a pubic hair drawstring. When the bag is complete, the drawstring wraps itself around my wrist and floats behind me at shoulder length. The bag may be useful if I ever find food, but I sigh as it wraps itself around my wrist again. It is a stubborn and ornery hair - a hair with its own agenda. I have misgivings about our continued relationship.

Grama Ans snaps her teeth at me again and stares with serious attention. 'It's time for a lecture; pay attention,' that look announces. I straighten up. Grama Ans first motions to the two baby-beasts playing, then to the one lying between us. She cradles her arms like a mother-with-child. Then she points at my stomach with her crooked boney old finger and shapes a big round belly with her hands.

"I know they came out of me," I growl. "So what's your point?" I'm starting to get irritated with her, just like I knew I would given enough time.

She grabs the closest creature, the apathetic one, the only one not fighting for the keys. Grama Ans carefully presses it up against my neck and scapula, smashing us together. I reach to take it; she slaps my hands down, squeezing us together again and again.

"What?" I ask, irritated with her. "What do you want me to do?" Then I remember my dream in the upside down forest. "You don't … no! You aren't asking me to nurse it, are you? Because I can't. I absolutely will not." I remember what happened in that dream. "You're out of your mind," I raise my voice as I brush the thing away from me.

Grama Ans falls to her knees facing me, our eyes level.

"Get that away," I insist. "I have nothing to feed it. Stop pushing it at me."

But she persists, smashing the spiritless little revolting thing into my shoulder holding it forcefully against me. It squirms in protest. "You *at here* same," she repeats over and over, "*resonate tap. I in tots* your baby. You *at here* same."

I twist my upper body away from her. Reject the pairing. "It's hideous and wrong," I assert.

The baby at my shoulder bites me. Hard.

Grama Ans pushes the beast into my hands.

She is staring at me with a look I've seen before – a penetrating, piercing look. It is the look of someone taking the time to really see me, which makes me uncomfortable. I extend my arms to hold the thing facing outwards, away from me. "It's their fault, you know." I tell her. "The soldier sliced me open because he saw them. He knew they were wrong and because they were with me, he got scared and cut me." She looks disappointed in me. I slow down, but feel even more defensive. "Can't say that I blame him. Look at them." I jiggle the apathetic monster. As if we practiced the timing, the wrestling firstborn beast removes the golden key ring from its mouth and burps. "There is no way I'm bringing them to the white light with me. They'll just get me into more trouble." Well, that ought to be clear enough.

Grama Ans responds with great seriousness, "*Whats thy teat?*"

Even though I should be used to her non sequiturs, I'm thrown off guard by the question. What asinine teat is she talking about, I think testily. My patience races to its end. "I can't understand your folderol," I dismiss her and lay the creature down so I can fuss with the drawstring at my wrist.

.

Grama Ans retorts just as smartly, "*Fox must beseech a lie* choice for those mired *sworn sleepiness. Each anal ambition not salute. Delete the foe a siren. Among love. Tears want. Proclaim sensibility* over your circumstance. Don't seep yourself *a lenient ad irk my root* others wrong. You *rage worn.* Untwist yourself."

Even though I am irritated at her I lean forward, eyes blinking, trying to absorb her words. I almost got that. I almost, almost understood her - but not quite. I sigh and cluck and one side of my mouth stretches up and back and I shake my head 'no'.

Grama Ans sighs, too. And stares at me. She picks up the apathetic creature and puts it in my hands again. Then she pantomimes a big belly. She opens the belly like a door and pulls out an object. 'Oh, nice,' she pantomimes.

"What is it?" I ask.

She pantomimes a box.

"The object is a box?" I ask.

She pats the imaginary box approvingly and looks over at me significantly. "Did you get that, dunderhead," the look says.

"A box?" I ask her. "Pretty box, nice box."

Grama Ans smiles at me with delight. I'm happy again. Now we're getting somewhere.

She pantomimes opening the box lid and with a flourish pulls out an invisible something pinched between thumb and forefinger. She locks eyes with me then motions with the three remaining fingers to the monster in my arms. Then she acts like it is ugly, raising both hands up in front of her and wrinkling her nose in disgust.

"Yes," I agree with her, "that's what I've been saying. It's wrong."

She digs into the imaginary box again, another flourish, another imaginary something pinched between thumb and forefinger. This time she points to the monsters dog-piled up between us. Eyes locked with mine she continues her theatrical message. This second air-flourish she cradles and rocks and strokes then lays the pretend baby down to the side of her and then nods her head at me. This look hollers, "Did you get it?"

"That one, the imaginary one at your side, that one is pretty." I interpret. She nods, eyebrows arched, excited. "But mine are ugly," I repudiate.

She leans away with a huff and raises her hands. "No," she barks, each word distinct. "No, don't *trice jet*." Then Grama Ans plucks the apathetic beast out of my arms and strokes it and bends her face towards it while eyeing me. 'Ah, now' she pantomimes 'this one is pretty, too.'

Now I huff at her.

"Fruit-less rev-er-ie," she chants, her voice like a drum, gaining strength in my head. My eyes hook onto her mouth. I'm seized. In a moment my body melts, heavy and mellow. Vision softens; I stare, but not at any one thing. Attention is snared. Half-way between trance and attentiveness, I understand the beat if not the words. Warm. My cheeks are warm. My mouth drops open and my eyes feel like pushing out. Penetrated. Caught am I in her rhythm.

"Fruit-less rev-er-ie's

cast off

and that

con-jures-space

and thus

they came

Stim-u-la-ted.

They came -

came forth

quest-ing.

Re-cup-er-a-tion-sought.

Do you think

you can re-cover

what you will

not see, my sweet?

Huh, not me!

156

Mus-ter you must

the cour-age

to see them.

Mus-ter you must

the cour-age

to know them.

Mus-ter you must

the cour-age

to want them.

"Wow," I think.

"Did I just

un-der-stand?"

And she says, "Mus-ter you must

the cour-age

to see them …"

I'm not sure how many times she said that last part before I shake my head and un-trance myself. I can't quite hang on to the words. Her meaning fleeing from me like it's scared. So, disappointed I growl, "I don't know what you're getting at." Then to reclaim some control I go further than I want to - putting myself at odds with her. "That monster, it still looks wrong to me," I say. Eyes unblinking we clash wills. It's all bravado on my part so I drop my gaze first.

The silence is strained like jelly through cheesecloth - pressure provided by her. I'm merely miserable.

Finally I offer Grama Ans, "Well, they don't bite you." In admitting that one, tiny redeeming factor, I also admit some validity to myself. "Whatever these things are, Grama Ans," I continue, "they behave themselves around you." I feel I'm being generous but she just sits there staring at me with torch eyes bright with expectation. Feeling slightly bratty, I mutter under my breath, "So you take them," and I frown.

She gives up on me for a while and pays attention to the wee savages. She handles them carefully, playing snuggly-warm with them. Somehow it disturbs me to see their hideous faces slacken into drooling pleasure. To distract myself and reclaim some of her attention for myself, I fill the air with words, telling her how awful everything has been since I last saw her. She grunts and nods and even that little bit of off-hand attention makes me feel better, like someone cares. I settle back on my arms, acting as slack-faced and drooling with pleasure as the little beasts.

Between grunts to me and playing with the beasts, she picks up small sticks. I'm trying to figure out why she's fussing with the sticks. She examines each one, sniffs it, bites it, pinches it, and then stacks it into a little pile that gets quite large. She rearranges it, but it's no sculpture. It's still just a pile of twigs. Even though we've only met twice I already know it's unlike her to fuss. She doesn't waste motion.

Calmness is something I notice and in her presence I too have been twitch-free. This is unusual. All of The Family is rampant with insistent motions. We are a family of jerks and vellications - repetitive lip rubbing and foot circling and fingertip tapping fingertip - and counting. One aunt must step twelve times before passing through a door (half-steps, circles and sliders are permissible, or so I'm told). Grandma must always cross her ankles after she sits. If she forgets, she must re-stand and re-sit again two times (one to erase the mistake and one to replace it). We are a family of obsessive fussers, of motion wasters, of re-arrangers. On the other hand, Grama Ans has an innate

158

stillness - is poetry with motion. I'm unusually serene in her presence and value that. I wonder what she's thinking about that causes these ripples of movement in her. Am I distressing her?

At least the little ones are quiet, entranced by her movement. For that, I'm grateful.

She reaches over the babies and hauls the urn over their heads and sets it next to the pile of sticks. Strong that old biddy is. Then she takes out her eye. I scoot back. I hope she's not going to try and grab mine again.

Instead, she holds the eye over the pile of sticks. Her eye is a blazing torch. It stares at her, alive even out of the head and ferocious. She gives her eye a gentle squeeze and shakes it. Embers fall from her hand. Smoke curls up. She leans over - she really is quite flexible - and whispers into smoke, blowing it downward, gentle puffy smidgens of air onto glowing embers. They expand, redden, and crackle into flame.

Now the stick rearranging makes sense to me. She was making a fire not fussing with the damn sticks. I didn't know; I've never seen a fire built before. Fires have always been there before I realized I needed one.

~

Grandmother enters the mansion with stamping feet and shaking head to get the snow off. I'm directly behind her holding onto her long coat for balance as I take my boots off. We had a fine time on our walk.

"Oh, child. I'm chilled to the bone."

"Your cheeks are pretty; red like ripe tomatoes."

"Thank you, dear." Her voice is sardonic and confused I look up at her. She examines me. "That's right," she gentles both her eyes and her voice, "you love tomatoes."

I smile and nod, happy again.

Our butler intones. "We've built a large fire in the drawing room, Ma'am. The room is quite warm."

"Superb, my good man, superb." Grandma steps out at a lively pace, our butler has to scurry in quite an undignified manner to get to the door before she does. I snicker to myself. Grandma sinks down onto the hearth and holds her hands out to the fire. My-Good-Man barely gets a pillow under her rump before it hits the hearth. She must be freezing to sit without a thought to dirt - and on a hearth; and she forgot to cross her ankles. There is no fussing before the fire, no fretting. It's a good day.

She leans as close to the flame as she can get and blows on her hands to boot. The fire flares up when the extra air hits it and with a cry Grandma falls backwards knocking me to the floor.

I throw my arms around her to cushion her fall and rub my cheeks in her hair. I adore this woman. Right now I feel close to her and am filled with love. My laugh tints the air. I hug her tightly. She looks at me and smiles even as tears fill her eyes.

~

It never dawned on me that Grama Ans was messing with sticks to build a fire. Relief trickles as I realize how much I value her lack of fussiness. A feeling rises in me, a feeling of connection. I sit on my hands to stop myself from hugging this old woman lit by firelight, her eyes full of appreciation.

Now that the fire is burning, light casts a larger circle and I can see the urn quite well. The urn is covered with ... well I'd like to say erotic depictions, but they look obscene to me. I like them. Here I sit naked. Grama Ans is naked. All of the birthlings are naked. Somehow all of this naughtiness strikes me funny. Grama Ans spits into the urn, then tilts it and rolls it toward the fire. There's a lot of something rolling around inside that urn.

"Help stumpy," She tells me, *"Teach net do veneer yes sin."*

I sniff, hoping it's food rolling around inside the pot. My nose detects nothing but the ugly creatures are getting very excited so I am hopeful. She snaps her teeth to gather my wandering attention then adds, *"Aptly dominant storm,* shed your *lately forgets.* If you *mute halved,* they *roomful wind* you."

"What?"

The little monsters, greedy to the core, scramble and bite and fight to get to the urn. Grama Ans thinks they are funny. Nevertheless, they stay back from the fire when she says so. Then she dumps the urn over and the dirt is warmed by a big pile of not-quite-soft rice. The creatures hum and vibrate with excitement but don't eat until she hands them each a mouthful. Although I hint at my hunger, I get nothing. They eat every grain of rice – the birthlings and she. I am disappointed, but try to be a polite.

She does talk to me as she feeds each little one. When they finish eating Grama Ans pats each in turn and lays them down to sleep. The two with eyes (firstborn and apathetic last born) stare at her with an odd ugly innocence. They stare unblinking, fighting their heavy lids until they are asleep. The blind second-born gropes for the hairbag to rub between fingers and thumb in a slow circular motion - a physical mantra. It seems the hair bag is soothing. Watching those fingers move even settles my gut. The tiny second-born drifts off to sleep, too.

Grama Ans gently pries her keys from the firstborn's grip and returns her keys to her pouch. She stares at me as she does this and I know she is deciding whether to trust me or not. I determined then and there I will not take anything from her again that she does not offer first – even if it means I have to find another way to get out of here.

She motions me to hand her the clothes-sewn-into-a-bag-with-drawstring and I willingly hand it over to her. She gently tucks each little beast inside the bag, kissing hands and feet and faces first. They grunt and snortle. Then she ties the bag shut and hands me the drawstring. I guess she wants me to take the fat-bellied baby-beasts with me. I don't want to. I'm not naturally good with them like she is and I'm not interested in learning those skills. I'd rather she keep them and this is what I motion to her but she is relentless and eventually I take the hair-string. If I must take them, inside a bag is the best solution. I put it behind me and lean against it.

We sit for a long time staring into the fire. We bake and mellow and drift into comfortable companionship, which is water for my parched soul. Right now, I don't want anything else. Beneath my back, soft snores rise and fall. I feel like snoring myself. She shifts her weight as if getting ready to stand.

"Don't leave," I blurt, "please. I'm lonely."

She smiles at me. "You're not *lacey bluenose* you *an areole*. You're *lacey bluenose* you *allowed defiles. Lyon* you can fix it, *Heard Tear*." She speaks so tenderly it wrenches me.

I reach up and scratch the back of my head hesitating before putting my request into words. "Do you have to go? Could you stay with me for a while?" Dispassionate was the tone I was striving for. I'm disconcerted to hear it come out of my mouth like a whine.

"You already know *whatnot sin equates the rot*," she croons to me. "*Here I snit it* your newly sewn *tug. Cues oxen* for hiding. Ontogenesis is *anorexia rebel skene*. Nor can change be placated *battery yen. Ether* is no *formable writhing root*."

I'm bitterly disappointed. Even though I didn't understand all she said, I know in my gut she isn't going to stay with me. This ugly death is probably something I am supposed to do myself. "I have to go alone?" I grizzle. "What about the other people? I'll find them. I'll go with them."

She looks alarmed. "*Daresay gore then out* you." Grama Ans points to the bag and to me; to the bag and to me. "You're *snideArchfiends; two tall hint* be *bevy sold kerosene sight.*" She makes a face at me.

"I'm not taking them." I insist. She hugs herself and points to the bag and to me. "No," say I. She pantomimes a mounded belly, oh no, not this whole spiel again. Irritation rises in my thudless heart and bitterly I ask her for the two lockets.

"No." she states unequivocally. Well, that at least was clear enough. She pantomimes an offer to trade my eye for hers, though.

"Plus the lockets?" I ask. I am actually willing to consider it if it gets me "home".

"No, *hee jute sty,*" Grama Ans resists. "*Ether* is *on thee* …"

I put up a hand in protest, interrupting her discourse. "Ether is on thee?" I mimic her and question her all at once. "You know, we're not sprouting on the same twig here."

Grama Ans closes her eyes on a sigh as if in pain. Boney hands cover torch eyes and after a pause rub all over her face. I recognize that motion. She's trying to comfort herself by rubbing her face. I'm transported back in time when I sat in my lonely, grieving corner rubbing my face in a vain attempt to bring Da's memory closer. It moves me, her face rubbing.

I lean into the space between us and take her hands from her face so I can rub my forehead against hers. We brush back and forth, rotting flesh against old leather, offering each other comfort and caring. She looks at me eye-to-eye compassion shining in her milky orbs as brightly as light ever shone. Her hands cup my face gently. How could I have ever have mocked those hands or fled from those gentle twisted fingers? She feeds her purposefulness into me - kindness flowing into my chin and cheeks as her rusty voice slows to a crawl. I know she is trying to tell me something. I can hear clearly yet understand next to nothing. I can tell she aches for me. I don't want to cause her pain. I long to perform for her, not to earn love or approval, but because I trust this woman. But there is nothing I can do. I can not take the filters from my ears. Lord, I try to.

"*Enclose stilly; ether* is *on thee eight whirl.*" Tears of compassion dim the flames in her eyes. Each word is enunciated clearly; hands gently cup my face. "*Thousand lesser critics sick, wee stone,* you *the Christ ego trims thrusting wrath* you *pomade Utah.* Do not *upheave runes, anew hooded. Sustainer dupe* yourself - *near* yourself - *need fond tie to a vital haven* you *sin it* own time." Then she draws back an inch so she can see more of my face.

I take her hands from my cheeks and cradle them in my own gently massaging them. "I know it's important, but I don't understand. I am truly sorry." I don't know what to do.

She smiles at me sadly then lowers her lids to dim the light and motions for me to sleep. I lie down, head on the bag of monsters and stare into the fire. She picks up the urn and pounds it into the ground. It makes a dull reverberation. Then with her rough, rusty, voice she sings and drums me into a dream.

~

In front of me is a great tree limb on the ground. It has seven holes in it. I am curious and approach the limb. Up from one limb-hole a monstrous head appears. It spits at me and then drops down from view. I am startled at the interaction and offended. Suddenly another head appears, another monster, again it spits. In my hand is a branch. I swing at the beast. It disappears before I connect. And this keeps happening until I am enraged.

I feel a gentle hand on my arm and swing around with a snarl. It's Grama Ans. I try but fail to stop my swing. The branch connects to the side of her head. With a sickening dull thunk her head caves in.

"No," I cry, empty devastation inside.

She picks herself up from the ground and pats my cheek. "Begin drum powerfulness they find center. *Loud wit* be self-indulgent for you *hope to rest* just because *if shot." She tells me as she motions to her face. Then as she backs away from me she gives one more important sounding piece of nonsense. She says, "*Be *the lost romanced,* whatever wisdom is mine *lip whirl wise* in your heart *rid damn unto* your dreams. *Yet ye named a hero to try make gut slit* hear the id. *Is hit* can do for you, *Wee Stone. Yare* you *aping* attention? *Instil* you *well?"*

I know she wants something from me so I nod my head and pop up on my toes. I smile at her in encouragement and lean forward, open body, open arms, hands open. Yes, yes. I insinuate I understand and will comply.

But I've fooled no one. She knows I am a smiling, nodding idiot. She waves me off and turns to go. Then swiftly, she turns back and taps my breast bone above my heart, "No eternal list," she whispers. I feel it tingle all the way down into the organs that lie beneath. Shivers race up and down my neck. She turns on her heel and sets off down the road. "No eternal list," she yells back at me without looking over her shoulder. I tremble anew and my fingers burst off my hands like ten little corn kernels pop, pop, pop. . . .

Further down the road, still not looking back she yells again, "No eternal list, dreams yet."

and my hands plop one, two onto the ground; then my arms land beside them and my eyes shoot out from my head and my nose slides off my face. Then my ears start dribbling down to my chin and then I can no longer see her or hear her or touch her. I feel my head start to wobble and open my mouth to cry out.

~

All parts of the yew are poisonous except the
fruit.

-Journal Entry, May 15, age 24

Chapter 15 – Silent but Not-Quite-Alone

When I awake I know without opening my eyes that I am alone with a bag of snoring monsters. Grama Ans is gone. I can leave, too. I can leave the monsters in the tied-up-bag.

But just as surely as I know Grama Ans has left, I know she will be disappointed if I abandon the little beasts. She believes in me. Grama Ans believes in me. Why, I'm not sure, but I know she believes I will eventually do what is right. And she believes that I am the one who is supposed to take care of these things-in-the-bag.

I heave a sigh and mull over the repercussions of hauling them along with me. Now, I'm not trying to earn Grama Ans' approval and I could care less about the wellbeing of the little beasts. The only reason I'm considering accepting this burden is because I want to safeguard a fresh, new feeling of connectedness I sense inside me.

Because Grama Ans finds me worthy I am able to suspend my feelings of unworthiness; because I trust her. And with unworthiness suspended, I can also catch hold of a feeling of self worth - just barely. I think I believe in me. Deep down, in the dark of me, I think I believe in me. If she can believe in me, then I can, too.

The most amazing aspect of this is that when I am able to believe in me, then I can also connect to other satisfying things that I have no names for. These other satisfying things are also deep down in the dark places of me. At this point in my life, or rather death, feeling connected to anything is compelling. Feeling connected makes me warm in a very cold place and it radiates out.

Even when I died the first two times and floated in the white light and felt like I was one with everything all at once, I didn't feel connected to me, me. Everything else was too overpoweringly present.

This third, dark horrible death exposed something that was missing in my good deaths and that surprises me. Here in this bitterly awful place, I have connected to something valuable. I like this me-knowing. So, I decide. "I will bring the three beastie burdens along on my quest to find the white light. And I will keep this feeling alive." It makes sense, I reason. "When I find the white light, then I will figure out what I can do with the creatures." It would be much better to ascend with no regrets.

<And with no monsters>

Slowly, careful not to wake the little beasts, I stretch the kinks out of my muscles and I roll to my knees. That's when I notice two round balls and a mound of something on the ground next to the embers of our fire.

I look closer. The balls are eyeballs. In the dim light I recognize the milky one. It's hers. Then I recognize the other one. It's mine. I feel my face and confirm my eye is out of its socket. I'm not surprised. Nor am I horrified. Resigned is more like it. I think I knew I would have to trade eyes at some point in time. She was so persistent even in her gentleness. I don't know why it is so important for her to have my eyeball, maybe hers is wearing out. But I like the old dame. I've done her wrong. And she rescued me, because I'm more and more sure that the distraction she provided with fire and light was all that saved me from being split open by Soldier's sword. Considering all this, I decide I can spare one eye. Hell, everything is rotting on my body anyway. If she can use it, I donate it willingly. I pick up her milky eyeball and brush it off. I stare at it and it stares back at me. With a huge sigh and a bit of a shudder, I lift my lid and push it into place. The gory dangling parts wake up and wiggle themselves into my socket, hooking up to parts in me, rolling around, seating itself, settling in. I feel like I have sand in my eye and tears flood and spill over wetting the eye and my face. I force myself not to rub at it, to let it settle.

When I open my lid, it's no longer dark. The torchEye lights up this aphotic world. I can see quite well. I can see far off. In fact, I can see further than I ever have and around corners, too. And I can more easily feel my connection to the deep dark places inside me. This eye is special. But it makes my brain hurt, because I'm not used to processing this much data. Narrowing my focus to bloody feet limits the brain-ache. Maybe the eye trade is not a total disaster after all. I feel less frail or maybe not so vulnerable. I turn my back on my old eye so I am not tempted to trade it out again. Even though the new eye is handier, I am comfortable with the limits of the old eye. I understand those limits. Since comfort is tempting, I focus on the mound.

The mound on the ground is rice. Hunger gnaws, but my gut tells me it was left for the ones I'm supposed to care for. I move the mound closer to the embers to warm them up. I have to pick dirt and twigs out of the rice so it is clean for the little monsters. Soon there is movement in the bag and I lift it from the bottom and tumble the three out. They lay on the ground with voluble complaints.

"Where is the pretty lady?" The firstborn asks.

"I'm hungry," says the grumpy second one.

"No, you no get to wipe my face," the firstborn resists my efforts.

"Stop pushing me," growls the second at the firstborn who rolled away from me and accidentally bumped her sister.

"You no wipe face. I da boss of me," demands the first.

169

"Why it sssso light? Ssshut offffff that eyeball." snarls the second.

"I decide what to do," claims the firstborn.

"I'm hungry," yells the second, turning from pink to red in an instant and standing and stomping her foot. This one has quite a temper. I step back.

"I hungry," the firstborn rubs her fat feet against my ankle; "and I pretty." She flutters her eyelids at me, trying to charm me into feeding her, I think. It's ridiculous.

"I'm hungry." The second born kicks at me and kicks at her sister and bites her own arm. "I hungry, Iiiii hungry, Iiiiii hungrrrrrrrry" Each word is louder. The beast launches itself at the ground, a tantrum of heel kicks and shrieks and slapping hands and twisting, rolling arching anger.

The third one just stares at me throughout this whole spectacle. It makes me uncomfortable so I look away.

There's food for you after you go potty and clean up." I'm calm even though I'm yelling the words to be heard over the screams.

"Thissssss isssssssss ssssshameful," the wrathful one cries with bared teeth and narrowed eyes. She's gone from red to almost blood red. Her hair stands up like licking fire but shorter and it doesn't move quite as much as fire. It's not beautiful, not pretty at all. It's alarming.

"Go potty first," I demand; "then I'll wash your faces, then we eat." I am going to hold the line on discipline. I'm in charge.

"Sssssssshut up," the second born screams.

Her older sister, the leader of the three, dives on top of the screaming beastie. She hangs on despite the scratching and biting. "Shhhhhhh, Hissie. Shhhhhhhhhh, we gonna eat. Yessss, we are.

Shhhhh, good girl. You a good girl. I better dan you, but you ssssstilll a good ssssister. My good sssssssisssster." She wraps her short fat arms as far around her little sister as she can, which is not far because the firstborn is just about as round as she is tall and her arms are short so they barely get around her own body; but she's strong. She wraps her short fat legs as far around her writhing sister as she can, too. Firstborn is so much heavier than her sister, so her weight alone dampens the tantrum.

Slowly the second born lies still, merely sobbing, the biting all finished.

The firstborn rolls off her sister and looks up at me. "I da best. I calm my Hissie. Hissie like sssssssshhh sounds. Sssssss ssssoundsss make Hisssssssie feel sssssafe." She stays close enough to her sister to continue to rub Hissie's arm.

"Well, thank you," I acknowledge the older sister and she smiles. This firstborn likes attention, wants to be important. "Now go potty," I reiterate sternly.

The oldest girl spreads her chubby legs and says, "No pee-pee. No have pee-pee." And she's correct. There is no anatomical place to get rid of waste. I glance at the other two girls. As far as I can tell, they are the same.

"Feel ssssstupid now?" sobs Hissie.

"Stupid there," The firstborn points at me. "I not stupid. I smart."

The third just stares at me.

It feels like I'm losing control and that frightens me. Hell, I don't know how to be in charge. I pause for a second and look in my deep, dark place to feel that connectedness and remind myself why I'm doing this.

"Hey," I say to the wee ones. "I'm bigger than you, I'm smarter than you, and I'm tougher than you," They look at me with an array of expressions. Maybe I'm just reminding myself that I'm bigger and in charge. "You don't have to go potty," I gruff; "but I will wash your faces before we eat." Then I spit on the bag and hold them down with a hand on their chests and scrub their faces.

They are not as patient with me as they were with Grama Ans' washing efforts. They chew on me and push each other and try to get to the food before I'm finished splitting it into three equal servings.

One word exclamations accompany each beastie I plunk down. "Sit," I say to the firstborn. "Stop," I command Hissie, the second born. And when I plunk down the apathetic one next to her share of the rice, I demand, "Eat." I expect the dang beasts to dig in, which will afford me a short stint of peace. What I get is:

Hissie says, "I want dat one," pointing to the oldest one's pile of rice.

"No, no, dis is miiine. It's the best. I da best." The oldest one huddles over her pile. "What'll da big one think if I not have da best?"

Da big one? I think she means me.

Hissie jumps on her sister, kicking at her and trying to snake her hand under her fat sister's belly. "My rice," Hissie yells, turning red.

Oh, no. "Quiet!" I say, maybe not as calmly as previously. Everyone freezes. I look around. Two pairs of wide eyes stare back at me and one pair of empty sockets (Hissie's). I don't think I can do this, I think. Then I hear a noise that squeals on my nerves. I shudder.

"Feed me," the noise comes again, generating out of the apathetic one's mouth. "Feed me," she meows in her squally voice. One sharp fingernail finds it way to my ankle pore - just one pore. She hooks into my pore, to get my attention, I suppose. Her eyes widen disgustingly and are damp. "Food coming now?" she whines in her squeaky, irritating voice.

"Feed me first. I da oldest. I important."

"My rice, my ricce, my ricccce," Hissie flushes and raises her voice.

"Feed me?" the youngest squalls.

I remind myself, "I'm doing this to safeguard that fresh, new connectedness to me. This new-connection-to-me is worth it." Repetition calms me so I am able to quiet the ruckus outside myself, too. Sitting next to the rice piles, I settle the beasties between my legs and anchor them in place. Then one-by-one, I feed them. This, at least, keeps a modicum of order. I like order. I'll do anything to maintain order.

They remind me of demanding baby birds: mouths open, heads tilted back, those with eyes focused on the food, all of them squawking. "Feed me; that's mine; feed me, it's my turn; feed me?" They gobble and gorge and eat until they finish the rice and cry with pain. Apparently they have no ability to self-regulate and I haven't learned yet when to stop feeding them.

I have to rub their bulging bellies to quiet the two oldest. The apathetic one just stares at me again. Although her stare bothers me, it's preferable to that voice.

They eventually fall into an overfed stupor so I place them back in the bag - do it carefully - am desperate not to excite them. Grama Ans will come back, I reason, to bring more food for the babies. "When 'the pretty lady' comes back," I whisper as I slip the bulging-bellied Hissie into the bag. "I'll turn you over to her. She's better at this than I am. I'm wasting time here, you see." Leaning over close to Hissie's ear I give it to her straight. "You're foreign to me. You're too difficult."

173

"Dat'ss ssad," Hissie mummers; "sssssso sssad."

"Shhhh," I soothe her. "Slide in here. Yesss, jusssst like thissss. Ssssh …" I tie the end down tightly.

"Want out." Hissie speaks up, but she is still mostly stupefied. I sit next to the bag most of the day. Too soon they rouse themselves and as they do, they become much more vocal.

"You ssstoopid. You sooo ssstoopid," the two oldest yell abuse at me.

'Stoopid' seems to be the worst insult they can imagine. I'm not the only one they abuse. They yell at, fight and wrestle with each other, too. The bag rolls around the forest floor, bouncing into me and into trees - but mostly into me. For my part, I stare at my eye in the forest duff. I stare until I can't bear any more.

It's the bag banging into me for about the hundredth time that finally breaks my false calm. "Enough," I yell and get up and stomp around. "Aaarrrgh! Ahhh. Ahhh. I'm, I'm going for a walk."

The bag gets very still. "Don't leave us," the oldest one begs. I recognize her voice. Her voice trembles. It almost touches my heart.

I grab the bag and hang it from a tree. "I'll be back," I rasp. Guilt makes me utter that rash promise. "I'm off." I stomp into the woods even though the beasts beg me not to go. "I need time to myself." I yell my justification at them, then whisper, "That's not wrong."

I'm calm when I return from my evening stroll. There on the ground next to the old fire is a mound of rice. Grama Ans has been here. I smile, feeling close to her even though I missed her. The bag is still in the tree and wiggling. Complaints issue from it. My smile fades. I guess I hoped Grama Ans would take them. She took my eye - that's gone. It's a relief not to have to keep staring at it.

Eye gone, rice here, no fire - just ashes - and no old woman, but beasties are here; my responsibility; beasties in a bag made from a wild pubic hair. And I'm in this rocky death place - that's what I know right at this moment. I'm still bleeding from my chest hole. I still don't need to breathe, although I want to. There's dirt and rocks throughout the rice so I pick out the bad stuff and divide the mound into three equal piles. Only then do I untie the bag from the tree. When I empty the bag I notice the beasties have grown.

"I'll wash your faces and then you can eat," I say in all politeness.

"Go stuff yourself," the mean second born says. She must not have enjoyed her day-in-the-bag.

"Wash me-face first. I da oldest. What'dle the others think if I don't lead?"

I wash the apathetic one's face and battle with the mad one. Then, finally, I offer a grain to each in turn until it is all gone. Again, I take no grain for myself. Between bites the two oldest endlessly yammer at me. When they finish, I rub their distended bellies again and stuff them in the bag to sleep.

"It's dark. Go to sleep," I bark at the bag.

"Not sssssleepppppy, No! No dark! No sleep," they yowl until I lay my head on the bag. After one hearty kick to my head, the babies are quiet.

"Hmmm," I muse, "I wonder who kicked me." And I smile because I'm quite sure I know who it was. I'm learning about the character of each and that's good.

The night is still. I close my torcheye and all goes black. It's quiet, just a few snores and grunts from inside the bag. I might have snored a bit myself that night.

My head bumps up as someone in the bag twitches. The ground is warm beneath me. Day is breaking. I crack my eyes and see dawn rise up from the ground.

Again there is a new mound of rice. Yawning and stretching I roll to my knees. The grumbling starts up as soon as my head leaves the bag. "Just a minute," I grump back at the bag. "I gotta pee." To myself I admit irritation - missed Grama Ans again! Wanted to ask her to take them. Wanted to ask her where the other people are; if there's a town where I can get help? I must get going to the white light. Can't just sit around all day and feed these things.

"I might be running out of time," I grumble as I divide the rice into three equal piles. I open the bag and let them crawl out. Spit on the bag and wash their faces. Sit with them. Manage the fussing, because there is fussiness going on. Although the mounds are the same size as before, there is not enough food to satiate them. They've grown. They're more persistent, too. They don't wait. They grab handfuls. They eat every bite and then, when the last grain is gone, they complain that they did not get their fair share. Not a great start to another long day.

With mistaken generosity, I let the two oldest remain out of the bag to play. They fight with each other and kick dirt on me. They cry over jabs and poke and tattle and point fingers. They are grossly unhappy.

"It's time for a nap." I announce, fed up.

"No nap; not tired," this from the leader, of course. She steps closer to me then yelps because the second born, Hissie, pinches her.

"Quit stepping on me," The ill-tempered one says with another pinch.

"I not step on you. I step right here." She moves her big foot off her sister and slides her eyes towards me to see if I noticed. "I no step on Hissie-baby. What'dle others think if I step on Hissie?" She folds her fat, short arms in a gesture of innocence.

"You bad," Hissie growls, flushing; at the same time I say, "You need to apologize to Hissie."

"I not bad, I good," she tears up.

"Don't be so sensitive." The first-born's need for approval nettles me for some reason. "If you step on someone, you need to apologize." My tone is sharp, condemning. It hurts my own ears to hear it.

The firstborn waddles closer to me, eyes wide with sincerity. On the way, she steps on 'Hissie-baby' again. "I no step on. I do nothing wrong. I a good girl. I … ouch, ouch. Stop dat, Hissie-sissie."

The second born, already flushed pink with anger, turns red. "You step on me, you oaf. You step again."

Oaf? That's an odd word for a baby to know.

"You big, clumsy, paddle-footed oaf." Hissie pushes her older sister. With detached wonder I note her vocabulary improves in direct proportion to her anger, which revs up, up until Hissie attacks her older sister completely out of control - a little tornado of flying fists and kicking feet. It happens so fast, I don't even get my mouth closed.

"That's enough." Finally I roll onto my knees and crawl over. "Stop this fighting. Ow!" (bite to the collar bone). I separate them; get punched in the cheek. "Hissie-sissie, ow, stop." I pull the little monster into my chest, wrap my arms around her, suffering pinches all up and down my forearm. Finally I fall on the ground and roll on top of the wiggling beast. "You," I huff and puff at the firstborn, "Get in the sack. Now." I have to be careful not to crush the beastie underneath me.

"No nap." The oldest one whines, the voice of them all, even as she waddles with her fat belly jiggling towards the bag. "Not tired. No nap." She lifts up the sack, still grumbling, and waddles inside and sits next to her apathetic sister. I am left with only one angry wiggling baby.

"You need to settle down," I say to Hissie.

"Let go, let go, let go, let go, let go …" rapid fire, staccato words.

Brute force is not working. I try reason. "Hissie, you need to calm down. Do you promise to behave yourself if I let you go?"

"You hurting me. Too tight. You hurt me."

From the bag, the waddler sticks her head out with concern. "Don't hurt sissie."

"No, no. I'm not hurting anyone. Get back in that sack." Then to Hissie I gentle my voice, "Okay, I'm letting you go. Shhh, shh. There now. That's right. Settle down." I get to my knees and take my first hand off and am bit, hard, right between the fingers on the webbing. I bare my teeth in pain and make a noise, a hissing soft yell.

Hissie freezes then cocks her head - has a funny expression. She sits up, bringing her head closer and gently puts out a hand to stroke my chin. "Like it," she says and trundles off to the bag, lifts the edge and ducks inside.

That fast, it's over. I'm alone with bared teeth and throbbing webbing. Bewildered I am and missing Grama Ans. So do the little ones.

They don't nap; how could they, they just woke up. Instead they roll around inside the bag and wrestle. I look every where but at the bag. Wish I had better company than these uncouth mordacious bumpkins. Maybe I wish I was alone.

No. I most definitely do not want to be alone. I want to be in proper company.

I'm anxious; don't want to miss Grama Ans this time, but feel like I must move, go, make progress. I crawl over to the bag, lift the edge and look inside. Hissie's got her finger up her sister's nose. I don't want to know why. "Come on out of there," I command, looking away, trying not to laugh. All three crawl out of the bag. The oldest two look towards me, a question implicit in the tilt of their heads.

"We're going for a march," I tell them.

"I march good. I da best marcher. What's a march?"

Hissie rolls her eyes at her sister and we share a chuckle. The apathetic one just stares at us. "I da best marcher," Hissie says with a smirk.

"No, no; I da best marcher." The oldest raises her voice anxiously looking at me.

So I pantomime how to march. "Like this," I say.

"I know dat," she says with exasperation and lifts her knees and her paddle-feet plop, plop in the dust. "See. I march good."

"Well," I consider the motion; "you are pretty good at marching in place. Let's see you march in a circle. Let me see Hissie march, too." Then I turn to the youngest. "Do you want to march?" I ask.

"Idunno."

"I'm marching," Hisser announces.

"Uh, huh." I acknowledge; "good job."

"I march better," the vain one pipes up.

Yeah, yeah, yeah, I think.

"Let's try marching," I suggest to the youngest.

"Idunno," She squeaks barely moving her mouth as if the word sits heavy as a stone on her tongue.

"Are you too tired to talk?" I ask with an edge. Somehow this one's lassitude irritates me. Out of large blank eyes she stares. I shudder.

"Hold onto the bag-hair and keep together," I command. I'm a great commander because they all grab onto the bag-hair. We shuffle single file around the trees. I figure the exercise will tire them out, but I don't want to go far and miss Grama Ans.

"No more," the youngest stops.

"Keep marching," I command.

"Iiiidunno," she sits.

I'm reduced to idle threats. "Well who-knows-if-you-dunno?" I say to the youngest. "If you don't march, you don't eat." And that gets her up. Eating is the only thing that motivates this dry, depressed torpid beast.

We march again but make almost no progress because they cannot behave themselves.

"Wrong, wrong; what'dle others think if you march wrong?" the firstborn shrills. "Do it like me." She pulls at the hair-bag and causes Hissie to trip.

"Sssssstop it, Ssssssiss."

"I'm hungry," this of course, from the youngest.

"Hurry up. You slow." Tug, tug, push, fight, wail, pinch, "I hungry" whine, kick, "Stop it!"

How can Grama Ans derive satisfaction from this group, I wonder. I don't like them. To tell the truth, although they are little and mostly defenseless, I am strangely afraid of them. So I keep them marching ahead of me until I cannot fight them anymore. I yell for silence but they are totally out of control. The world around me has gone mad with chaos.

"No more walk."

"I walk."

"Want food."

"I hungry, gimme food, now," the oldest one joins the youngest one's constant chorus.

"Hungry," adds Hissie.

"Hungry," said by I can't distinguish who since they're all yowling it.

"I want hug," whines the oldest one.

They want too much. What about what I want? I want some peace. Want some consistent behavior. "Quiet." I yell.

If I must keep them with me, then I choose to have the minimum interaction with them. Marching is too much work for me to deal with. I pick them up and push them in the sack.

They don't like it and Hisser kicks me so I let the bag bump onto the ground and drag them for a while. When I lift the bag onto my back again, they are better behaved but I feel ashamed of myself. I try to justify my meanness but I'm fooling no one, not even me. I cannot ever do that again. I've never been a mean person, didn't know I had it in me. They bring it out in me. I wonder if the creatures and I will ever do anything right again?

I'm tired, so tired of them already. Inside the bag the haranguing starts up again.

"Let us out. Let walk. You no ever let us walk. No fun. You mean." I recognize that voice - the leader's complaining voice. The others follow suit.

"Mean."

"Hungry."

"Out, out, out, out."

Honestly at my wit's end, I am back to my original thought. If they get tired enough, maybe they will fall asleep. I let them out. We march, they fight; I walk and carry; we march; I sling them in the bag over my shoulder; we shuffle on together moving in and out of the trees with them attached to me by the hair, complaining at me, depending on me. Until it is late and dark, then I herd them back to our campsite to eat.

There is no mound of rice waiting for us. Grama Ans has not come back. But other things found their way to us. There are two new beast babies asleep by the ashes. I had almost let myself forget I gave birth to seven monsters. Now I have, what … five to care for? If I'm lucky, the predacious one will stay lost and continue digesting the one it ate.

Hissie spies her sleeping siblings. "Sisters look!" Hissie yells with joy and runs to the sleepers. The youngest one plops on my foot. I look hard with my new far-seeing eye. The forest lights up. No food. I search to the left. No rice. Swing my eye to the right. No hint of Grama Ans' footsteps or presence although I can see where the two new beasties wandered into camp, one following the other one. One of them shuffled their feet. But no Grama Ans. Deep in my dark place I know that Grama Ans is not coming back with rice or her crazy advice or company. We are on our own. I hadn't planned for this. I look at the beasties, spotlight on. They don't understand the situation yet.

"Turn that light down," Hissie gripes at me. "Babies sleeping."

"I hungry," Squeals the youngest one with her horrid voice.

"Me, too," the leader says, her voice subdued. I think she's reading my face and can tell something is wrong.

"Hungry. Eat. Eat now," the young squealer whines.

"I saaaid, turn down that light." Hissie roars.

I look away from the group, a worried frown furrowing my forehead. I guess I thought we'd stay until … what? … until Grama Ans came back and told me what to do, took control of me, took over my charges … I was waiting for that. But maybe, maybe I knew that wasn't going to happen.

<Perhaps no one's going to help>

Maybe I can find some people here in the dark rocky place. Soldier said there were others here. Some where along this internal dialogue I began wringing my hands and mumbling out loud.

"Wha' wrong?" the oldest asks. She catches on quick, that one.

Two little faces look up at me with worried expressions; the youngest one's face is blank. There is a thrum of unhappy whines as they watch me. I cannot let them know I am lost or it will be worse for me. Must decide on a plan. This requires boldness even though I feel foolish doubt. I scoop the three awake babies close and tell them we are not eating tonight.

"We have to start along a path before we find food," I reassure them; well, lie to them. They are subdued, thus are more compliant than usual. "Let's go now," I smile.

The firstborn looks up with concern. "Bring dem, too? We need dem."

"Yes, yes; I'll carry the lot of you." But they look up at me with worried expressions; I'm not sure they trust me. I talk to them

183

about my life. I make up stories and even hum a bit as I put them in the sack with the sleeping two. I nestle the bag in my arms instead of slinging them over my shoulder. They like this position and they like the humming so I continue that. One by one they fall asleep and the worried chatter fades away. I walk until I cannot carry them any more.

Then I lay the bag at my feet. I am at a crossroads; eye turned on full; two ways to go.

<The babies are heavy>

Dear God, I am tired and hungry and too burdened. Please show me the way.

One of the babies cries out in its sleep. The bag twitches. One rolls over, the rest roll over, too.

<I need direction>

Two ways to go. "Must find a clue," I mumble to myself and crouch and begin scrambling around. I run in ever widening circles looking for a footprint or trail marker or any indication of which way to go. I run down one direction then come back and run down the next. I circle round and round, spin, look up with my torcheye to try and find another way. I sniff. I lay on the ground with my ear pressed to the dirt trying to pick up vibrations. I lay still reaching out with my other senses, the new-deep-down-in-the-dark-places senses, the ones that have no names but are coming alive because I have the far-seeing eye to help me look inside and the connected-to-me-feeling is warming me up. Even these new senses cannot find a clue.

Ear pressed to the ground, flattened in the dirt I lay still.

<I'm tired. Dear God, I am so tired>

I hear a grunt and a scratching rustle in the bag but I'm too weary to swivel my head to look. "Directions, a clue, a tiny bit of help

184

please, please; show me what I need to do." My prayer puffs the dust.
<Dust thickened>

Under my cheek the ground vibrates with footsteps. The oldest baby bends her knees and lifts my arm. "I ..." I start to say... start to say what? ... start to explain, to complain?

"Shhh." The oldest says and slides to the ground under my arm. She pats my arm into place and snuggles into my armpit.

I shake my head; well, rock it back and forth on the ground. "I ..." But all I get is a snore in return.

Maybe tomorrow I will know what to say, know what to do. I'm scared, too much responsibility.

<Not enough of me>

I'm lonely. I push up off the ground and carry my fat bundle to the bag and stare, too tired to decide what to do. Bag of beasts, bag of babies, bag-o-trouble.

<Lonely>

Leaning down I lay the fat baby on the ground and open the sack to check on the others. They don't wake up. It's for the best. There's no rice here, nothing to feed them. Too tired to pack them away again I lay down to sleep spooning the five. We are tucked in close – the six of us. Hairbag lifts itself and covers us.

The bark is poisonous.

-Journal Entry, May 15, age 24

Chapter 16 – Act Better Than That

I awake via a bite on my nose and start the day with a scold. "Don't do that," I grump at the eldest one. My nose hurts.

The eldest one blushes as the others laugh at her. "You no talk mean at me," she whispers. "What'dle the others think?"

"What will the others think?" I ask her with derision. I can't decide if I'm angrier at her because she bit my nose to wake me up or because she is so pathetically worried about what her siblings think about her. "Get a backbone," I scold meanly. Ugly I am.

"No backbone. You lack-a-bone. It's well known. So don't moan …" one of the new birthling sings and jigs in place. The others laugh and point at the leader. Waddling-What'll-They-Think screws up her face to cry. I caused this. My meanness.

"Why can't you act properly?" I castigate them all. More meanness, tone ugly. Their faces fall from smiling-anticipation-of-my-waking to confusion, uncertainty and shame.

"What?" I growl at them. I cannot stop my mouth. To my dismay I realize I sound just like The Aunts. Inside my head is a whole litany of admonishments. Chides and denouncements line up like little bats waiting their turn to fly down and dive bomb the creatures in my care.

Don't want to be like The Family, I realize. For the first time I see clearly the effects of Grandma's oft repeated condemnations. This is no way to treat a child. In an instant I understand how little sensitivity Grandma had – her almost disgust for naiveté – because she did not prize innocence. Maybe it even scared her. Control was more important to Grandma, to The Family – control and predictability. This is a surprise to me. I have always assumed that acceptance is what everyone craves.

Meanness seeps out but I have no examples of decent guardianship to fill myself. Although it's a dilemma, I'm sure of one thing: I will not act the way Grandma acted towards me because upon seeing her point of view, I comprehend it is not for me. No more smiling innocent faces will fall from eager delight to shame.

Without thought – as if by some long damped instinct – I reach out and tweak the oldest one lightly on the nose and apologize. "I'm sorry I growled at you. It hurt, your bite. Were you trying to wake me up? Well, I'm awake now and I have your nose!" These last five words were said quickly and on a rising tone. I pull back my fist with my thumb peeking out between two fingers and I laugh as I show "the nose" to the oldest bumpkin. Her eyes widen in shocked alarm and she feels her face. When she realizes her real nose is still on her face and that I am playing a game with her, she breaks into an ugly howl of delight and dances around, eyes twinkling. The others dog-pile on top of me in utter mayhem.

"My nose, take my nose."

"Me, me."

"In the soft night glows; parent doze, we all knows that in the throes of repose wisdom grows; now I suppose that my nose is pretty as a rose …" this ditty is sung by an extremely ill-favored but loquacious new baby.

"Take mine."

"You can't have it."

"I get yours."

"I'm hungry," said the youngest creature - the only one not in the jumbled mass on top of me. She's watching again. She looks too listless to have actually spoken. But speak she did. I'd recognize that voice anywhere. "I'm hungry." And then there is a chorus of cries from the others.

"Hungry, hungry."

"Eat. Now, eat. Now!"

Whimper, cry, push, shove, bite, they lose control of themselves and unwanted chaos engulfs me again.

Sometime later they are relatively calm, complaining, but waiting to get their faces washed with my spit and the bag. I will do this but not because they are unacceptably dirty. I do it because the routine comforts them. I'm learning the difference between establishing stability and demanding consistency. "Everything will be okay." They look up at me with ugly hungry faces.

A longing blooms. It's delicate, my longing to ease the hungers of these unlovely things in my care. My longing is frail because also inside me a dread blooms. It's strong, my dread of spending time with the babies because - my confusion, the noise - all of it takes energy I don't have.

This longing and dread interweave and I'm not the same. I am more vulnerable. Beneath my trembling hands the pubic-hair-turned-into-a-bag undulates. I look down at it. The hair loops itself gently around my wrist bone and I don't feel so alone. Such a simple thing, a touch.

189

So I touch back and pat the others. Everyone gets a pat. I feel better.

Here we sit in the middle of a crossroads. Which direction I take is very important. This I feel with every resounding part of me. I bring the bag to my face, hold it there for just a moment. Then I spit on my old clothes and reach for the first face to wash.

I'm stuck with them, I think with a smile. Waddle/Whattle-the-other's-think-of-me/Whaddle thinks I'm smiling at her and is happy. She smiles back at me. I grab her chin to keep it steady as I wash. She scrunches up her face, but holds still.

Since I want to be a different kind of guardian than Grandma, I realize the babies must be let out of the bag. "Today," I announce, "we begin searching for food together." This is my choice - the direction I choose. "First we walk. When you get tired, I'll make you a sling."

"What is sling?"

"Want sling."

"Sling."

"Hungry," The apathetic youngest one intones.

"Hungry for sling, that's the thing, ding-ding-ding-a-ling ..." this from the ferociously ugly one. Darn birthling is a creative little rhymer. The whole noisy gang starts singing ding-ding-ding-a-ling (except the youngest, of course). I'm grateful for the distraction. 'ding-ding- ding-a-ling' is better than 'food-food-food'.

So, they want the sling first. Maybe I shouldn't give a lot of options right up front, I think.

I loop the bag around my neck then load them into the sling and rest my arms around them. They like riding this way, able to see. Since we did not find food at the crossroads, I make a game of pointing out odd rock formations. They like to play. The oldest one points out an odd formation to me and I make up a humming song starring it. Soon they are all pointing out formations (except the apathetic one) and I build a trail of words about each formation, creating an oral map of where we traverse. Every time they point out something odd, I add it to the song, starting from scratch, singing it from the beginning each time. I am surprised at how well I remember it. We are all actually paying close attention to where we are going.

Here I am.

I'm stuck in Hell.

Along the way

Don't see too well.

Well, here I am, I'm stuck in Hell; along the way don't see too well.

Dark lights up

I meet a crone.

With torch eye cups

I'm not alone.

The dark lights up; I meet a crone with torch eye cups; I'm not alone.

I'm in some pain.

What can it be?

There's creatures seven;

Don't look like me.

I'm in some pain, what can it be; there's creatures seven, don't
look like me.

Met man with sword.

He seem quite kind.

Had lost an eye

But he didn't need mine

Met man with sword; he seemed quite kind; had lost an eye but
he didn't need mine.

The lord with sword,

He slipped, I'm gored.

My stomach's flayed.

Since been restored.

The lord with sword, he slipped I'm gored; my stomach's
flayed, since been restored.

Oh there's a rock

Looks like a frog.

It's coated with mold

Might slip, don't jog.

Oh there's a rock; looks like a frog, it's coated with mold; might slip, don't jog.

And there's a stone

With quite some dash.

It looks like it

Has a big moustache.

And there's a stone with quite some dash. It looks like it has a big moustache.

...

That's all for now,

I do avow.

Will only say,

"Let's take a bow".

That's all for now, I do avow; will only say "let's take a bow".

And then I bow down and pretend I'm going to tumble them all to the ground. They love the ending and say, "Again. Sing it again." The rhymer-baby and I sing it to them for hours as I look for food.

"Sing it again." Whaddle carols.

From Hissie-the-irritable, "Whaddle quit crowding me; make her stop."

"I wanna face dat way," whines the other new baby. "I wanna find a rock. Wan' you to sing 'bout my rock."

"I'm hungry." These are the only words the youngest one, the apathetic one, says.

"Hold me dis way, I don't wanna sit da way you face me," Hissie again.

"I'm hungry."

They still push and bounce around inside the sling, but at least they do not bite me, which is a step in the right direction. The skinny-one-with-the-overbite (the rhymer) hums along with me. We do a nice duet.

Even dead leaves can kill if consumed ...

-Journal Entry, May 15, age 24

Chapter 17 – Guiding Me - Me - Me

"Oh, no. Big fat stinking oh-no." We are back at the crossroads. Walked for stupid hours and we are back at the crossroads. There's my bloodPuddle, our footsteps, this is where we slept. And that is ... what the hell is that?

I look closer, turning on my eyeLight. Footprints ... not-our-tracks - ah, dang it - if I had just stayed put, I would have met up with other people. "There are tracks," I point out to the others. "Look at that," I grump; "they walked clear over at the edge. Were they hoping I wouldn't notice their tracks? Are they avoiding us?"

Why would they ...? Well, there are two important points. One, there are signs of life other than these creatures-I'm-toting. And two, they didn't go the way I went. They took the other road. Dangblastit ... that's the way I should have gone.

Hisser stands up in the sling and puts her hands on my shoulders and yells in my ear, "HUUUUUUUUNGRY, EEEEEaaat NOOOOOOOOW!"

I want to scream at the monsters and hurl them as far away from me as I can. I thought we were getting someplace. We seemed to be better. I thought I could handle this. But I am right back where I was

195

this morning: angry, mean, barely able to control myself. Very disappointed. Very discouraged. Trying not to chuck it all up.

Damned hair is tugging on my wrist, too clingy.

I put them not-too-gently down. Whaddle, the oldest, immediately takes off exploring those other footprints. She's standing underneath a tippy rock. "Come back here," I yell. "Might be dangerous, you little fool."

They're hungry, I keep reminding myself. It's a worthy attempt to restrain myself from screaming or hurting them. "We walked far today. Aren't you sleepy?" I ask. The desperation coloring my voice acts as fuel on their fire.

"Stop humming!" Hissie snarls and lashes out at the ferociously ugly sibling. The ugly-rhymer won't quit humming our song. Quite ornery, this ugly one. "Let me go, let me go, let me go." Hissie says this to me. I am holding onto her arm, trying to stop her from acting out what I'm feeling.

The two youngest raise their voices in order to be heard over the ruckus. "I'm hungry," says the apathetic one with her great empty eyes trained on me. Her brother, the other new baby, plucks at me and whines, "I wanna ride. I tired. Why you holding Hissie. I wanna hug. I wanna."

Everyone wants a piece of me.

They're tired. I walked them, hoped it would tire them out; but I don't think it works like that. I think that when they get overly tired … Oh Dear Rotten Hole! …

"I wanna hug," desperate whine from the new boy;

"Stop humming, let me go, get outta my way," cranky Hissie;

"hummmmm.mum.mum.mum.hummm, mm, mmm …" naughtiness from rhymer;

"They can't control themselves" that's my thought. "Stop," I command. "I'm serious, STOP," louder. "Whaddle, quit walking away from me. Hissie, stop hitting."

"Hey!" I yell, losing it; utterly losing it. "I said stop and I mean stop right this stink'n, Freak'n MINUTE!" Two breaths, I tell myself; just take two deep breaths. Through smiling gritted teeth I try to sound calm and reasonable, "Right here is where we are sleeping tonight." Relax my fists. "Hey, hey, Hissie! I said stop it. Sit your butts on the ground and SHUT UP for a minute." I'm teetering on the thinnest of edges; my shoulders are so rigid I'm afraid they'll pop right out of my skin.

I need a beastie break or … I need to get away for just a few minutes.

"Hair," I grab the bag and loop it three times around the gang "you are in charge. I'll be right back." I'm panting, which is fanning the fires of desperation. I have got to get away. Right now!

With huge strides I stalk off, but I don't go far. Just out of sight, just so they can't see me press my back into the wall and yell a berserker cry as wide-mouthed and silently as I can. I press back, am going to push right through the wall. Stretch my mouth wide; unhinge my jaw, wide; open, open, fill my mouth with yell; and bellow dumbly until my eyes squeeze shut and my jaw clicks. My hands are claws and I shake my burden out through them. Shake. Unhinge my fingers. I yell until my neck hurts and even my upper lip hurts from the intense wrinkling. I utter no sound but I roar, back pressed into rock until I am too worn to persist.

My mouth is stuck wide. I have to shift my jaw to the left, really stretch it before it will unlock so I can close it. I take one breath and all tension leaves me. I sink to the ground, not enough strength to remain on my feet. "I don't think I can carry on," I think on a sob.

When I open my eyes, the second born is standing in front of me all lit up with commiserate emotion. This one is always angry. This one knows just how I feel.

I didn't want anyone to see.

I stare, not knowing what to do. Am empty. "What?" I whisper. God damn me, I think; what do you want?

It shows me what to do. She stretches up her arms.

Pause.

I'm numb, have nothing inside me, not even resistance. With rubber bones I extend my arms half way. Our fingers touch. I can move my fingers. I clasp her fingers in the tips of mine. She steps forward. I stare again. I guess I'm deciding although it doesn't feel like my brain is thinking at all. Maybe I'm not thinking.

I reach my hand to the back of her head and pull her closer. She turns her head and bites my forearm, but it is soft and more desperate than mean.

I find I have enough in me for this task. I pick her up and since she is facing me anyway, I give her a squeeze. She latches on, buries her face in my chest, clutches me. Now what? Because it worked before, I give another tentative squeeze and that seems to be what she needs. She doesn't let go. I guess we could just sit here all night. It would be all right with me and seems to be all right with Hissie, but I hear a commotion start up on the other side of the wall so I get to my feet with the used-to-be-angry one still held awkwardly in my arms.

I guess I have some energy after all. Not a lot. I have never been so physically tired. But I have more than I did before the scream, before the squeeze. I walk back to the gang. The apathetic one is sitting on the hairbag. Her brother, one of the newer siblings, is tugging on the bag, "I wanna sit. Give me. I wanna have it."

The ferociously ugly rhymer is licking Whaddle's eye goo. When they see me, half of them dissolve into tears. The apathetic one remains static, which I have come to expect. It seems I have another crisis on my hands. I sigh and then wade in.

~

"What are you doing, Smudge?" Russell's voice is calm, not shocked at all.

I loosen my jaw so I can answer him. "I'm chopping up this bush," I spit the words without turning to face him. I just keep slicing the poor flowers off.

No sound from Russell.

This is the third plant I've attacked. I also killed a holly bush and a climbing wisteria. Whack, grunt, whack.

"Why?" He asks, so unruffled I want to move him to emotion.

I spin and raise my weapon. He neither blinks nor steps back. He's Russell, steady Russell. He doesn't see me as a danger, doesn't see me that way. All of a sudden, the impulse drains out of me. I look at the blade in my hand. Don't know what to do with it.

"Do you feel better now?"

I look away from him to consider it, "No. Not really. But I felt better while I was hurting them."

Pause.

"Did you really?" Was all he said with a half-surprised/half-interested look on his face.

And I stopped to consider my answer. I hadn't actually felt better, but I did lose myself for a time and that felt just fine. I scowled at him. "Yes, I felt better," I growled.

"Where do you hurt?" He asks me and holds out his hand. I hand the blade to him without noticing. He hangs it from his belt alongside his other implements. "Where in your body do you hurt?"

"Here," I point to my jaw.

"Ahh, chewing sweet grass helps that. Where else?"

I smile. Can't help myself. It's such a Russell-thing-to-say. "I'm tight, all in through here." Neck, chest, even my stomach is clenched.

"I know the perfect spot," my wise friend says and leads me off to the far side of the pond. We lay on our backs, hidden by the tall meadow flowers, and chew the sweet white bases of grass and we watch the clouds float by and change from one shape into another and listen to the endless "zzzz's" of bees and hear the water lap and feel sun-like-syrup run down our faces. We don't answer when Rob calls or Uncle Eck. We don't answer when the other gardeners summon Russell. We don't do anything but drain out the poison.

"I'm sorry I hurt your babies, Russell."

"Mmm," he grunts. "Hep, this is much better."

It was, too.

~

Touching them helps the beasties settle. I sit down and gather them to my lap. I wipe away tears and rub bellies and croon to ease hurts. My hand is gooey after wiping Whaddle's eyes. The creature produces prodigious amounts of goop: eye goo, nose muck, ear drippings. I think she is allergic to being hungry.

The ugly-rhymer starts humming again, I lightly place a goopy finger over her mouth as I push down on Hisser's chest to keep her from attacking. The ugly one licks my finger and thrums with pleasure. I give it my palm to lick. The beast licks it clean.

"I wanna hold your hand," the small whining beasty-boy says and tugs on my arm. He moves my hand to rub over his face. As soon as my hand lifts away, the ugly one scoots over to Whaddle and licks her face. It's disgusting but skinny-rhymer-with-the-overbite likes licking Whaddle's goo and Whaddle seems to enjoy the attention, too.

They sit up, hands clasped on each other's arms, feet-to-feet, both humming enjoyment. The apathetic one just lies still watching us all with cold bleak eyes, which leaves two hands to manage two babies. Easy.

The humming eventually attracts the whiney-boy's attention. He throws my hand off his face and sits up. "I wanna lick, too" he whines. No one seems to think it is disgusting, except me. So I concede. If that goo can be harvested maybe they'll stay calm. Maybe it'll ease their hunger.

"What do you think, Whaddle? Do you want to share your goo?" I ask the leader.

"I good. I share goo. I da one. I da best." She loves attention, craves respect. This works in my favor right now.

"Whattle the others think?" I ask knowing full well what the others already think.

"Want goo. Wanna have some," says the boy as he reaches graspy-hands towards his sister. "Why I no get any." In-out, in-out he grasps his fingers. "I wanna." His whine is no match for the manipulations of his sibling, though.

"Whaddle's the best." The ugly-rhymer croons. This one knows exactly what to say - is pretty sophisticated when compared to the other beasties. "Whaddle a hero."

Whaddle sighs with joy and turns her face towards the ugly one, again. The ugly one keeps licking. That one is smart.

201

"Want some now," the boy whines.

Whaddle points to her brother and bosses, "You wait." Petty little tyrant.

I let this go on for a few minutes, then say, "Who's next?"

Whaddle points to the apathetic one and asks, "You hungry?" The youngest gets to her feet and scurries over. I've never seen her move fast before. She meows a pathetic, whiny sound and her eyes get disgustingly wide at the idea of food. It's the only time I've seen expression on her face. It turns my stomach.

The boy wails his disappointment. "Not fair. I wanna lick."

"Each of you will get a turn licking Whaddle's face." I reassure him.

"Wannit now. Wanna lick now."

"Shh, shh. There, there now," I rub his belly and offer other nonsense. Wish I had some sweet grass to offer.

"How I doing?" Whaddle keeps asking at each new turn. It's curious to me how a boastful, vain creature could have such a puny identity. Whaddle is very sensitive to our opinions. It is an interesting contradiction.

"Your goo so smooth," charms the ugly one from the sidelines.

The tyrant Whaddle says, "It's your turn again," and points to the ugly charmer, which will cut short I-Wanna's turn.

"No, no. My turn still." He grabs onto Whaddle's arms and won't let go.

"Don't lick so hard," his sister says "You make wrinkles."

That makes me laugh; what a character she is. I tuck my chin so she doesn't notice me laughing at her. She would hate to appear foolish, which is, in itself, pretty hilarious.

Whaddle's tiny arms are not strong enough to push her brother off. I-Wanna, the boy, has long arms so he holds her head still as he slurps away. "Dis not work'n for me," Whaddle states. "Don't hold me." But her tiny arms can't push him off of her and he's not letting go. Ever resourceful, Whaddle leans back and her great weight pulls her roundness out of his arms. She rolls away from him, tucking her tiny legs and arms flat against her belly-like-body. She rolls around and around getting her goo all dirty, keeping her goo to herself. I-Wanna-Turn follows after her, but cannot get a hold of her. Whaddle taunts him, "I no like you slurp. You have 'nuff. Go away."

He charges up to me, the impotent one, tears of frustration overflowing his eyes. "No fair. My turn all gone. No goo. Hungry. No goo." The ones in my lap are agitated, too. Afraid they are going to lose out on the treat. Cry, yammer, pout.

Whaddle sings out triumphantly, "Whaddle is great. Whaddle in charge." The overbearing little fart.

I grab I-Wanna and whisper. Whispering adults always catch the attention of children. Whaddle stops rolling, beasties stop twitching, and I-Wanna stops crying and listens. "This is what you do," I say on a breeze of a sound. "Walk up to center stage and say you are going to let everyone lick your eye goo …"

"I no have eye …" he interrupts.

"Huh, huh" I huff and put up a stop-hand and give him The Look. I guess all adults-in-charge-of-children develop their own version of The Look. He quiets right down. "As I was saying," I continue on a whisper, "go center stage and say you're going to let everyone lick your eye goo. Then, when your sister resists the idea, you let her convince you that it's her job. Then complement her. Got it?"

He nods.

"Okay. Go do it."

And he does. Perfectly.

Whaddle is horrified by his announcement. She rolls up and bumps into him. "I da one, I da one. My goo. Eat my goo. My goo good."

He plays it perfectly. He let's her convince him that she should be the one to supply the goo. He helps her stand by pushing her onto her big red (kind-of freaky) feet. And he tells her, "You so sweet I can't compete with you." Quite a nice little ditty.

Whaddle is completely won over. She is so delighted she dodders in a circle on those long paddles of hers. I enjoy watching her go. I enjoy watching the show. Her brother gets his turn. Before the next creature can start, Whaddle must receive a compliment.

I help them come up with compliments since their vocabularies are limited. "Pocket Venus you're a genius," or my personal favorite, "You're sweet and kind and lovable all the time." This is how it goes:

"I dunno what to say." A squealing voice, one pointy fingernail scratches my leg; the youngest begs me, "Give me pretty. Say pretty let me eat." The most words she's ever spoken.

"Okay, okay. Ummmmmm. Okay, say this, 'You are so round that you astound and pound for pound you are renowned.' Make sure you say, 'you are renowned' really loud. She'll like that part the best. You got that? No, no, try it again. Yes. Yes. That's it. Go try it. Yes, it sounds very good. Go try it before all the goo is gone."

And then another one sidles up and says, "No goo. Hungry. No goo." cry, yammer, pout, or something similar.

To tell the truth, it's kind of fun making up stupid rhymes and silly sayings. I don't even have to keep the creatures on my lap. The compliment-process demands they take turns naturally. Not many fights break out. They are occupied. I'm entertained and Whaddle loves being the hero. Her head seems to swell with each compliment.

As the others lick her facial drippings and tell her how wonderful she is, Whaddle gazes off in the distance slack jawed and with a dumb look of satisfaction glowing on her face. I'm grateful for my ringleader even though she is loud, obnoxious and gooey and vain.

Finally, Whaddle runs out of goo, but everyone is calm. We settle in for some sleep. All around me, tiny heads lay on my lap. The sweet weight generates a modicum of enjoyment. The creative one chews on the wild hair and blind-Hissie rubs a pinch of my skin between forefinger and thumb. I-Wanna grumbles about who got the longest turn (it wasn't him, of course) and Whaddle half-heartedly gripes about a rock under her hip but at the same time they stare at me with unguarded and heavy-lidded desperation. They need me to help them nod off, which I find oddly disarming. "Droopy eyes, sleepy eyes, gotta dream of starry skies," I sing nonsense to sooth them and a warm ember glows in my gut. It stirs me.

The ugly one picks up the song and hums nasally. Hissie stirs. I pet Hissie and put a finger over the other's mouth. I'm learning how to distract each one. They are all five different.

"I a hero," Whaddle whispers dreamily to me.

"Make her sssstop. Pleasssssse." Hissie is getting upset again at Whaddle's endless recaps of how wonderful she is. The others are fading, almost asleep. Whaddle's stomach rumbles. She never got to eat. The rumbles are keeping both her and Hissie awake. They are lying right next to each other. And me, of course, Whaddle's stomach rumbles keep me awake, too.

I peek under my lids at the five of them and Whaddle notices. "I make goo," she tells me, revving up again, "I make goo and feed all the babies. I a hero. First I just make da goo ..." She loves an audience.

"Please close your lips and go to sleep now," I request again, but she won't quit talking. Hissie covers her ears and turns pink. Not a good sign. Around Whaddle's round noggin I wrap my hands and haul her up into my arms right next to my face. "Just tell me," I whisper to her "and let the others sleep." I wink at the angry one who harrumphs and closes her eyes with a snarl.

"Poor little rumbley belly," I rub Whaddle's tummy, but Whaddle is silent now, gazing off in the distance as if she doesn't hear me. Her ears are just holes in her head – folded skin punched into her skull - inside out ears. "Hey, where are you?" I tease "I think you're listening to your stomach rumble more than you are listening to me." Actually, that may not be far from the truth. Slowly she falls asleep, but I am awake now and continue to rub her tummy.

The five creatures are attaching to me. They crave my attention and that scares me. What white light sign or signal might I miss by giving them the attention they demand? The more attention I turn to them, the more they seem to need, need, need and the less time I have for searching for clues.

By habit I pour what-if-scenarios into my brain and my brain responds with buzzy anxiety.

<What to do when the white light is found>

My hands start to tremble and I clench them to keep them still.

<They are too dependent>

My chin wobbles. I tighten it.

I'm going into the white light, I reassure myself. No way am I missing it

<Beasties need, too>

Hand them off; yes, that's the best solution.

206

<Who'd accept them>

If I find the people who travel here in this third death, and if they are acceptable then I could…

<Soldier would hurt them>

Soldier is not a candidate - he's no guardian. But there are others here, if they are reliable They can at least help me, advise me, tell me what they think I should do. If they are not like Soldier …

<if, if, if>

Grama Ans, she would be best solution to these scallywags.

<She said "no">

But, she said no and left me behind.

<She's gone; crashed - perished - gone; she's gone>

"Left behind," I mutter; "ugly words they are." Words forced out between taut lips. Everyone in my world is worried. No one has a clue what to do except Grama Ans and she's gone.

So, I must think. I have two goals. I need to find someone to take care of my charges. Then I can find and call the white light.

Oh, and another goal - I must find something to feed them. I don't think the goo will be enough.

<They need>

I look in my arms at vain and gooey Whaddle and rub her grumbly tummy. They are demanding, but she, at least, was generous today. I have come to recognize their distinct differences. Whaddle helped out today.

<You can never let her out of your sight, she'll get lost>

She is independent, Whaddle is, but she won't stray too far from the center of attention. Her vainness may keep her safe.

<That second born, has issues>

I'll admit, Hissie needs lots of socialization.

<Quarrelsome and violent; no one will tolerate her>

Distraction is the key with Hissie I think as I glance over at the blind girl. At least, I think distraction is the key. I can teach any new caretaker that skill.

<The third went and got itself eaten>

I barely remember the third one, but I remember the fourth one. The fourth is the predacious one that ate the third and then ran off; so these two creatures are gone. I guess that's for the best. Unconsciously I rub Whaddle's belly again.

<That skinny-one-with-the-overbite is too ugly>

It's smart.

<It's a hermaphrodite>

That is very different from the expected.

<No one is going to want that>

S/he is a good rhymer. Funny. S/he discovered Whaddle's eatable goo and s/he caught on to the song first.

<And likes to hum, sweet bleeding ears, it loves to hum>

Yes, it does enjoy the sound of its own voice. I smile and note I'm not vibrating any more. That boy, sixth born, is a bit of a whiner.

<Demanding little bore>

Never seems satisfied.

<Unacceptable, pesky>

Yep, nothing gets past the boy. He's vigilant, I'll give him that.

<And then there is the youngest ...>

I shudder. This one repulses me.

<Great empty eyes>

Empty except when it comes to food ...

<Shrill and cold>

... she gets under my skin.

<She is a problem; would have been nice if the predacious one had eaten her>

My lids are heavy. I'm so tired. I feel like moaning and I gently rub my feet together, but carefully so as not to disturb my charges. I look around in satisfaction and am surprised to catch the gaze of the youngest birthling.

<Those eyes>

I shiver and stop rubbing my feet.

<Soulless eyes>

I frown at her and motion for her to close her peepers. She stares a moment longer and then shuts her lids. Is she asleep?

<Or just waiting for me to fall asleep so she can stare some more>

I massage Whaddle's belly. It rumbles under my hand. While the first-born tries to be larger than life the last-born strives for less-than-living. She never moves when she can stand, never stands when she can lean, never leans when she can sit, and never sits when she can lie down. She sleeps if she is given half a chance. I don't know babies very well.

<Snort; don't know babies at all>

Never would have suspected that a baby could be depressed.

<Depressed and wrong>

While Whaddle craves attention, that last one …

<would sooner be unconscious>

My eyes dart over, checking on her lids. Still down; that's good.

<She's a desiccant; dries everyone out just by being nearby>

I don't like her. But I didn't like Grama Ans at first either and that's turned out fine.

<Took your eye, has Momma's locket, and saddled you with them>

Whaddle snortles. "I'm going to lay you down now," I whisper as I pat her tummy one more time. "Actually, it's easier on me that the apathetic one demands very little of my attention." I whisper-croon the words to Whaddle as I place her slack body on the ground next to me, "I like the break she offers," I sing-song to the boy as I shift sleeping bodies into spoon positions. Hissie shakes her head so I rub her arm. She snuggles back to sleep. I sing nothing to the youngest one as I place her on the outside, furthest from me, but nestled into the hermaphrodite. But guilt nibbles at the corners of my heart. I lay down at the far end. "Tomorrow I'll do better. I promise," I whisper to the roof.

210

<That's an excuse>

Yes, I admit to myself with shame.

... and the seed is lethal ...

-Journal Entry, May 15, age 24

Chapter 18 – Stories Are More Gold than Truth

"Why you no quiet?" the easily-angered-Hissie screeches at Whaddle, her question more a yowl than a voice.

I just got to sleep not more than fifteen minutes ago.

Whaddle's tummy must have started rumbling again. She's no longer underneath my hand. I cannot rub the tummy. I wave a shushing hand instead. "I need sleep," I think on a wail.

Of course the shushing hand does no good. I open my eyes and now there is light enough to see the other beasties are awake and watching their sisters fight.

The creative one reaches around to his naked hindquarters and grabs his cheeks and kneads them, such is the rising tension s/he feels. When I turn my eyeLight on him/her I see his poor little butt cheeks are bright red and mottled.

"Please everyone, shush. Go back to sleep." I really don't want to have to get up.

"Hissie is loud cuz Whaddle's proud," the ugly-one explains how the upset began. "Whaddle needs help."

213

"Let the two of them work it out," I begin, but I'm rolling over because I can tell the heat is rising. Hissie strikes her sister. "You need to stop," I suggest, too passively, just like I heard when Rob hit me in front of Uncle Eck. No heat behind Uncle Eck's command and no heat behind mine; no starch in the order, no sign of follow through. I'm still on the ground. I may be odious, but I cannot bring myself to move and stop the fight. "You don't want me to have to get up and come over there," I threaten, my warning is as empty as my order.

Of course they ignore me. When Hissie slaps Whaddle over her head, I finally heave myself to my feet and get between them. "Alright! What's this about?"

Whaddle proudly says, "I got extra toe and finger. See."

This statement is not what I'm expecting. Have to admit, I'm confused. "What?" I ask. Then I look down and see the extra digits and for some reason those extras bother me. "Euwe," the though flashes across my brain, "That reminds me of my extra long big toe. People hate that kind of thing." Some disgust must have flashed across my face because Whaddle defensively grabs her extra digits in her other hand and begins a long-drawn out story about how useful it is to have extra fingers and toes when swimming.

"Swimming?" I scoff. "You've never been swimming."

Hissie says with no little heat, "She no lie; she braggart." To her oldest sister she says, "You try to say too many toes is better than my toes?" And Hissie turns bright red. Any minute now she'll start kicking.

"No, no." I interrupt, desperate to end this and get back to sleep.

"You expect me swim?' Hissie screeches. In the background the creative one chimes a melody as s/he anxiously milks his butt cheeks, "We don't swim. We don't swim. My, oh, my, Whaddle you are dim, not to know that we don't swim."

"You're not helping," I shush him/her.

Whaddle pipes up in her tiny voice, "But I like to swim. Am good at swim. Maybe if I show you how ..."

"What did you sssssay?" small-boned Hissie interrupts, screeching the question again and again every two seconds until I bend and pick her up and scratch her along her jaw. This has calmed her down before.

'What in skunk-liver's name is going on here?' I demand in a funny voice, trying to deflate the situation. Hissie slugs me in the chin, wanting down, wanting to attack her sister. I hold her away from my face. I want to retaliate, but that will just make her angrier. I round on Whaddle taking my sleepless frustration out on her. It's safer than getting mad at Hissie. "Are you causing a ruckus again?" I demand and Whaddle scrunches up into a tight little ball and whispers that she wishes she was invisible.

The ugly-creative one huffs at this as if in agreement, but Whaddle's eyes are as big as two moons. With a snort of dismissal for Whaddle I look back at Hissie and try ouci-kouci-kou'ing her. "You're a good girl, aren't you? Aren't you a good little girl?" I say in a baby voice trying to calm her down.

I-Wanna asks, "Is Hissie you favorite? I wanna kouci-kou. I wanna. You only love Hissie?"

And the whole area gets quiet. The other beasts glare at Whaddle for starting this whole problem.

"What you gonna do to me? You no want me?" Whaddle shudders. All of the other beasties shudder, too, except the ugly-creative one. S/he pads away from Whaddle and starts a deep-throated rumbley sound and he winds his long skinny body in and out of my legs just like a cat. For just a moment s/he doesn't look hideous all stretched up on her tiptoes, weaving an enticing pattern and perfuming the air with her rumbles. Hissie swats at me with her foot and I put her down, confused emotions bludgeoning through me. Did I just act like Grandma again? Did I just reward the mean-Rob-Hissie while crushing poor little Whaddle who did nothing to deserve it?

The creative creature licks Hissie's huge ear and they both close their eyes in delight. The other babies take their cue from me and gather around Hissie and the creative creature. Their backs shut out Whaddle.

I can see the despair in Whaddle's eyes as she looks at the row of backs facing her. "I no know how to live lonely," Whaddle says. She's scared and I cannot unglue my mouth to reassure her or my feet to go to her.

Wanna, the envious one, hops from one foot to the other staring at me with eyes widen with fear, "If dis can 'appen to Whaddle, it can 'appen to me." He hums with agitation until the idea overwhelms him and he takes off running. He runs until the wild hair he is still holding pulls taut and then the poor thing falls on his backside. His legs keep running though.

I force words past the lump in my throat. I speak to the gang at large as if telling a dirty secret. It hurts to talk and my voice is scratchy. "I was never supposed to talk about this." I say but avoid their expectant eyes. "All I ever wanted was to be welcomed by the rest of The Family. I tried to act right but inside me was a coiled spring. Just sitting beside The Family wound the spring inside me, coiling it tight until I had to jump up and run in circles and hop and bound off to some far corner of the grounds. . . . " Here Wanna sits up, his legs stop peddling. And Whaddle nods as if in recognition of such a coiled spring.

"... It was during one such 'unwinding' that I fell into the pond. ..." Here the babies look wide-eyed at me.

I muse, lost in memory, "... It was a shocking surprise at first, of course, but then as natural as all-get-out my legs started paddling and

216

my ears came out of the water as did my nose and then I was swimming. I was quite good at swimming."

"Me, too. Extra toes help me paddle," Whaddle haughtily takes over the story. "Those same toes dat Hissie point at and snicker 'bout. D'hose extra toes giff Whaddle good grab at pond. Whaddle feel grand 'bout swimming around da pond."

"Braggadocio," I sputter and laugh, "what are you talking about? You have never even seen water in your life." Having said that to her, I start remembering again, "But Whaddle is correct. Swimming in the pond did feel grand. I felt grand swimming and rolling down a hill, and climbing a tree. I felt wonderful until I got back to the mansion. Grandma didn't like the idea dirty pond water on her rugs. The Aunts shuddered and said I had unnatural aspirations. The Uncles pooh-poohed the idea although I know that they must have played in the mud as kids. The house boys who I had seen recently in the pond kept quiet on the subject since Grandma said it was uncouth and no one who valued their jobs spoke up against Grandma. And Rob, whose father had almost drowned one winter when he fell through the ice, hated the pond. Rob hated water he couldn't see through and he especially hated the idea that little, weird, whispery me could do something that he was afraid of."

Whaddle shouts triumphantly, "Just like Hissie. Hissie scaredy, too."

Hissie leaps from my arms and pounces on Whaddle teeth bared and toenails extended as well - sharp and tearing. Hissie rips into Whaddle persecuting her rotund sister with screeched denouncements. Although there is no doubt in my mind that Whaddle is going to be torn apart, I still can't move my feet.

I can't move because Grandma didn't move when Rob jumped me. Grandma wanted me to behave. She was tired of my in-her-face-wildness and she wanted someone to get the message across in a way I couldn't ignore - but she didn't want to lower herself to that level. Of course Rob got out of hand. Just like Hissie is too rough.

There is inside me an urge to preserve Whaddle, but before I act, Whaddle begins to fight back. Whaddle lets out a huzzah that makes all of us jump. Amazingly the rotund tyke gets up from being pushed over and runs to a pillar-like rock. Hissie roars after her, anger not satiated, fixated on catching Whaddle. Whaddle runs up the pillar and then flips backwards in the prettiest somersault ever seen in this third death. Hissie is blind. She follows her sister by sound, so she doesn't notice the pillar. She runs straight into it. Hard. Stunned. And before she can register what happened, Whaddle lands from that pretty somersault right onto Hissie's backside and grabs her neck.

Wanna and the ugly one, naughty little monsters, giggle uncontrollably. The youngest watches apathetically. I'm horrified. Whaddle will break Hissie's back.

Whaddle, stretched out over Hissie's neck, reaches around and digs sharp little baby claws into Hissie's cheeks. Then Whaddle reaches over and bites Hissie's tender nose with pointy baby teeth.

Hissie's howl echoes around the cave. Everyone scatters as Hissie's rips through the middle of the group like a wounded tornado, spinning, bucking, and bleeding. "Stop this, stop this, please move to stop this," my own childish voice echoes down through the years. "You see it happening. Don't hide from me. You see. Why do you let this happen again?" I cry out in pain as Hissie sets down near the youngest for only a moment then is off twitching, lurching, and jolting until she bumps into my legs. I'm scratched by Hissie's flailing feet, but that's not what caused me to cry out. I unstick my feet and retreat, turn my back, busy myself winding up the bag hair, try to distance myself from the hoopla. Once again I feel agony at how I am shadowing the faults of The Family. Once again I am failing and cannot move myself to change the pattern.

Hissie is a juggernaut and through it all, Whaddle hangs on and digs in (those extra fingers and toes coming in handy once again). Ironically, the same pillar that stunned Hissie in the first place got a second chance at her. Hissie never sees the post she runs into. Whaddle does though, and jumps off just in time. Hissie proceeds headfirst into that pillar and then sits for a good five minutes trying to stop the world from swimming around in circles and trying figure out what happened.

The surprising thing is that I did not cheer for the bulbous baby that fought the bully and won. Although the others muffle snickers at Hissie's expense when she sat stunned, I could not bring myself to salute Whaddle for a whipping given in self-defense, for a tyrant brought down a peg or two, or for the birth of a hero's soul expressed for the first time.

Hissie wails and gnashes her teeth and cannot endure the trauma. She sits in the dirt and throws a temper tantrum, her ugly lips pulled back so she can scream with not a thing to block the sound. Although I cannot bring myself to comfort Whaddle my heart breaks at the Rob-like-baby-Hissie. Just like The Family always did, I pick up the beast and support her. And just like Rob always did to The Family, Hissie kicks me and punches at my face with her feet and bites me.

I hold her tight and tell her I don't like the hitting. I soothe Hissie until she buries her head into my chest screaming in short sharp bursts now, but not so loud that she can't hear me soothing her. I know she is calming down because her skin fades from the blue-tinged pale of hot anger to red, to pink, to a faint flush of color, which indicates slight provocation. After a bit more snuffling and nose rubbing against my chest bone, she calms herself to the point where I can put her down and steady her until she gets lined up with the bag and grips it with one of her prehensile feet.

"That's enough for tonight," I declare.

"What happened when you was kid?" Little Miss Apathy asks shocking me as much as if one of the tunnel rocks had uttered the words. "What Grandmother do?"

I'm so surprised I answer her. "I fought Rob that day after he attacked me and I whipped him. But no one would look at me." I still couldn't look at Whaddle. "Rob was more feted than ever. He became even more obnoxious, but skittish, too."

The youngest birthling tugs on my leg and repeats her question, "Not Rob. What Grandmother do?"

"Grandma snarled at me," I say, my voice like a child's, heavy with confusion. "Of all the people in that house, I thought Grandma would support me. Instead she was angry at me for losing control. She said, 'We are pillars of the community. We do not behave like thugs...'"

Whaddle huffs at that, "Rob acted like thugling all da time."

"That's what I said." Finally I can look at Whaddle. She is indignant for me. I failed her in every way and she is indignant for me! "Well, Grandma could hardly argue with that so she changed the lecture immediately. She said, '... and we certainly don't go out prowling around by ourselves. We don't track mud into the house and we are all old enough to act with decorum.' She said a lot of other things, too."

The youngest birthling is silent now; that empty look in her eyes is back. Where are you, little one?

Whaddle is confused. "How can dis fight be Whaddle's fault? All bad is Whaddle's fault? Do me not say 'no'?"

I kneel down in front of Whaddle, still not able to hug her, but I can look her in the eyes and I can talk to her. This is a precious start. "Whaddle, you stand up for yourself. Don't be like me. If someone bites you, bite back. If someone picks on you, yell it out. Draw attention to it. Make people listen. Whaddle, I never went on another adventure."

Here all of the babies plunk down on the ground and cry. They wail. And then they start biting, and pinching. They are hungry, they are tired, they need this and that right now. I sit on the ground with them and clean under my fingernails and say nonchalantly, "Except," I say this very quietly and the babies's volume turns down. "Except during the long summer days..." Now they shush each other and push a bit and tug on the wild hair-bag to creep a bit closer to me. "I never went on another adventure except during the long summer days while lying in the sun, stretched out in the grass. I dreamed of swimming."

Whaddle cheers. And now I lie down slowly and turn away and they get up and lay down in the crook of my stomach, straining to hear this part. I speak slowly and drag it out unmercifully because they want it so badly all the while tucking them in and rubbing their foreheads.

"I lay there in the sun with Whaddle and our too-many-toes twitched when we slept. This was the only proof that we swam in the pond when we dreamed. Twitch, twitch. Sometimes Whaddle would dive under the green water with its bits of refractive matter and chase fish. I usually stayed on top of the water, but Whaddle could hold her breath for a long time. And Whaddle's irises would open wide in the darker depths of the pond bottom. Whaddle could see as well in the green underworld as she saw at night on dry land. No doubt about it, the fish were faster than Whaddle. They saw her swimming and darted hither and thither, but Whaddle had innate cunning and awesome dexterity. In our dreams, Whaddle and I ate fish aplenty. That's all."

The little ones sigh with relief and we all fall silent for a short while. I'm not sure they realize that the last part was just a story, something I made up. I think they believe it is real, silly beasts. I smack my tongue to the roof of my mouth and slow my breathing and deepen it. The sound lulls them back to sleep.

... but not that scarlet voluptuous fruit ...

-Journal Entry, May 15, age 24

Chapter 19 – Walking With the Light On

Childish whispering tickles under my blanket of sleep; don't want to wake yet. However, my attention is caught by the edge of conspiracy in the voices. Somebodies are up to no good.

Morning dawns when I lift my lid. Light fills the room.

There are only two little warm bodies lying next to me, Hisser and the youngest one. Three guilty faces peep around a corner: guilty-consternation = Whaddle; guilty-ornery = the hermaphrodite; and guilty-pouty = Wanna. "What are you three up to?" I croak, throat dry and thickened with sleep.

Whaddle steps forward hands folded behind her back, the perfect picture of false innocence. "We play quietly. Let sleepyheads nap."

Wanna pokes his head up over Whaddle's shoulder. "We okay. Not doing nothin' wrong."

The ugly hermaphrodite pokes its head over Whaddle's other shoulder, "Go back to sleep." All three nod with false sincerity. Nothing could have gotten me to rise more efficiently.

"Sooo, what are you up to?" I ask as I roll to my feet, which wakes the other two. They drag themselves after me like twin moons as we approach their siblings. Three pairs of eyes widen in alarm. I squint mine. "What ..."

Resigned, the ugly-creative one says, "Darn it."

Whaddle, always the optimist, bounces on her toes and answers, "Whaddle da 'splorer. I find it. I da hero."

Of course, Wanna finds something lacking in the scenario. He complains, "You always go first. Not fair. I find it if I go first."

The ugly-creative one explains, "Would be there now, but hair wouldn't let us." All three beasties frown at the hair looped around my ankle and intertwined between them.

"You found what?" I croak exasperated. "What did you find?" Whaddle points over her shoulder. Wanna slaps her finger, knocking it down. The hermaphrodite sighs. So round the corner I go. Of course it's the crossroad path I didn't choose yesterday. We take two steps past the area where I had my silent berserker rage last night and see a tunnel. I never noticed it. Right here, where my back was pressed against the wall is a low cave entrance.

"Whaddle," I ask, "What's this?"

"Whaddle find cave. I wonderful. I, Whaddle, will mount the cave."

"Mount the cave?" I grin.

"I go in first," she crows with puffed up chest.

"Me first," her brother butts in and pushes forward. "Me, me, me; I wanna."

"Let me just take a quick scan?" I suggest. "It's dark in there, pretty intimidating. Wanna backs off immediately, but Whaddle only reluctantly nods her head and steps back out of my way. "Excuse me," I gently brush little crowding bodies aside and sink to my hands and knees to peer in. My five beasties squat, too, huddled all around me.

Wanna-the-envious pushes Hissie out of his way so he can see better. "I wanna look. I wanna. Out of way, sis. I wanna, Let me. Let me." The push is too hard for the sleepy Hissie and she stumbles and bangs her hand on the rock.

With no conscious thought, I reach back and bring Hissie forward before she revs up. The creative hermaphrodite and the youngest step out of the way. Whaddle, too. Hissie's skin flushes pink, her eyes squeeze-shut and she bites me, but not too hard and not too long. "Whaddle-ssssisssie," I sssay; "don't dassh offff until Iiieeeeee seeeee ifff it'ss sssafe." Hissie sighs, Whaddle pauses, and I smile at the creative boy/girl, who smiles back at me.

"Hair, some help here." I request and the hair leisurely floats and snags a loop around each baby-bumpkin head.

Wanna opens his mouth to complain but my words are already on their way out, "Ohh, what pretty crowns you guys have. I can't decide if I like Whaddle's or Wanna's crown better. Hmmmm, let me think…" And the two preen for me as I scratch Hissie's chin.

"See, me. Mine is fine," my homely rhymer sing-songs.

"Miner is finer," Wanna whines.

Before I turn my eyeLight to full blast I face Wanna and, in a stage-whisper, I tell him, "Hissie is mad at you. Better watch your back."

Wanna's eyes grow wide and he spins in a circle, crouched down, hands to the ready, taking stock of this danger. I've got to hand it to Hissie, she's got strong boundaries and if anyone crosses a boundary, that bull's going to charge.

225

Right then and there, as I kneel on hands and knees, I decide I need some of Hissie's attitude. All my life I needed to draw boundaries and defend them, too. "Whaddle, step off. I'm going in first." I command so forcefully, Whaddle jumps back, respect dawning in her eyes. Heck, I even impressed myself. Feeling strong, I fill the little cave with torcheye light.

The cave is small, not much space, but deep. I glance at the others then shrug and motion for them to stay back as I crawl forward. Interestingly, there is a stool in the cave, placed midway between entrance and back wall. There are no lights and no footsteps inside. Everything is covered in dust. Someone placed the stool, but hasn't been here in quite a while.

Although the stool is squat, the ceiling is also close. I cannot sit on the stool as my shoulders would touch the ceiling with no room for my head. Over the stool I crawl and halfway across, I see a mirror on the floor, which is odd. I look closely at the mirror and see myself in full rotting detail. Euw, not good. Then I focus behind my reflections and see my behind. There is a mirror on the ceiling, too. From behind I appear much less tattered than my front-self. That's when I feel a tug on my leg and look down unsurprised to see Whaddle standing next to me, short little arms held up.

Amused my hands snug under her delicate little armpits, bones fine-spun like a bird's, and softly grasping I lift her up and plop her onto the stool. She bends over and looks into the mirror. I expect her to be horrified at her ugliness but am disarmed when she likes what she sees in the mirror. She reaches out in delight and when her hand hits the mirror, she is confused and looks up at me. I point out my reflection and her eyes widen in wonder and she explores and finally learns the concept of reflection. What a delightful process to witness!

Whaddle rolls her head up and sees her behind reflection and wiggles her backside. "Yep," she coos, "dat one works, too." And then, with a look of dawning wonder and enchantment, she stares forward and dips her head a number of times and then she falls spellbound staring into the mirror. Even with an overabundance of vanity, I cannot see why staring at her reflections would spellbind her. I lower my head so it is directly behind hers and still, all I see is our reflections spun out a number of times.

"Look dat," her voice shakes and so do her fingers as she smashes my face next to hers and points at our reflections. Tears course down her face. She lifts her little arms again and then, when I lift her, she buries her face into my shoulder and clutches at me and sobs. I pat her back awkwardly and finish crawling over the stool and sit with her clinging to me. I am confused by the tears. I saw nothing in the mirror that would disturb.

I-Wanna-do-it enters the cave whimpering. He awkwardly pats his sister's heaving back. Hissie crowds in, too. There really is not enough room in this cave for five of us - the rhymer followed on Hissie's heels. All three are uttering little thrums of distress. For once Hissie doesn't react to being crowded. "Wha da matter," Hissie mewls.

I shrug my confusion to them and hand-soothe Whaddle's fat little body. Before too long, the ugly one reaches up and pats what s/he can reach. And then Hissie joins in, too. Only the sluggish one, who is still outside the cave, is not trying to comfort the sister. I have to swallow down my sentimentality at this show of caring. They are learning.

Finally Whaddle stops bawling and turns in my arms to face her siblings. Her facing is shining, beaming, exultant. Not at all what I expected to see. She squeaks and squeals and waves her fat little arms. The others draw back and then start hopping up and down in excitement. Wanna crawls up onto the stool.

"Me next," the creative one demands, followed by Hissie. Since the lazy one hasn't entered the cave, she makes no claim to the stool. I assume she's fallen asleep out there.

"You alright, Whaddle?" I rub her face. "You had me a bit worried back there."

227

She smiles her ugly toothy grin and pats me on the shoulder and tries to wrap her too-short arms around me. Then we both turn to look toward the stool as we hear chaos erupt - probably a fight to see who gets to look into the mirror first. I roll my eyes and we share a grimace, then I set her down and I crawl back to the stool.

... that ...fruit – small and plump with a
charming little depression cupping its moit.

-Journal Entry, May 15, age 24

Chapter 20 – Somewhere, Understanding Builds

"So what did you see in the mirror that made you all so happy?" I ask. They trade looks and giggle and pat my arm.

"You no see? Seventh mirror - see good all the way - what we gonna do!" Crammed into the cave with barely room to move we all look towards the mirror again. Wanna's on the stool. I'm on the far side of the mirror closer to the back of the cave. I'm leaning in and looking hard with torcheye on full. There are only two mirrors, one stool, and the five of us in the cave. Four little faces look at me in the mirror. Four little expectant faces, four laughing faces, everyone is laughing at me - except me; I'm frowning.

"There are only two mirrors," I counter, somewhat disgruntled and sweep the cave with light one more time. "Where did you see seven mirrors?" They laugh so hard they bend over. "What?" I ask them charmed by their giggles in spite of myself. "What?"

They just laugh harder. "Sssstop, sssstop pleassse." Hissie gasps.

Me: "No really. What do you see?" Truly, I don't see seven mirrors. I stick my head close to the floor and light up the area beside the mirror. "No, nothing. Count 'em. One, two mirrors."

"Ahh hahahahaha, tummy hurt," Whaddle chokes out propped against my bum so she doesn't fall over.

"Cheeksss ssssore. Sssstop." Hissie falls to the ground right next to Wanna-on-the-stool who's kicking his legs in the air and yelling, "We see, what we are gonna do. Ooh, my neck, my neck tight. No mo' laugh." For once, the rhymer can't sing anything. S/he is too busy laughing.

"What's the joke?" I pull my head away from the mirror to see them rolling on the ground. "You laugh like Grama Ans," I grumble to Whaddle. She has her legs in the air. No one believes my frowning forehead. Maybe it's the smile stretching my lips or my hiccupping stomach. "You're teasing me, right?"

"Ahhhhhhh hahahahahahahahahahahhaha."

I wrap my arms around my stomach and bend over. A snort escapes. It makes them laugh harder. Tickles my fancy, too. "Hee hee hee," I gasp laughing as hard as they are now. "You really only see two mirrors like me - don't you?"

"Haaaaarrrrrrr"

"I 'plain it to you. I sing it straight for you," laughs the intersexual ryhmer. S/he stands up and waves her/his arms. "Tah dah …We innate, you negate disassociate, one irate make two absentee-rate with one infant mortality rate - crime rate, crime rate - ate - hate." The other babies are clapping and cheering. I'm completely lost, haven't got a clue. The ugly singer continues, "In the mirrors, seven times we see da whole blind date, recriminate, desecrate, relate, reinstate, innate, maturity date, then eight. Whaddle's got goo and see in seven mirrors, too. Tah daaaaah." S/he ends with a big flourish and bows.

The others laugh. "Now you understand," Hissie says as she reaches for me so she can stand. She pulls me down on all fours.

I chuckle but warn, "Careful there. And no, I haven't a clue what just went on."

"Me, me. I wanna stand. No mo' stool. Help *me* stand."

"Ooooooonly two? Hahahaha. Yesssss, nooooo seeee seven." Whaddle's still hysterical, but the laugh is developing an edge to it. I close my torch eye to concentrate on what I'm feeling. Gentle little warning in my gut. The laughter is edging towards something other than fun. Things are on a downward slope. Time for a distraction.

"Hey, gang." I plop to the ground and grab Whaddle's arms so I don't knock her over. I need a distraction. "I'm going to walk to the end of the cave on my bottom. Look, I'm butt-walking backwards. It does the trick. Hissie and the others are laughing-real again, not that edgy laugh. They all hit the ground and try to coordinate 'cheek'-walking.

I scoot myself towards the back of the cave, followed by a quick-to-catch-onto-cheek-walking creative baby, followed by an uncoordinated Whaddle, followed by a butt-scooting Hissie. They are having fun. Hissie unbalances, falls, turns red.

I'm too far ahead with too many bodies between me and disaster. I need another distraction. "Did I ever tell you about the time Hissie outfoxed Rob?"

Hissie freezes in her tipped over position. "I foxed Barb?" Hissie asks.

"Rob," I correct. "Cousin Rob. You don't remember outfoxing him?" I hide my face in my hands and shake my shoulders like I'm laughing. Got to give myself time to figure out what this darn story is going to be about. "Yup," I sing-song, "Rob was a bully and he just

231

walked right up and took a piece of Hissie's dinner. Well, as you can imagine, Hissie wasn't going to stand for that."

Everyone nods, even Wanna who is frozen mid butt-walk - one cheek raised in the air - and wide-eyed to boot.

I nod and think, "Hey, I'm getting the hang of this distraction-thing." Out loud I say, "Hissie decided that she was going to reclaim what was rightfully hers." I laugh as if the story is so good I cannot continue. Four little faces tilt up looking at me with excitement. Four little faces deeply enjoy this story. In a flash I remember the look of smiling satisfaction on Grandma's tilted up face as I stuttered a promise to trade away another glittering piece of my soul. Grandma's comfort was all I strived for back in life because along with her comfort came ephemeral acceptance. That tar-like acceptance stuck me fast to a stick that beat my spirit everyday and I was less for the doing of it.

These four smiles are so different I want to stop and gather them to me and fuss the dirt off of them or clean Whaddle's eye goop or feed them something. But there is no food and all I have to offer is my story. So, overcome with gratitude, I struggle to keep my story light and entertaining and spanking along at a great pace – good and right, for once, wreaking innocent storyline havoc on disgraceful abuse. They are happy. I have made them happy and I am more for the doing of it.

With a start, I realize I am different than Grandma. I am a different sort of guardian. Children ought not be treated as I was treated. I think, maybe I am doing a better job of stewarding these five than Grandma stewarded me.

I glance over my shoulder and see I'm almost at the back of the cave, which is not rock. I turn my eyeLight a bit brighter and see that the back wall billows. I scoot backwards just a little as I further the story along. The little funny kidlets scoot forward, adjusting around me. I scooch back one more time. They adjust again. Now I can clearly the back wall - it's fabric. I finish the story and bow at the waist as they applaud. Then I exclaim, "Hey, look. It's a curtain behind us." I lower my voice to a whisper, "Where did it come from?" The babies seem amazed by the curtain. In their whole lives, the only fabrics they've seen are my clothes made into a bag to carry them. "Other people made this curtain," I tell them. "Maybe we can meet some of these great people on the other side of this curtain. Would you like that?"

"Heeelllllllooooo," Waddle sings out. "Any bodies out there?"

The multi-gendered creative child lends her vocal talents to the callout, "Is someone behind the curtain? Iiiiii'd like to know for certain because I swear, if great people are there, I'd do more thaaaaan stare …"

"I here," from behind the curtain we do hear a voice. It's a voice we've all heard before: a squeally, monotone, nail-scratching-on-chalkboard voice. It's the voice of the youngest beastie.

"How'd she …" I begin. "But we all thought …"

"I so very amazed," Whaddle utters with great huge eyes.

Wanna and Hissie trade glances then shrug at each other.

"You were sleeping outside the cave," I trip on my words; "…way across, outside the other entrance… way over there." I point.

The youngest, behind the curtain, squalls, "I hungry."

"Oh dat's a surprise," the boy/girl giggles.

I call out to the youngest, "How did you get out there?"

She's silent for a long time, probably gathering her energy to speak another sentence. Finally she says, "I walked around. Followed da road."

"Come on in," I invite. Silence is my response. I scoot backwards towards the curtain and the beastie hidden behind it. I keep scooting (and the babies keep adjusting around me) until I can lean

233

over and move the curtain to one side. Sure enough, there she lies, just outside the cave with her back to us.

"Hey you," I waggle my fingers at the giggling boy/girl. "Could you move a bit so I can find out what your sister is doing out there?"

The smile falls off the homely mug. S/he pulls back his/her teeth and cries, "I Eggee, not Hey-you."

"Ok, whatever, could you move your knee ..."

"I Eggee, I Eggee, I Eggee, I not Hey-you. I Eggee." Tears dampen his/her cheeks.

"Shh, shh, Eggee. I'm sorry I didn't listen better. What a good name Eggee is. I like it. Eggee. Do you like it Whaddle? Hmmm, yes, quite nice. Eggee fits you..." My hands gentle when they land, stroking, soothing and my words fall into nonsense. Maybe I heard the nonsense once when I was very young and cared for. "Okay, there, there now. It's alright. Shhhh, shh. Oh baaaby, it's alright. Okay, there, there now ..." and Eggee calms and Wanna starts to cry so I calm him, too. Waddle rubs her head on my leg and purrs. I pet her cheek. Today I don't mind touching their goop or wrinkles or prehensile limbs.

Whaddle asks, "Why Idunno scared all time?"

"I ... Idu-who?" I ask.

"Idunno," Whaddle nods towards her youngest sister, the apathetic one outside the cave, outside the group. "Why Idunno scared all time?"

"Well," taken aback I pause. "Where did that come from?" No one answers. "You want me to tell you about Idunno?" I'm madly searching my mind for a story, but it's gone blank. I can think of nothing to say about her. "Well, you tell me …" I think I am clever as I sidestep and deflect. "… What do you remember about Idunno?"

"Idunno scared all the time."

Now this is not my understanding of the youngest beast, but since the others are all nodding, I go with that idea. "That's correct." I encourage "How did you figure that out?"

"Why Idunno scared?"

"Why scared? Why scared? Why scared?" Revs up Hissie.

I jump back in. "Idunno suffered a psychological trauma – uh, someone hurt Idunno's feelings very deep hurt – very bad." I am surprising myself. I have no idea what I am saying until I hear it, but what I am saying feels right. This *is* the only thing that could have happened to Idunno. I hear myself continue. "Idunno sustained a physical trauma as well, which also causes stress. Poor Idunno. Do you remember what it was?"

"Rob mean."

"Hurt Idunno."

"Idunno cried."

"No Momma." They chorus back to me a multitude of answers.

"That's correct." I urge them to continue. "Poor Idunno. What happened after her momma died?" A story is unfolding, not the reverberating truth, but something that is grafted onto a true root base.

"Idunno no sleep any mo'. She cold."

"Wait," I grimace, "She sleeps all the time; are we talking about the kidlet?"

Whaddle says, "She skinny. Me hungry; me eat; me fat; me have lots of friends." Whaddle can't seem to get off her original thread, "No friends. All like Rob not Idunno. Why? Why no friends?"

"Cry inside. Poor Idunno cry too much. Dry out. Idunno sad." Comments Hissie

"No momma!" Cries s/he Eggee. Okay, they are all getting distressed. I've got to come up with something fast. I'm still racking my brain when the-creative speaks again. "Grandma mad at Idunno. Miss pee-pee box?"

In the past few hours, the beasties began to develop anatomical elimination parts and they have been pretty obsessed about bodily functions ever since. Ah, now I have an idea. "That's right, Eggee. That's exactly what happened. Idunno was so sad she forgot how to wake up and go potty in the special place. She went potty on Grandma." Here the little beasts giggle and roll about. They love anything naughty and, I admit, I enjoy their ticklement.

"But everyone at the mansion loved Idunno." This last part I say as I lean back using my stomach muscles to hold me in place so I could speak to the baby outside the cave. As always, she lays with her eyes closed, silent and unresponsive. "Idunno," I cajole with my voice. She rotates her head, opens her lids and stares at me with big empty eyes. I shudder. Eyes to disappear in, or rather lose your way in. Since I'm not getting through to her I turn away, sit properly and speak to the rest of the gang, "Everyone at the mansion loved Idunno so much they went and got special help so Idunno was not sad anymore."

"No!" they clamor. "No help. Secret."

"All mean," Wanna whines.

And Hissie pouts, "Rob mean. Hurt Idunno."

"Oh, no." I exclaim in mock horror. "Idunno's family would never put up with that. They love Idunno."

"No help," Wanna clamors.

"Secret," Whaddle says simultaneously.

"Mean." Hissie shouts.

"Idunno sad. Not right." Eggee mourns at the same time.

"Well, you are all correct. It's not right." I love how they jump to Idunno's defense. Their sincerity catches me off-guard and I find myself choking up - how silly - even as I continue with the story. "No family should ever keep a secret like that. How will a problem ever be solved if no one pays attention? Did Idunno's family just look away? Pretend it wasn't happening – that Rob wasn't hurting Idunno?"

"Yes," Wanna says.

"Secret," Whaddle reaffirms.

"Ah, yes, a secret." I mourn. "That wasn't right at all. Idunno deserves better than that. All babies do." They bobble their silly-looking heads and I snort before continuing. "Yep, it's not right. Grandma got mighty busy whenever that bad stuff was happening. It was difficult living with Grandma when she found other things to notice."

My torcheye brightens to monitor their expressions. It lights up what I'm trying to hide from myself, too. I'm mighty busy, right now, telling this story so I don't have to deal with Idunno.

"Not right!" Whaddle empathizes and pats Hissie in commiseration. "All babies d'serves better dan dat."

I close my eyes because it looks like they are all accusing me. I know it's my own imagination, but I close my eyes anyway; don't want to see. With the light off, my nose picks up the smell of a banana.

"Wha…" Eggee begins.

My eyes pop open. Banana smell wafts into the cave; it's close by. As if connected by a string, every head in the cave swivels towards the entrance. Idunno sits outside the back of the cave, on the hairbag, calmly pushing the last bite of a banana down her hatch.

I'm bowled over by eight baby feet all in a hurry to get out of the cave. With my head on the ground I see Idunno tilt back her head and gulp the banana peel in one huge swallow. She disappears in a sea of bodies. Hands windmill. Something oblong is juggled up into the air. All ten hands are grabbing for it. It falls and rolls towards me. My sweet heavens, it's a pear!

My stomach lurches and hunger claws, claws, claws at me. Movement is my name. I roll onto hands and knees, scurry towards the pear stuck under the curtain. I dive for the pear; am beaten by inches. Hissie has it but not for long. Eggee tackles her. Wanna dives over both of them. Whaddle wrestles with Idunno for something. In one huge swallow the pear disappears down Wanna's maw. Whaddle has swallowed something, too, and Idunno is licking her face. Maybe there is more.

"Idunno, where did you get the fruit?" I ask crawling again, baby hands and feet underneath me; need to be careful where I set mine down. I'm out of the cave, but still crawling. My voice is sharp. "Idunno. I'm talking to you."

She turns those great empty eyes my way and says, "Found them in the white light."

Words to halt all breath. She couldn't mean "white light" as in my white light. She must mean light, just any ol' light, but my voice is hoarse as I demand, "Show it to me."

"Mo' food?" Eggee asks.

"Where food; I wanna some," whines Wanna.

"I find it," boasts Whaddle. "You no need show me. I find it."

Idunno just sits there, the laggard. "Idunno," sharp bites my voice. "Get up. Show us this light."

She huffs a sigh, not of exasperation, not of resistance, but for the effort she will need to expend. For her, standing demands great effort. Right now I hate her for her slowness.

She rises, teeters a bit, then after an agonizingly long time she steps; pauses to consider her next move … "Idunno!" my harsh voice echoes in the tunnel.

Eggee turns reproachful eyes on me and frowns. I've got to get a grip on my patience.

Idunno teeters another agonizingly slow step. Behind us is the cave. Behind that is the crossroads. It looks like a single road ahead of us, for heaven's sake. How hard can it be? She takes an age to remember. I'm bouncing on my toes. Eggee sends darts my way again. Idunno turns back towards the cave we just came out of. I open my mouth to complain as she stops to peer into the dark. Whaddle puts a warning hand on my leg, so instead of complaining I up my torcheye to high beam so Idunno can see better. I guess it helps. Idunno shakes her head 'no' and rocks back on her heels to consider alternatives. "Shouldn't you turn around so you can see if that's the wrong way? Oh, for goodness sake, turn around and look, will you."

Hissie kicks my shin. Whaddle takes hold of my hand. "You got to be quiet," she tells me. "Let Idunno 'member."

Idunno takes chilled molasses time to spin around and look at her other two options. "We just came from the mirrored cave path." I pop up with advice, "It can't be that way. Can it?" When Whaddle jiggles my hand I look down at her. "What?" I ask defensively, "I'm just trying to help."

She shushes me. When I look back to Idunno, nothing changed. "Idunno!" exasperation forces me to speak.

Hissie spins, bright red. "Sssssso help ussss, ifffff you no be sssilent, I gonna ..." I hold up my free hand and hunch my shoulders in acquiescence. Eggee's back is tight and straight and turned decidedly against me. I vow to keep quiet no matter how long it takes, but it seems like it is taking forever and I really need to get going towards that light.

"Breathe," Whaddle suggests so I start panting.

Two tottery steps down the road, the one I didn't take last night, starts the mass migration. Finally we are on the way. It can't be the white light that Idunno found; it can't be that easy. The others crowd in front of me. Whaddle uses her grip on my hand to keep me behind her. It dawns on me that they think I'm too pushy. Ha. That's rich. Slightly offended, I snort derisively and try to unpeel my captive hand so it isn't until just now that I notice an extra light on the wall in front of the gang. It's subtle, the light, and it's not coming from me.

"You meanie som'times. Yo voice hurts." Whaddle pats my hand, the one still captured in hers. Some part of my brain must have registered the words and the pat, but I am caught up in the mystery of that light. Something about that light. I lean forward and dim my torcheye. Chatter dies down as the others take in my expression. I've got to go look ... I've got to ... I push my way to the front of the line and creep to the corner ... I peek ... another corner, brighter light ... it *is* soft and bright ... I half run, ziz-zagging around a third corner.

What I see is miraculous ... it stops me cold. Even my thoughts freeze. I am entranced.

Ahead of me a table stands; amid a pit of stone. Simple mortise-tendon joined, it stands like a throne. Rough-hewn, wooden, sturdy block - four legs and perfect top. I take in every detail, but my eyes keep going up.

Atop the table is a bowl. Bowl sits.

Clay bowl. Dry but not a fired trough - somewhat fragile. Within clay, thumb prints. Indents all over. Not proudly displayed, not smoothed out, just there – testifies creation. No hidden message. Cognition absolved – just a bowl. Naiveté delights.

In bowl lays fruit. Oh, this fruit is ripe ...

...is lusciously fragrant. No apple ever was so enticing on twig, in clay, or grounded. No peach was so ladened with scented promise, no mango ever so boldly colored yellow-green-red and oozing tongue-come-to-me-sap from the small gash in its flesh. This kiwi skin is roughly haired, begging to brush over tongue and teeth. The banana I can smell better than I can see. And yet it is not the bounty, nor bowl, nor table that holds me in thrall.

It is the light.

Shining down from a single source hidden from view onto table, bowl, and fruit is a heavenly white light. Soft yet it frees all sights for viewing. I've seen that light just twice before. I am here. The light has been called (and without harming Grama Ans). I can go home.

Breath catches, a hallelujah chorus of thanks rises in me even as the baby-beasts pile up behind me, bursting into action upon sight of food. They tangle in the hairbag, pulling me into the fruit-scented-air.

This is it. This is what I have been striving for, needing, wanting. I suffered for this and begged for it and yet, as the five little hoodlums hop into the light and clamor to be picked up and claw at the table, my feet are rooted and I'm bent like a bow - stomach out and back bent stretched by the hairbag that is pulled taunt, wrapped around my waist and tangled around many baby parts. I cannot move my feet forward.

Reluctant to even consider my hesitation I find my knees too heavy to lift. This light is what I need, what I have spent my whole third death looking for. Actually, it's what I've been striving for since I was sent back from my first death. For thirty years I hungered for this light. Here it is. Right in front of me. All I have to do is enter it and I am on my way to the heavenly death I love.

Is this a terrible spell that I am the only one who can't move? My fingers twitch. Fingers climb the air and wrap slowly around the hairbag drawstring. I pull myself forward, upright; drag a foot forward so I don't fall. I can move. I can. Go feet, go. Move into the white light.

The stinkers demand fruit be handed down, to be fed, to get some. Hissie kicks the table. Whaddle strains on tiptoe pulling at the table edge. No one is tall enough to reach, but that doesn't stop them. Even apathetic little Idunno's eyes stretch wide in that off-putting look that masks her face – that desperate, whiney, pathetic look - that says food, food, if I'm good I might get some food. "Table grew up," she mews pathetically. "I reached before. I can no reach now." Hissie kicks the table again then starts biting it. All this done before I can shuffle feet forward. And then the light begins to fade out.

The dominant light is now the one from my eye. Hurriedly I enter the spotlight around the table, but feel nothing – no warmth or bliss, no connection. Now, from inside the glow it is just a pretty light – more yellow than white, actually. I am too late. What have I done?

Numb, not knowing what to feel, I pick up the peach for myself - it's too sexy to feed to the little ones - and am jostled. The peach is knocked from my hand to the ground where a fight ensues. I grab both kiwis and a mango to distract the fight and I step out of the faded-light and yank backwards with my stomach, which wrenches all five away from the table in a tumbled heap in front of me. They squirm and roll around trying to get at the table and back to the fruit and the fallen half-eaten pieces. They really are little scamps.

They bump me again and I lose the fruit in my hands before it can be divided up fairly. Hissie gets two fruits in one gulp. The other kiwi is smashed as Eggee and Wanna fight over it. It's ground into the dirt during the scuffle. As they shove each other Whaddle licks the ground getting both smashed kiwi and dirt. Since Whaddle and Hissie eat all the available fruit, they congratulate me on my find. The others chew on the hair, trying to get free and get back to the table. So fast did bedlam erupt, there is naught to do. Now the food and the fight are resolved except for complaining. And I got nothing. Arrgh.

Glancing up, I note both table and bowl of fruit are fading just as the light faded away. The creatures cry out in surprise and disappointment. Clamoring starts - pleas for food, moaning and mewing and demands. I am berated for not getting more fruit. I am berated for yanking them away. I am berated for every decision I have made since they were born. Tiresome little beasties! That's when I realize I enjoy their company – quarrelsome and unattractive and noisy as they often are.

"Come on," I say gruffly, trying to hide my contentment with them. And careful not to step on them, I start walking amid a cacophony of protest down a maze of tunnels ahead. Finally I figure out exactly what I am feeling. I feel notLonely. I feel replete. Their irritatingly sweet little complaining voices satiate the echoing void that was inside me. They are mine to take care of and I can no longer be ashamed of them. Though I don't exactly know how they fit me, fit they do. And I realize I am not going anywhere without first making sure they are taken care of.

They just need a bit more time to grow and learn to take care of themselves. I push all deeper information away and start to sing a silly ditty to calm the tumult. I'll find the white light again soon. I'll find it and they will be ready to be on their own. This is not a disaster. We found the light once. Now I know it is here. One-by-one my little birdies settle down to march and tilt their chins to sing with me. Not hungry at this moment; I need nothing else.

PART THREE – *"INNAR"*

Although it alone is not poisonous …
-Journal Entry, May 15, age 24

Chapter 21 – Dangerous Back Trail

It is one thing to survive, I think. But it is even more impressive to grow despite stunting conditions. And my babies are growing. I'm … *ammm* … well, proud of them.

"Who's dat?" Eggee, the creative, asks with head tilted and a frown of concentration on her/his homely mug.

Everyone quiets and we hear a delicate sound wafting along the air – childish laughter and the screams of excitement heard only when children play tag. Where there are children, parents are not far away. Where parents are, I can find answers and maybe even supplies. "But, which way?" I wonder out loud. It's echoic and hard to pinpoint the laughter's direction.

Eggee listens hard - has a good ear that one - and says, "Dis way." And we follow without question. "Look dat," Eggee points to the ground.

I shine my torch-eye and see footprints. Adult footprints pointed in the direction we are now headed. "That's good," I say to the five little concerned faces looking up at me. Finding more people is a good thing."

They don't look so sure.

"Start walking," I firm my voice.

"Idunnooo…" a surprising dissonance from the youngest one. First time she's ever offered an opinion.

"Just start walking." I give Whaddle a gentle push.

The oldest resists. "I think we listen to Idunno. Som'ton don't lookee right."

Since I'm a bit fixated on my plan, I don't listen very well. "Wanna," I address the boy, "would you like to lead the group? I bet you could do the best job." I'm manipulating and it feels slightly slimy, but it works. Wanna pushes out his chest and looks around to gather in admiring looks.

"I lead the gang," Whaddle says, but her voice is hesitant. Hissie looks concerned. Eggee, who usually lives out loud, is reaming his/her rear end again. S/he only does that when anxious. Idunno has sunk back down into torpor.

With hesitation reflected on every face, Wanna deflates. "I not sure 'bout go'n dis way," he mutters.

"You lead the gang," Whaddle encourages her brother much to everyone's surprise. She ushers us all into a line. "Wanna, start walk'n. Eggee, you help. Wanna you gotta push Idunno to get her go'n. Hissie, walk proper! What's the matter with you all? Go on, walk like I tell you."

The hairbag gives me a tug and I find myself marching with them. "Well this is an unexpected turn," I mutter under my breath and

246

twist my head to keep track of Whaddle. It's disconcerting to have her lagging behind us instead of up front.

Eggee says, "Lift up, please. I need up to cuddle Idunno. She loves me."

I look at Idunno carefully, trying to see what the others see. Her expression is completely deadpanned, almost slack-jawed. "Whatever you say," I'm skeptical; but I pick the two up.

Eggee continues, "I lick her ear. It calm Idunno so she no worry."

"Whaddle, dangnabit!" Hissie yells to the back of the line; "get up here with us."

"Yes," I support Hissie in this. "What are you looking at? Quit dawdling." Then to Wanna, who has dropped out of the lead. In fact, he's behind me, too, and treading on my heels. "Wanna, please, back off. You almost made me trip. And Eggee, could you please loosen your grip; you're hurting my arm? What is up with you guys?" My little beasts are acting strange and it's starting to get to me.

"Wanna!" I accidentally step on him, then lift my leg and hop so I don't hurt him, but he grabs hold of my straight leg and almost climbs me. We topple, Idunno, Eggee, Wanna, and me. I twist to land on my back so the two I was carrying are cushioned by my chest. My leg, however, is pinning Wanna. "Is anybody hurt," I gasp.

"I wanna up. I need ride," Wanna demands as struggles out from under my knee.

"No, Wanna." I resist the whiney request but raise my leg; "I'm not carrying you. And I'm not lugging you either, Hissie; you both stay down. Eggee, Eggee! You need to let go of my arm, I'm trying to get up. Whaddle, where are you? Ouch, Eggee, that hurt. Let go of my arm. Ahhh! Okay, that's it! I'm not carrying any of you. Wanna and Hissie, start walking. Eggee, let go of me and grab Idunno's hand. Hell, drag her if you have to. Whaddle, get up here."

We stumble along for another hundred feet or so. Whaddle walks rearwards, looking at our back trail. Nobody's talking. Not even Idunno squeals to be fed and that worries me. And they shush me if I try to talk. Silently, Wanna and Idunno keep lifting their arms to me, supplicants to be held, but I feel a strange need to keep my hands at the ready and so keep shaking them off.

The skin on the back of my neck is prickly and in response to nothing, little shivers of dread race across my shoulders. I light our back trail, eye blazing, have done it repeatedly. We all crane to see but there is nothing behind us except fruit poop. My creatures still have not yet learned the skill of "holding it".

I turn my searchEye to the roof overhead and along the walls. I see nothing to concern me but I have to admit, I'm spooked. Subtly, so as not to alarm them further, I sniff the air. If I had stand-up ears, they would be swiveling all around my head, but I don't so instead I reach out with my new feeler-sensors.

All I sense is me.

"This is not going to work." My voice is low and deep. The babies jump at the sound of my words as if they were shocked by static electricity. "Stop doing that!" I exclaim and I jump and jiggle to get the tension out of me. "*Ammm*, we can't keep walking along when we all feel so over-strung." I scan the surrounding area for a place to hunker down. "Whaddle, we'll be right here. Would you please take the hairbag and brush out our trail like this? Stay in sight. Everyone else, pick up two big rocks - like this - and bring them to me."

And now, with my back to the wall and surrounded on three sides by boulders, I spread my legs and arms wide for the five to settle in and be surrounded by me. I cover them completely with the bag and they become pressing little soft statues. Intense stillness falls over the group and I strain with every sense I have to find what is out there. But

I close my eye. Fear of the dark is less worrisome than drawing something to us with the light.

There. I hear a smudge of sound. There it is again, the softest of padding, more a caress across ear hairs than a sound. What ever is out there is casting around our back trail. Predators do that. Hunters. Danger does that. I stop my breath.

It's getting closer and I am glad my heart doesn't work, otherwise it would be pounding out of my chest. But my lower jaw is tight with tension and I don't even realize my teeth are bared. The padding edges along our outermost boulder, so silent, slowly. Something is following our trail despite our attempts to hide it. I'm scared and not ready for this. Not a peep from the little ones.

There is a tiny scraping sound along the second boulder. This is the point where the hunter could go the wrong way. I strain my ears, my eyeSense, collect nothing. Is the hunter standing there, waiting for a clue? Go the other way, I silently urge - the other way.

I feel rather than hear movement ... as if the air currents are stirred ... but cannot tell if the hunter is coming or going ... just moving ... slowly ... another stir of air ... My back is hunched and neck down. I tighten my leg muscles in reassurance and close my hand over one of the rocks we gathered.

Just on the other side of the third boulder - right there - one more step to get round it - the predator is coming on a whisper of a sound. I turn my eyeLight to full blaze, hoping to blind whatever it is. In front of me is the soldier. Unblinded. No weapon in hand. Not even surprised by the sudden light.

"Oh, it's you," he says. "Got the locket?" He sounds nonchalant. He's not even breathing hard. I am. I'm breathing again and sound like a wheezy old racehorse coming in last.

"You! What the ... I think you enjoyed scaring us, I mean me." He has not rotted at all. In fact, if possible, he has gotten taller, more starchedPressed, older, cleaner, more angular and more commanding. His eye rakes over me and I can see by his expression that I look worse than last time.

I glance at his sheathed sword and recall my flayed stomach. I am spiked with adrenaline so I answer his original question rather sharply, "No locket." I look him square in the face and I know that I will not put up with any sword-play; I will fight him. I am in no mood to deal with him. "I have no food, no locket, and no time for this. Why don't you just move along?"

Soldier is surprised at my tone, but not offended. In fact, he seems intrigued. His lips move over the words "move along" as if he is tasting them, as if he savors them. He looks at me again, with more interest. "Are you alone?" He asks.

"What's it to you?" I retort, uncomfortable with the question. If he was indeed hunting us then he would have seen more than one set of footprints. He's playing a game and I don't like it.

Smoothly Soldier glides one step forward, too close, into my space and squats, rocking onto the balls of his feet. "Interesting bag" he comments. "Can I see it?"

"I'd rather you left it alone." I rejoin, but he reaches out towards the bag. I lift my rock and brandish it at him. Adrenaline is a fearsome thing, I think, because I am awash with an impulse to belt him with the rock - right upside the head as he squats - to protect my own.

He smiles at me, all charm at the forefront. It's an urging smile, a disbelieving smile, like he can't believe I am being so unreasonable. But it has an edge to it that smile, a soupcon of challenge, maybe? Between forefinger and thumb the soldier gently pinches a corner of the cloth and pauses to look at me with a question.

I'm horrified by my urge to violence even as I determine I will bash him if he moves again. Is this violence appropriate? Am I being too much like Rob? I was too rough with Grama Ans, she didn't deserve it, but the Solder is dangerous.

< He's also clean and well-groomed and unarmed; has he crossed such an unpardonable social boundary that he warrants the rock>

As a compromise I say again, out loud and more firmly, "Please leave that bag alone!"

He doesn't move, not an inch. Including not letting go of the bag. I decide that maybe Soldier did not hear me.

I speak louder. "I said," quite loudly this time, "please don't touch that bag!" But the soldier gives his wrist a twitch and flips the bag like a wave towards him as he rocks back on his heels.

I swing and miss. My creatures are exposed. They sit still as toadstools. Hissie is white-blue with rage but Eggee and Wanna each hold on to an arm and Whaddle sits on Hissie's legs. I drop the rock and spread my hands and arms over them like a puny shield. I will preserve them no matter what the cost to me. I will not shirk.

All he says is, "They've grown since last time." But I read in his eyes that my instinctive gesture of protection enrages Soldier. Now I know for certain, there is something wrong in him.

"Yes," I clip answering his comment, trying to keep his focus on me and away from the little ones; "they're getting quite ..." My voice trails off. He reads my eyes, too. He sees my ploy, my trying to distract him. It is a rejection of him, of sorts. All this skitters across his face. Because of the new eye, I read him clearly. Soldier's hand twitches and the cold that was in his eyes radiates out to cover his entire face, freezes it into prim condensation.

That's when Whaddle scooches forward, before I can stop her, and grabs hold of the bag. Sissie-Hissie spits with choler, "Give us that you thieving fathole, you shriveled-mewling-cockroached-ginkoberry!"

251

The Soldier flushes while I am shocked to the core. I feel very Grandma-like with my hand to my chest and my mouth O-shaped. "I've never ... where did she learn ... please excuse ..." Pandemonium ensues. Before I can stop them, Eggee and Wanna jump forward and kick at the soldier's knees.

"Ow," he yells and falls backwards onto his clean, starchPressed butt.

I grab the blue-white Hissie and hang on with considerable effort. She's gotten stronger. I lift my legs to encircle the agitated fiends so they can't follow Soldier as he scoots backwards. They are intent on gaining control of this strong fellow. For my efforts I get bit. I can't believe the filth streaming out of Hissie's mouth and the others echo a chorus of the more obscene segments of her monologue.

They keep demanding Soldier return what he stole. The Soldier has already let go of the hairbag and my naughty creatures are reeling it in. So he didn't really steal it. And yet they keep demanding Soldier return what he stole. He has never taken anything else from us.

"Sssssshhh ..." I try to calm the tumult.

Soldier finally scoots out of kicking range, but he is still within cursing range apparently. My little monsters don't stop the abuse. He stands up.

"I came to help you," he intones with injured dignity.

A tendril of giggle climbs up my throat at the sight of such precise dignity juxtaposed with pink cheeks and hands-brushing-dirty-bottom. It is not funny. I know it is not funny. And I, of all people, know how to maintain a respectful façade.

Dangnabit, I am as out of control as the dolts I hold back. Emotions are banging around inside me. His injured dignity fills me with glee so strong I have to bite my cheeks to keep from laughing at him. It's not even funny, but ... I bite my upper lip and lower my face.

"It … is … not … funny," he grits out and I look up. Now he reads the laughter in my eye (not the torch eye, the other one) and stomps his foot. "I was going to tell you directions to the white light," he storms.

A smile tilts the corner of my right lips; I cannot contain it. "Thank you," I respond - all chuckle removed from my words, "we found the white light. We know where it is."

"What are you implying?" He grates out. "You don't need me?"

He's angry, so mad his fingers are twitching over his sword. I pick up a rock as unobtrusively as possible. He notices. "I was trying to help us both out of here," Soldier grates out; "But you, you think this is funny? *I* don't want *you*." An odd thing to say, but it doesn't feel good.

"You are a waste," he rants, his words straighten the smile from my heart and lips. "You dross, junk, rubbish - I toss you away, you stinking offal dump. You're garbage. You want to be alone with your loves, with your monstrosities?" He tosses the words at me. "Well, your loves don't want you. They are just using you." His face is contorted like Hissie's face. At this moment Soldier is ugly as sin. "You small insignificant garbage pit stinker," he spews.

My dead heart feels again like it did the last time it was metaphorically ripped from my chest (during my second death). I recognize this feeling. The old wound rips open. I finger my throat scar.

He sees the pain darken my cheeks and smiles in satisfaction. Both have been hurt: his pride, my spirit.

Soldier bites deeply once more, his spite damaging more than his sword, "You think anyone wants you around, swill? You think you have anything to offer? You are rubbish; you know it … everyone knows it."

My grip convulses from the direct hit and Hissie wrenches free. She leaps at Soldier with bright red skin; her hair is doing its fire imitation; her fingers are in claws; and even though her teeth are bared, she manages to snarl nasty words at him.

Soldier screeches and runs off. I barely catch hold of Hissie's leg.

My little savages fling words after him - insults and demands for him to return what he stole. They are high from the clash.

"Me Eggee," Eggee says, "and me Soldier, too. Say bad words, Hissie-sissie. Kick me, Whaddle." They replay the battle in front of me.

"Watch me, Idunno," Whaddle demands." See me. I da Hero." The others stroke Whaddle's pride because she needs it and they are, sometimes, very kind to each other. For my part I sit and stare at the rock that somehow is clenched in my hand again.

I rub my head against the rock and relive the whole pathetic, trashy story of my second death.

... I would beg off partaking of it, proximity being so dangerous.

-Journal Entry, May 15, age 24

Chapter 22 – Flying to the Sun [Second Death]

Overworked at eighteen I had a crisis of faith. Oh, not a crisis with God, how could I? No, my faith-disconnect was with The Family. I had, by that time, achieved all of their set goals and more. I was the "perfect child". Achievements accomplished, credibility established, amazing results compounded - glory reflected all over The Family like a fox's shiny coat in sunlight. I was ready for my reward; need made acute through anticipation.

Minimally I should be deemed acceptable in the den. That was our deal: I excel at everything The Family prioritized and, in return, I am embraced. But by age eighteen, no acceptance had been received. I only received privilege. Inclusion was not forthcoming.

It came upon me slowly, the realization that I could not earn what I desired most in life. Long had I suspected there was a basic flaw deep inside of me that I was not privy to. Seemed everyone in The Family could see this flaw even as I could not. Seemed this defect rendered me insufferable. Seemed I was going to have to find inclusion outside The Family. Realization made its way up my fingers as I pounded violin strings and things stirred in my heart.

255

I was playing beautifully, sitting stiff in my chair. My fingers were on the strings feeling the music but my ears were listening to Rob in the background getting ready for another of his parties. Rob was laughing with Uncle Eck - teasing the older man about being tied down, while he, Rob, was going to brashly sample all the delights of the weaker sex. Uncle Eck's voice responded with, "Boy, you're untamed and uncouth. Ought to be ashamed of yourself." But his tone said, "You are just like me, like I was, like I could be again if I put my heart into it." And the men laughed with hearty camaraderie.

"Are you going to hold your breath through the whole piece?" Grandma asked sardonically. Such was my fellowship.

I tightened my lips. Rob had invited me to this party. He'd never done that before. He asked me to join him just before he skipped out on our violin practice - before Grandma settled in her chair with primly proper-crossed ankles. A quick kiss on the cheek, a naughty comment, which Grandma called him to task for, and he skipped out on us. I was left so she concentrated on me. Music flowed up my fingers.

I wanted to go to a non-business-party. Rob asked me. He never had before. Fizzy inside, I felt the music fountain.

"Concentrate, Child. Really. Keep care to the composition." Grandma sat like a pike was shoved from her head through the chair. "Stop, stop, just stop. Now, start again, please. How will we put the piece to rights if you don't breathe?"

I fussed in my seat. He'd probably never ask me to a party again.

"Eyes on the strings, Dear. Whatever are you looking at? There, there, you hear that. I hate to rail at you but you missed the pause again. It's not in the sheet music, but try it. Listen for it. No, start over. "

So I listened to Rob and Uncle Eck laugh and I put in the damn pause. I was flawless. Music flowed around me in staccato barks covering a range of frequencies as if a fox was singing - in through my ears, up my arms, bark, bark, pause, barkbarkbarkbark.

Grandma complained, "And what was that? You're imposing too much of yourself onto the piece, dear. Lighten up on the phrasing. For once, try playing it as the composer intended." She was never so happy as when she could pounce on a fault - real or imagined, it made little difference.

I played nimbly. Heard Rob whistle, light-hearted to be escaping the clutches of her machinations. He would be gone soon. Having fun. Doing wrong. Escaping the den; prowling in the dark. Acting the fool. Crescendo. It makes me angry.

At eighteen years old I still indulged in anger on occasion. On this occasion I was angry at myself not him. Here I sat like a caged fox, panting to be patted, the tormented kit belonging nowhere. Chasing my tail and receiving paltry compensation for doing it. What I really wanted was to make music in concert with my pack; but I was willing to find a new pack to yap with tonight. I wanted to sing with the moon, drink until I got the bed-spins. I had never done that.

I looked down at the music making its way up my fingers and realized I would not play my way out of violin-hell. My bejeweled tyrant and I were finished. I unclenched my jaw and firmly placed the hourglass shaped instrument in its bed. "I'm going to the party," I told Grandma and before she could stutter her shock or marshal her face into something that would stay me, I was off and running and yelling to Rob to wait. I determined to surround myself with noise and stimulation and people crowded together.

I was the yowling frenzy at the heart of the song. Went headlong into swelling frivolity. I was away, not looking back at Grandma or Uncle Eck or anyone. Unluckily I barged into the next thing without thought about what I really wanted. My escape was as useless as staying to saw at strings in time to Grandma's tyranny.

For a fleeting moment I did have fun. Jostling elbows pressed all sides as we entered the doors. I was groped immediately. Danced. Thoroughly over-stimulated myself. Rob went off on his own prowl. Someone yelled in my ear, stepped on my toes. I had a drink. It was spilled. On me. Was handed a glass of something clear. Elbow was gripped, thrust up. It was drink-it-or-wear-it time so I quaffed that drink. Coughed. My back was pounded - with approval. Howls of merriment were raised in salute to me, all around me. Was given another drink. Felt warm to the center with excitement I wasn't thinking at all. Was having the time of my life.

Saw Rob talking by a plant so I made my sloppy way over to him. That's when I fell in love with the tousled hair archeologist Rob was conversing with. In an instant, above all rational, two dark eyes had me tumbling out of control, down into love, in thrall.

That night and the fortnight that followed was captivating. I grabbed onto my passion and held it close enough that nothing could interfere. Swamped by feelings I swore, "You delight me." My love touched my leg in response and shudders of sexual energy coursed through me. "Do you know," I asked, "that we could be anything together?"

"Yes," my love whispered in my ear and it was enough. In that one word everything I wanted to hear was said and I swelled with the possibilities. I swelled so full, I floated up towards the sun. It was the second time I flew to the sun.

Even now I wonder if Rob fed his friend information to aid in my mind's seduction. Every word uttered by my sweetheart went straight into me. It is completely possible, however, that my own mind provided all the seduction that was needed.

For once, nothing The Family said or did registered. This was time apart. I was apart, had no desire for their approval. Nothing mattered except climbing into this person and absorbing everything I could get my spirit around. For once in a long, long time I felt connected and charged up.

I can see now that to a struggling archeologist with big plans and no reputation, I was manna from heaven - a grant to be won - sponsorship with benefits. I didn't listen to my archeologist's actual words. I didn't read the clues. I chose - I chose to believe that we talked about dust-encrusted-civilizations because they were far away and adventurous and that the subject was a code for our desire. I chose to believe our passion would rage underneath any subject we spoke about. The passion was the thing. Any subject was a social cover for our consuming mania for each other.

In the dark I held on tight and told my love, "This unbearable longing is tearing me apart." Oh, I was so dramatic.

That's why I left my home.

Drama.

When My Ideal said it was time to leave, even though all the money had not yet been secured and travel would be dangerous without it, I could not bear the pain.

"You are not really leaving are you? You're going across the world from me?"

"I must," came back a tortured whisper. "What do I have to offer you, you who have everything?"

"No!" I agonized. "Without you I have nothing." Oh, my gosh, I'm sure I read that line in a bad play somewhere.

"You can be part of it, an important part," My love offered while tiptoeing fingers up my stomach. "You can help keep me safe. I won't be long and when I come back, my reputation will be established. I need money. You have money. That is what will speed my return."

But paying for the excursion was empty compensation and time apart felt impossible. "No," I cried and pounded the walls like I had never done before, even as a child. "We'll have an adventure together." And my heart soared when I heard my words. Yes! We would flee all restraint and go adventuring just the two of us.

"I can't afford you."

"Cold words, sweet love," I pretended to be hurt, but those words meant nothing to me because I chose to believe they were uttered to keep me out of harm's way. "I must protect my investment." Oh, so coy. "Nothing you say will do the job. I will come with you. I will find the money to finance this dig and share your passion at the end of the world." It was a white lie. I meant 'share our passion' - for each other.

I didn't feel selfish; thought my archeologist would value me more when I participated in the work. I would see this enthralling place that my love treasured and maybe I would be swept away by it, too. We plotted together, tousled head-to-coiffured head, possibility-and-intent, the-means-to-an-end and finally-the-end-I'd-dreamed-for.

I had honor. Even with the justification of love, I did not steal. I need few things and had spent very little in my life so I was sitting on a plump little packet of money. Although Rob spent recklessly, I gave him a great deal of money and now, in this instance, he was quite generous back to me. I didn't ask how he came to lay his hands on that amount of cash. I didn't ask why he was helping me. I was wrapped up in me and what I wanted; what I needed.

Rob kept up a stream of encouragement, "Don't worry, Cousin. You're doing the right thing. It's about time you did something like this. Don't worry."

I am not a fool. I knew Rob wanted me gone above all things. We were connected much as he might deny it and he wanted that connection severed.

"Rob," I grabbed his shoulders, "don't let Grandma get too proprietary over your life, because she will and then you will become just like I was." He forced himself to look concerned and grateful and to pat my shoulder. Everything in him was eager to see me gone.

"We need a story," Rob warned. "They'll come looking for you, maybe even head you off. What should I tell them?"

Here I was stumped. I could dissemble, did it all the time, but I could never outright lie, not even to save myself. Could not think of one now even with so much at stake. It was Rob that finally cobbled together a semi-plausible story.

I would pack. I needed to anyway. Rob would pack, too. He would announce that we were going to visit an old school chum. The Family was grateful to see me get away from "that damned archeologist" so they put up no fuss.

I left the country immediately and it was almost a fortnight and a day before the lawyers asked for me and Grandma realized I was not only gone from her reach, I was gone from the country. Rob wouldn't let me tell him where I was going, so they couldn't manipulate the information out of him. Into the safekeeping of another's hands I delivered my life with no regard for my own safety or direction. To me, this precious act of trust was love expressed.

Instead of gratitude, my dear's voice was strident as I turned over the money. "I thought you were rich," my love chided me. We were on a bustling dock across the world. The raised voice caused a few heads to turn and I was embarrassed even though no one understood a word of our language and I understood nothing of theirs. "What is this?" The volume grew louder. "I can't outfit a dig for even six months on this pittance." It was a lot of money, but I hated the look of disappointment and was desperate to fix it. I smiled a sexy promise and stroked the beautiful hair. I could fix the problem physically even if there was nothing I could do financially at this point.

"Here," I was handed a small bill. "Go down that street right there and secure us a room. Don't get anything fancy. We don't need much. The third door down should be good enough." A bit abashed by the harsh tone, I pulled myself away. "I'll get things set up and then come for you. Be ready."

I dodged a man carrying a heavy box and sidestepped a tipsy sailor, then turned to steal another glance at my love's face. That face was already gone disappeared into the crowd around the docks. That face didn't need one last look at me. I stumbled down the road to a dangerous looking public house - third door down - where I managed to secure a room using pantomime.

There was no water in the room so back down stairs I padded and performed another pantomime for two pitchers of tepid water. I washed with one, but was so thirsty I drank the other. The night was spent alone. My bed remained empty and by morning I was exhausted from squashing unease and the nasty bugs that clicked along the floor in the dark.

Alone I was for three days. The only face I saw was the young boy with old eyes who brought me glasses of water. I had no money for food or gratuity. I gestured I would pay him later, but his eyes had seen too much to have faith in my promises and my rumpled appearance didn't inspire confidence.

When my tousled love finally showed up at our hotel, it was to tell me that we were moving inland. We didn't have time to pay our bill, he said. We didn't even have time to go out the front door it seemed. We snuck out the back. I told myself this is what it was like to be free from convention, iconoclastic, a bandit, but remembering the boy's oldYoung eyes, I could not overwrite the guilt.

The trip was well-organized. Our belongings were on the road ahead of us. Camp would be set up near the unsanctioned dig that was to be our home – tents would be raised by the time we arrived, the garbage pit dug, the water system put into place, the fires built. My poor busy dear was exhausted from all the arrangements and after giving instructions to the driver, spent much of the time we traveled asleep, which was fine as I felt ill from heat and stomach cramps.

We traveled five days. This was living as I had never known - dusty living with no way to get clean - I had scant knowledge of destination's end - was bounced around - Dear Heart brooded - but I gloried in it. I dove headfirst into the lifestyle. In fact, I took it further than I needed to. I didn't even wipe my face or comb my hair. Barely conscious of my motivation, I visited the edges of acceptability. I passed through smudged to stinky through itchy to disgustingly filthy. I visited my own sick, unwashed animal state and found some core of myself. Precious stank rose from my archeologist, too. I loved this time together when we offered each other the opportunity to see beyond the obvious, to find the edges of ourselves and to meld. I felt so ill we dared not embrace; but I often leaned my dirty head onto a shoulder stiff with agitation and imagined my sweet weight soothed the unrest. To me, these days together were divine.

Arrival in camp seriously dented my self-delusion. There was no denying that my lover's passion for me was not as great as the desire to grub in dirt. We stepped out of our conveyance and with only a motion and one word to the driver (I think it was 'unload') we marched to the dig site. Only one other time, from that moment on, did I ever have my sweet's full attention.

Possibly it was my fault. Despite my best design, I was uninspired by the land spread out before me. I could not get excited by buried pots and tidbits. But my lover was obsessed and it was as if I ceased to exist. It was night when I wandered alone back into camp and then through camp, trying to identify which tent was ours. My stuff was piled on the floor of a small tent with a single cot. A jug of water sat on a crate. I drank from it and fell asleep.

The next day I was discouraged from visiting the dig as I was too ill to help move dirt. "Stay put," I was advised, "and don't go exploring. It's too dangerous." I managed to hold on to belief that my love was concerned for me even though those beautiful dark eyes were on the dirt in the screen being shaken by two men in front of us.

Sometimes I silently stood at the top of the dig site and stared at the energy being devoted to old bits. It was hot in the sun, so hot I

263

thought I would fry. I always returned to camp and drank my water and tried to feel better. I'm not sure I ever ate. At night the workers trudged back to camp and cooked dinner and drank and sang while my sweetheart bent over the day's gleanings in a tent separated from mine by the entire length of camp. All of my illusions were fading. This left me plenty of time to concentrate on how dirty I was and how sick - even sicker than before. I scared myself.

That's when I composed three sweat-stained letters. The first was an invitation to my lover. I propped it on the-cot-across-camp while the object of my desire was digging in the dirt for shards of pottery. The note was to be a reminder; it held my final hope. I also wrote a letter to Rob and one to Grandma, confused letters, manic letters, illness-inspired missives. I never intended to mail them. I just needed to put thoughts down on paper.

I hid those last two letters inside my pillowcase and laid my head on top of them, feeling my body get hotter and hotter and my insides cramp and try to twist out of me.

That night, while the others worked late, I washed as best I could, water shortage be damned. I cleaned up the sty assigned to me. I waited until it got too dark to work, even with lights. I heard the workers come back to camp. I waited in my tent until the food was cooked and eaten and the camp was set to rights. I sat on my cot, in my tent, all alone until the drinking was finished, the last songs were sung and the laughing faded. I sat stiff-backed, hands on knees, head held high, in my best clothes. I sat waiting until the lights went out and the snores started and the sounds of the night became a chorus. Then I knew my lover was not coming to me, had no intention of seeking me out.

There was no cost to toss the last of my pride aside. At the very least, I needed to understand. Across the camp I slipped. Reached out with trembling finger tips and found the tent flap tied firmly shut from the inside. The light went off when I scratched at the door. I felt my throat close and could not call out.

That night outside the tent door I became aware that I was the most primal of creatures - wrong in every sense - outcast. Nothing was more frightening than that night when I realized that I was unsuited to every person alive. There was no place to hide from this knowledge.

Time grew fuzzy; so did my head. I remember gathering my sleeping bag, my pillow with letters inside, and my water jug. It was empty though. I must have been dehydrated because I swam in and out of consciousness. When I was conscious, I was sitting on the lip of the ravine at the edge of camp – the garbage dump. Everything useless and rejected was thrown into that pit.

Oh, my head ached for relief. But there was no relief to be had. Lying on my sleeping bag didn't help nor did burying my head deep into my pillow. No one came to check on me, but I really didn't expect anyone to come. With a small turn of my head, I vomited into the pit. I vomited quieter and quieter until, in morning's light, I floated up and out of my body. I floated high enough to turn my non-face towards the sun. Even I was not interested in looking at me.

Over the camp I floated as if seeing it for the first time. There was a strange ancient energy suffusing the entire area. I guess my archeologist was correct that this was an important site. Based on the energy field, I'm pretty sure it is too important for an unauthorized dig. The energy put out by the workers was much different. I followed it rather than the sound of voices to the far edge of the dig site. There they were my archeologist and the workers hard at work - so excited about their bits-n-pieces.

I floated down behind the busy tousled head and watched, just watched. One by one the workers started mumbling among themselves. They kept looking over their shoulders and grabbing for protection dangling around their necks. It took longer for my busy digger to get antsy, but it happened eventually. They carefully put down their tools and very subdued, walked back to camp. I followed them, had nothing else to do. Was curious. Wondered what was coming next. They trudged into camp and plunked themselves around the dead fire pits and stared at my tent. No one said a word, just stared at my tent. That was the day my lover finally came to visit me.

I lingered outside the tent, looking back at the workers until I heard a cry of anguish. My lover had examined the tent, left the tent, wandered the camp and, finally, found me. The cry startled me and I floated over to the garbage pit to see what was happening. My love stood over my body looking upset. The degree of distress gave me pause until I heard the words, "Oh shit." I knew then that love was not the cause of anguish. Just as surely I realized there had been no intent to kill me. I think my obsessed excavator just hoped I would get well enough to up and walk away or to gather in more money or good riddance. For the first time it must have passed through that dusty head that there would be serious trouble if I was not returned to my powerful family. My death cut off a lot of options.

My lover stuffed me head first into my sleeping bag along with my pillow and my loose gear. It was my razor, tossed into the bag with my other bits that scarred my throat. I didn't feel it, of course, but I could see right through the bag. I ended up under a broken, overturned hand cart. This is how my love thought to bury me, un-acknowledged, un-cleaned up and unprotected from the animals. Some day my deadStench would reach the camp and cause them to gag over breakfast. For some reason, that was the worst of dying and being disposed of.

Even dead it felt as if my heart was ripped entirely out of my chest. I couldn't decide whether to stay and keep watch over my dead body or follow the others around camp. That's when the white light came.

It was much different than the first time. Oh, the white light came, made a tunnel, pulled me into it, my two friends were there. Joy, connectedness, love-extraordinary all this was the same. Momma was there and so was Daddy. All very similar. I felt connected. It was beyond wonderful.

Instead of them telling me to turn around and go back, Da took me off to a beautiful room lined with books, scrolls, and papers and maps. Da pulled one book off a low shelf – the most beautiful book I had ever seen. As he opened it I experienced everything I had ever done in my life and every missed opportunity. I felt every repercussion of my actions and inactions, like ripples in a pond and each ripple caused a ripple of its own until I was flooded. I could feel the love, I was the love. I thought that I might also feel shame, but I felt only wholeness and understanding of what would have been a better direction.

Being with my Da, sharing my book with a soul that loved me, me, helped me finally feel secure. Here was my protector-in-truth. Da held my spirit and allowed me to heal and expand. Being here with Da was a whole soul embrace.

Of course, death was rapturous, especially while staring at my book. I was fascinated by my many sparkling facets. Nothing else was needed. I understood everything about how I had lived. Now I was whole, connected and sparkling and, I'll say it, Me-Us-Everything was magnificently compelling in every way. Nothing could be more perfect. I drank like parched earth - absorbing all I could, letting the rest run off around me, knowing that with every drop I took in, I was more able to absorb. Here at the edge of heaven I had time aplenty to become fully hydrated.

Da told me I was now ready to go back.

I cried out in despair so plaintively I broke the angels's hearts.

Already moving down the tunnel I grabbed at Da's protection. I knew he was devoted to me. I knew he would not let me loose. But loose I became. I was loose. Loose is all I was. Utterly, absolutely disconnected. Except for one moment of other-than-loose when my fury hyperventilated out of me, pants of resistance thundered, pyrotechnics strained the gates of heaven inward like great bowed craters. "I will not leave."

Then the moment passed and I was a keening wail too burdensome to bear once again. Floating. I was surprised to see my body laid out in a box on a cold slab, not in the garbage pit. Someone must have thought to deal with me properly.

<How will I ever make it on my own?>

During my first death I felt complete, so united, and so whole that when I returned to my fractured life, I could never find my footing. I just wanted to be complete again and spent my life trying to earn it.

Then I died the second time and felt connection again and I needed it even more desperately because I knew it might be taken away. To be everything and then be just a spirit constrained by a body with limited senses … well, it aged my spirit. Weary, that's a better word. My spirit was weary. That second-death-send-back left me too weary to manage. Wasted and scant as an unwatered dead cow in the desert, I could not concentrate on the teachings of the book of my life. What was most present was the fact that I wasn't enough and I tried desperately to make up for it.

My ears had filters. No matter what was said, I mostly heard, "You dross, junk, rubbish, I toss you away." I spent my tattered bits of energy trying to understand why I, alone, was such an unpardonable waste. If God and Da could reject me and Momma just watched, then so would all others betray me or abandon me. I choose to believe I was a fool to want more and my best course of action was to censor myself in order to hide the unbearable aspects of me.

Censorship was my vow to the dead body in a box. The cold shell was still wrapped in my sleeping bag, but someone had turned me around face-out-of-the-bag. That was nice. And had basted together my ragged throat wound. My head rested on my vomit-covered blanket folded up like a pillow. My hands were crossed over my chest and rested on my two letters. And on a table beside the box, a death certificate declared me dead on May fifteenth. Second death; hot death; burnt-up little shell …

…back into that cold body I squeezed myself. There was no reason not to, and besides, I wanted to avoid being buried alive. I imagine that would be a horrible way to die. But it was difficult to wiggle into my shell. The box was too small. The shell was too small. Life was too small.

<Insignificant garbage pit>

Once I was back inside my too-tight-body, everything felt suffocatingly close. I wiggled my arms out of the too-constraining-sleeping-bag and pushed at the too-close-box. The lid wouldn't move.

I panicked, I'll admit it. I tried to kick my way out of the bag - couldn't. I threw wild elbows trying to bang myself out of the box; which had no effect on the box. And I tried everything I could do to exit my body again. I even tore holes in the tips of my fingers ripping at the wooden lid trying to create an exit. Because I was banging around I did not hear footsteps enter the room, but I did hear a scream and then I fell silent and the door slammed shut and footsteps fled down a hall. I yelled and yelled but no one came to release me. My throat was too dry to yell by the time I heard footsteps again.

I tried croaking, "Help!" but it was a small sound.

The lid raised and I saw the side of a man's face. He was looking back at someone with a condescending smile. Then he started to lower the lid so I reached up and grabbed his arm and croaked, "Help" again. The doctor screamed, high-pitched and girlishly. He jumped back, which brought me to sitting position as I did not let go of his arm. The box lid hit me on the head and then fell off to the side. The two men stared at me as if I was a ghost. I scratched my head because it itched. Such a normal action seemed to reassure the doctor. He crossed himself and then stepped forward. He said something to the man in rapid-fire unknown language and I realize I was going to be saved from having to experience the dying process again.

But it took work as I was still very sick. The next time I woke, Uncle Eck was sitting by my bed. "I hate it here," he told me. "I hate leaving my home. I hate this God-awful place. I resent being dispatched as if I was a peon. Your inconsiderate actions are deplorable beyond all imagination. I will never forgive you for putting me through this hell." This was the first of three times he spoke to me in the weeks it took me to heal and travel back to the mansion.

The second time he spoke to me he said, "It's time to bring you home. You are not going to be sick right now, are you?" I shook my head no and he said, "Good."

It was the final time he spoke to me that I learned what happened during my three missing days. Although he made it ugly, Uncle's unworthy resentment comforted me.

"Someone notified the authorities," my uncle spoke in a cold voice, "when you were left for extinct in a garbage dump. The place was abandoned by the time the authorities got there. No one tried to revive you as they were all convinced you were dead. That's what they said in the letter they sent us; you were dead."

I wondered how Rob reacted to that news. Our plans gone so horribly wrong.

Uncle Eck continued, "The informant lived near the site and kept talking about your ghost. That's why everyone was so jumpy when you sat up in the transport box with bloody hands. Don't you want to know how they knew your name?" He looked at me anger burning in his eyes. I knew he anticipated hurting me so I just looked away. It didn't stop him. I didn't imagine it would. "They found the letters you wrote hidden inside your pillow. That's how they found us. Thank goodness your lover didn't think enough of you bury you in clean linens else those letters would have disappeared just as every other identifiable object. I hope you finally learned that you have no sense. Maybe you'll have the courtesy to behave yourself from now on."

At that moment, the doctor walked in and reacted to my uncle's tone. Doctor looked disgusted - at Uncle Eck, not me, which might have been soothing if I could feel anything. Not even my damaged fingers hurt. Not even my heart hurt anymore. In fact, my heart felt gone. But when I slept, I could hear the bedsprings bounce to its beat so I knew it was a metaphorically missing heart.

Doctor solemnly handed me my two letters, the sleeping bag and the blanket, washed now and folded tight; and bid me farewell. A sleeping bag, a blanket, two letters and a scar at my throat: that was all I had as souvenirs of my big adventure. I looked at the doctor from behind dull eyes and I saw him instinctively cross himself. Poor man.

We returned home without another word, Uncle Eck and me. My welcome was a ring of steely looks and one pair of open arms. Grandma clung to me. Rob swore in front of everyone he never suspected that I would run away, never believed the archeologist was so irresponsible, or that trouble would dog me so endlessly. I looked at him with my dull eyes and he shuddered, too. The family closed ranks around us and neither of us was let off of our short leash after that. I didn't speak for over a year.

Up to that point, not one thing that anyone ever said or did caused Grandma to lose her icy control, but almost losing control of me, snapped something in her. After my initial thank-God-your-back-hug, Grandma pushed back off of me and glared. That was the start of it. For a while Grandma was so furious I couldn't even see her. No one could.

Back at the mansion, lectures began. Lectures from the lawyers, from the aunts, from the uncles, even Rob had the gall to lecture me on my faults and duties and the dangers of living out-of-accord with The Family's way. If I want, I can still draw up detailed descriptions of the lives and failures of rounders: the singer who woke up a nation and died, the poet who wrote the truth but could not live with that pain, the musician who broke every rule and resonated the soul and who wasted away addicted and alone. There were lectures on the pretty girl who everyone wanted except the one she loved - he took one taste and nothing else. In my head I hear about the funny man crying so hard he could not live in the world, about the women who

271

grab freedom and men who gain power yet have no control over their desperate hungers. "Don't be like these people." the lectures warned. "These are fringe men - unmasked women. Men so defiled by their own impulses they cannot creep back into polite society. There is no place for them." "Loud women," the lectures label them, "Look-At-Me women, ridiculous men, dead people." These are the stories I fed myself for eighteen years to keep control of my hungers.

"Look what you've gone and done to yourself." This was the first thing Grandma said to me when her fires cooled and we could finally see her again. "Honestly, you have no sense." Grandma spun a unique brand of lecture. "I told you that you could never do it on your own … you need me … That's not possible ... Do as I tell you."

In an eerie echo of past denouncements, Eggee (pretending to be Soldier) rages, "Are you saying you don't need me?" then Eggee leaps over me and uses my shoulder to haul him/herself back upright. "Help, help," he screeches in a high-pitched imitation of Soldier. "Don't let those babies get me." S/he leans over me and hides behind me in reaction to his sisters and brother's reenactment - very focused is on the play in front of us.

And yet, even in the "heat of battle" his/her hands stroke my chin similar to me-soothing-Hissie. This unconscious soothing is not performed to manipulate my passions or insinuate I'm lacking. S/he is caring for me and because of that I realize I'm allowed deep feelings and it is okay to convey those emotions and the soothing hand offers a path out of the deep places should I decide to accept - it's my choice.

For eighteen years I chose to feed myself denouncing lectures, but now I can feed myself something new. I ponder this as Eggee repeats Soldier's tantrum (at high volume, directly into my ear) one more time. S/he's so excited, Eggee jumps up and down, using my shoulder to gain more height. It jerks me back and forth; but does not move me as much as my pondering moves me.

I can trust what I think at myself, *when* I think wisely. I do not have to accept everything that passes through my mind. What a paradigm shift. Oh, my soul - it is not necessary to believe what I think. I never realized that before!

I spent my life believing my thoughts *were* me, but they're not.

Sometimes thoughts are just habit. Grandma planted thoughts in my head and declared them truth. But they may not be. It's for me to decide. Books teach, but may not tell the whole story. Majority decree is not necessarily correct. I knew that once. A support system's opinions are mostly idea inertia based on history. They may not be fact. And if my thoughts are not necessarily true, then I, I, I get to choose what to do with them: embrace them or develop new ideas to live by and die for.

Confronting old beliefs is just about all I've been doing this third death of mine. And, I've been making wiser choices than I was taught. I flush a bit with pride and smile. Eggee smiles at me and shouts again. Hey, I'm the one who figured out Soldier was no good. Grandma would have approved of the dapper fellow. And the Aunts would have admired his uniform. And Uncle Eck would have slapped him on the back and offered drinks.

I stare at the rock in my hand and feel warm bodies push against me as they re-live their confrontation with Soldier. They were mad at Soldier because he crossed boundaries, but now they are having fun. They let their anger go. I admire that.

So Soldier was mad at me and said mean things and raked up old hurts - so what? Okay, I reacted to old refrains and fell to bad habits - I get to choose whether to unbelieve his words and try new ways.

"Hey, Eggee," Whaddle calls, "we play new game now. I da boss. I say new game." But the other four are enjoying the confrontation-with-Soldier game so they ignore their oldest sibling. "Quit running around, Eggee," Whaddle commands as she captures the intersexual. "Wanna, come over here. I show you how to march. I in charge."

273

Eggee complains to Whaddle, "You hold me too hard! You don't know what you're doing!" S/he turns around and winks at Wanna. Eggee is just causing trouble and Wanna gets the message.

Wanna pipes up, "Whaddle, you move too slow! Stop pulling on the hairbag!" He turns around and winks at Hissie.

"You walk'n silly, Whaddle." Hissie says.

The round-robin criticism hurts Whaddle's feeling so she responds with loud defensive proclamations all the while moving faster, not pulling the hairbag and changing her walk. The other four babies work as a team. They proclaim Waddle is walking too stiffly so my firstborn waggles her hips and lumbers her shoulders from side to side with each step.

"That's much better," they nod and snicker and compliment until Eggee complains again, "You are walking too slow and quit shuffling!"

So Whaddle blusters back, "Am not. Walking perfect. Hurry up now and walk behind me." And she starts marching faster even as the others chorus, "Too slow! Quit dragging your feet! Can't you go any faster?" They quickly walk out of my sight.

"Hey, get back here," I call out. "Stay within my eyeLight."

I hear Eggee as they make their way back towards me, "You have no rhythm! What da matta wit'cha? Walk like chickie-boom, chickie-boom." And so it continues.

Soon Whaddle is hunched over and lumbering her upper body like a bear while her lower body is goose-stepping. Whaddle jerks around to gauge the other's reactions before lurching forward to march in a wide circle around me. All the while she vainly defends herself, "Am too walking straight! This is the way I always walk!"

"Well," I think to myself with a snicker, "I've never seen anyone walk quite like that," and I snort at the whole slamdang farce. It's like watching my own lectures come to life right in front of me. 'Habitual self-denouncements welcome to stage center; now please play out a farce for my entertainment!' Did I honestly transfer my authority so surely to The Family's manipulations? Was I as much a clown?

Poor pathetic vain Whaddle. Thank you, dummling Whaddle. I'm embarrassed I let mind-plundering-lectures hold sway over me for thirty years. From now into the future I vow, "I hold this farce as a talisman against future thought-inertia. Going forward, I will choose wisely."

And right now I choose to drop the rock and, with merry compassion, hurry to Whaddle's defense. "Okay, now." I chortle; "We have had such perfect fun that I'm going to carry you all for a while. Good job, Whaddle, organizing this play march. Come on everyone, gather around. Can someone please hand me the hairbag?" Whaddle lumbers over with a sigh of relief. It makes me laugh again, but I hold it in, not wanting Whaddle to think I'm laughing at her. Eggee-the-creative catches my eye with an ornery smirk and I shake my head and wink at her/him. Oh, these beasties.

Once I have everyone cradled in the hairbag sling and the inevitable fighting for position is over we settle down to walk. "Which way?" I ask. This is the first time I have sought their opinion. Eggee pats my hand. S/he understands an apology when she hears one.

*I asked Grandma where Russell was buried
and she said, "Russell-who, Dear?"*

*"Are there yew trees around his grave?" I asked
her.*

*Grandma said, "Yes, of course, Pet." But she
was planning the dinner menu, so ...*

-Journal Entry, May 15, age 28

Chapter 23 – Finding Innar

The encounter with Soldier causes me to rethink finding others in this place. Perhaps all the people in this place (except us) are wrong. "Let's not march headlong into the next situation," I say to myself. The thought is so good, so non-inertia, that I say the same thing to the kidlets. I'll admit I'm feeling slightly proud that I am getting close to wise.

The hairbag undulates.

"Maybe we are better off, just the six of us. We don't need anyone else." I continue.

In an about face, all the kidlets want to follow the footsteps to see what's ahead. They feel stimulated, empowered and mighty. "Pleeeeease," Waddle begs. The others nod.

"Maybe we find food," Idunno says. She decides me. Although I am certain that we will not find food and I am feeling less powerful than the kidlets, if Idunno can stir herself to speak, I can carefully take this risk.

"Do you agree hairbag?" I ask. The drawstring undulates around my neck. "How about you babies? Are we going to stay aware." Every single one of them nod sincerely. I chuckle to myself. They will remember that commitment not-a-whit if there is food along this path. I am not stupid. But still, we start, again. We follow the footsteps and before long we notice a glow.

"I spy," Whaddle points. Ahead is a sign lit by torches.

The sign directs us to an overlook. Those of us with eyebrows raise them at each other. This is interesting. The aforementioned vantage point offers a very unusual view.

Among the view options is an informational placard. I choose to read it out loud. "This placard welcomes you into a three-angled cavern called, Innar. Stretched out before you," the sign educates, "is an expanse of level fake-turf with pretty rock brooks meandering throughout giving the impression of a well-watered meadow. The turf is gaily spangled with felt and silk flowers of every hue: pansies, lilies, and narcissus - a marvelous, radiant flower. It is always spring here at Innar. The meadow, lying in the very center of the cavern, is the navel - the cavern's crown jewel.

At the meadow's periphery, precipitous cliffs rise high and fall off on all sides. Near to these walls a lake is nestled, Purpus by name. The water has long since boiled away leaving the lakebed coated in deep mineral and alkaline deposits, subtly toned white and pink, contrasting the gay meadow and the imposing dark cliffs. Stonehenge-like obelisks called lava trees surround the lake bed. Our lava trees are branchless and leafless providing an unobstructed view of the wall-mounted steam vents mouthing off within the cavern."

"Talking back to each other," I whisper in aside to make them giggle.

"Throwing hissing fits," Eggee snickers and nudges Hissie.

Hissie pauses, then decides to giggle. I continue reading, "The cavern is lit and heated by volcanic action casting a distinctive reddish tone and keeping the space comfortably warm. If you enjoy the smell of sulfur, Innar's atmosphere will be to your liking." I wrinkle my nose at the five.

"Near to Lake Purpus is a sacred grove of tree molds – bark-textured cylindrical holes in the ground, perfect negative impressions of long-burnt trees. Please watch your step as some holes are quite large. The area of tree molds is surrounded by hot boggy flats and a rock grotto containing a chasm leading down into the molten earth and opening to the north. Deep beneath the whole cavern floor is a ring of sulphurous pools boiling a merry reeking tune. Please respect this unique treasure by using the trash receptacles provided throughout the cavern."

It seemed a bit contrived, but the babies are excited to go exploring and I'm willing to be distracted. We make our way down into the cavern and there, stretched out before us, is a fake-turf meadow just as described. Above the wall's constant hiss I hear a delicate sound wafting along the air – tinkling laughter, the music of children playing. To me their choiring voices are as sweet as the swans on Cayster's gliding stream. But I have been fooled by sweet words and well-pressed looks before, so I'm hesitant. The laughter beckons my little ones, however; so I follow them as they pick their way through the meadow. Yes, the flowers really are silk and felt and well-dusted, too.

I stop us all behind the lava trees and watch a group of pretty children frolicking along the "shallows" of Lake Purpus. My rascals array themselves behind me.

"I fascinated by des people," Eggee says under his/her breath.

"Dey are our size." Whaddle whispers, stepping closer. I put a hand on her shoulder.

"Dey have fun," Hissie reports wistfully.

"I wanna play dat," Wanna whines.

"Look, dat big girl da boss," Whaddle says intrigued. She tries to shrug off my hand. "Let go," she demands.

"Where are their parents?" I scan carefully. Only children leap and play tag. My little ones are excited and ready to abandon discretion, but something feels not quite right in my deep places. I tighten my grip on Whaddle. One laughing child kicks at the white lake bottom as if splashing up water. The small boy chasing her stops and grabs at his eyes and begins to cry. The other children laugh at him and continue to chase each other in the lakebed powder.

"That was mean," I caution my own kidlets. "Look at their feet and legs, burnt red up to their knees from the lakebed powder."

"Dey happy," Eggee notes.

"I wanna plaaaay. I wanna, I wanna …"

"Shhhsst," I quiet them. "Stay here," I command; "I'll go first, make sure it's safe." They nod consent. "I'm serious," I say firmly. "Whaddle, you're in charge. You make sure they stay here until I call you. You promise?"

"I good," Whaddle says. Then as I frown at her, she adds, "I promise."

I unwind the hair from me and it twines itself in and around them. Then I stride out into the open. The playing children of Innar see me and they cry with joy and turn towards me. I wave to them, but continue to climb the small hill away from the lake where parents should be sitting to oversee their children. There are tables, but no adults. Only small footprints in the whole area. A quick glace from this viewpoint shows there are no adults here at all. I start down the hill towards the lake.

I don't signal 'it's safe', but my little creatures come out into the open anyway. They have been amazingly patient of my delay. Gentle babbling flavors the air around them. They talk back and forth, encouraging each other to come out and play. They are too far away for me to hear their actual words, but I know them. What startles me is their walk. They each crouch in a weird hunched-up position with fingers dragging patterns in the dirt - all but Eggee. Eggee walks behind the others in his/her normal posture. Eggee probably told the siblings that this type of walking signals a desire to play. And they believed him/her. So ridiculous my little fools are. My lips turn upward as bubbles of delight rise in me. Ha.

The beautiful Innar children don't see my babies. They seem to have eyes only for me. "Father?" one calls out to me. "Mother?" queries another. "Do you love me?" many cry. "You have finally come to take me home," the oldest girl states.

I wonder if they have ever seen their own parents. I reach them and they crowd around me, tug at me, and tell me they love me. The slope is slippery - little round rocks roll under my feet reducing the friction. They tug, tug at me and we all slide continuously towards the lake.

"Hold me," they whimper. "Hug me." "Want me." "Accept me." "Know me."

I've never seen these children. I turn my eye-torch on high and look deeper, inside them and inside me. No, they are not from me. I do not resonate with them on any level. They call me many names, none of which are mine.

"Do you know who your parents are?" I ask as I struggle to stand upright.

"You! You? Are you?" They chorus.

"Not me," I apologize. "These are my kids." I smile as I gesture to my approaching babies. "They would like to play with you."

"I thought you were different," the Innar girl pulls back from me and snarls. "You cannot dump them here. We are already too many."

"What?" I am confused by this whole scenario. "I am not dumping them. I wouldn't. Wait. Are you alone?"

"What are you implying?" The girl snaps, mightily offended.

"There's nothing wrong with us." The other Innar children chorus like a well-rehearsed play. "It's not our fault that we're alone." "Please love me," a small boy implores softly while the rest parrot, "We did nothing wrong" and "Look at us; we're beautiful."

I angle towards my own and hold out arms to halt them. "Turn around," I say. "Go back. Hair, take them away."

The girl hisses her displeasure, which catches Hissie's attention and because she is the leader, Whaddle is also rooted to the spot watching her. Together they present an anchor the hair cannot budge.

My deep place is sending out messages. "We need to go." I say to the Innar children and they cling to my legs and wail - all except the oldest girl.

She stands up tall and in a very dignified voice she says, "We came to help you." She sounds disconcertingly like Soldier did at our last encounter. A small nervous giggle climbs up my throat. It is not funny. I know it is not funny. And I swallow it, but she seems determined to be offended.

"It … is … not … funny," she grits out and I'm confused. This is a horrible repeat of an earlier scene.

At least I can change the conversation. "Where are your parents? Do you need help?"

"You, you, you are our parent - we love you," the Innar children pull at me. We slide, off-balance, close to the lake now. There are too many of them. I pull my arms free and start sidling uphill towards my own crew. I signal my own kids to step back but they keep coming towards the lake, the other children, towards me. All the children keep coming at me.

"What are you implying?" The oldest Innar girl grates out. "You don't need me? You don't need us? You think no one needs us?" She's angry, so mad her fingers are twitching. This is too odd. I push a few of the boys off me as unobtrusively as possible. She notices. "You don't want us because you have them?" She spits the words at me. "You want to be alone with your monstrosities?" Her face contorts like Soldier's face did. Maybe they are related.

My five babies tug at the hair-bag trying to get closer to the Innar children. Now they are close enough so the hairbag can attach itself to my ankle. I place myself between my gang and the Innar children and try backing them up but there are too many children. I am not containing the situation.

I have never seen my babies smile quite like this before and my heart performs a strange little lurch, beating for a short minute, and then falls still once again. They are so hopeful, vulnerable. I almost don't recognize my own voice, "Back to the trees," I grind out.

Then the screams begin. "Monsters," a girlish voice shrieks. My babies stop and cower, wondering what unseen monster is upon them. What horrible villain is poised to attack these children?

The oldest girl screams again and the other Innar children start pointing to my five and run in panicked circles. The newly blinded boy is knocked over and run over and rolls deeper into the lake, then he disappears under the white powder. He surfaces sputtering and cries harder as he crawls up towards the bank. The oldest girl runs towards me, pointing at my kids, screaming with false terror, "Help us. Save us from the monsters. They are hideous. Kill them." The other Innar children follow her with grabby hands.

283

My attention is not on her. She is nothing to me. My attention is all for my crew. Shock and confusion transform their sweet little faces as they begin to understand that the horror is them. They are the fearsome things the little people are afraid of. The other children run by past me, except the blind boy wallowing in the white lake. They run by and push my babies to the ground. My little ones turn to me for comfort, but I am surrounded by pretty Innar children now. These pretty children tighten their arms around me, grab hold of my hands, wrap armNooses around my legs, and pull at me. I'm stronger, but they are many. They point to my five and ask me to destroy the ugliness.

"Stop," I command using force to twist out of their many grips.

Big-headed Whaddle utters a sharp keening sound then runs her sweet wobbling waddle towards the one child still in the lake – the blind boy. The others follow Waddle, jabbering and squealing. Well, they have to. They are all connected by the hairbag. Just as I am, I realize too late. I am pulled off my feet and land on my rump and am dragged down the slope towards the lake by the hair wrapped around my ankle. Such a ruckus – children screaming, me yelling to my gang and they vocalizing a strange assortment of sounds: I'm-not-a-monster-sounds, trust-me-sounds.

When they get to the powder-blinded boy they each put a hand on him or foot. They pet him and pat him and look to the other Innar children as if to say, "Look, we're nice." I can tell by their precious expressions my babies expected a change in attitude but I don't notice one. The blinded boy reaches up. Unfortunately, he moves his hands along Eggee's ridged back. The sightless Innar boy screams, which is just the impetus needed to catapult the pretty Innar children into action. They pick up rocks, advance on my now frightened ones, and pelt them.

"Hell, no!" I declare, then I shout a lie to get those horrible children to leave my babies alone. "If you love me, you will stop and we'll leave together." A few of the younger ones look back at me, but the lead-girl never hesitates.

My babies, shocked and scared and confused, are the ones running in circles now. They get ever more tangled in the hair and slip further into the lakebed to avoid the rocks. I am dragged by the ankle, cannot get to my feet.

"Stop!" I yell again to the children with the rocks, to Whaddle leading her siblings too deeply into the lake, to the hair dragging me so I can't get up. I scrabble in the dirt to find rocks of my own, end up with pebbles. Toss them at the Innar children, which slows them, but doesn't stop them.

Whaddle, in the lead, slips under the deep white powder. My other babies tumble on top of her. More rocks are thrown at my crew. There is a veritable rain of rocks. They are hit. The boy is hit. They all bleed. I cannot get to my feet, am constantly pulled in sharp tugs and jerks towards the lake. The children, emboldened, run past me; look down at me; mouthing stinking words about killing the beasts - about loving me.

Those children. Those faces. Those terrifying, set in hard lines faces. Children's faces are soft and plump and have big eyes. They are made for lighting up in smiles or screwing up to cry. They were never ever made to look like this – tight, focused in hatred. How could any child learn to set their face like that? I cannot look upon it. Thank all Saints they are quickly past me.

I roll over to hands and knees and crawl backwards, feet first. Going in the same direction as the jerks and tugs. Once I'm moving fast enough, I make it to my feet and move, arms raised. I descend upon the Innar children from behind: hips knocking them down, arms chopping, legs sweeping them. Rocks fall to the ground. I am yelling louder than anyone. "Damn you, stop!" A large rock, one I am too late to block, trajectory at Hissie, is almost upon her. I yell, "Duck!" and she ducks just in time – just as the blinded boy stands to run. The rock hits the side of the boy's face and in sudden, utter silence he huffs once and then falls. All I hear is my own panting breath filling my ears and far, far away I hear my footfalls as I race into the lake. It's … too … late <pant> it's … too … late <pant> No!

285

The babies are too deep. The boy has fallen below the surface of the powder and it has closed over him. I try to mark it, but there are too many in the lake, too many going under, too many to keep a marker for. But I try. Losing even one is unthinkable. My God! They just wanted to play!

Under my breath I pray. I beg the hair to shorten up and to remain strong, to not burn through, to not break and not let any more sink beneath the surface.

They scream, my ungainly ones. I hit the powdery substance. Out too deep, the minerals burn their eyes and their throats and their skin and my legs – oh, God, it burns. Shuffling my feet to search for the boy under the surface of this white hell distracts me not one bit from my work with the wild hair. It's as if I have two minds, both fully absorbed with its separate vital task without impacting the other. So I reach and search for the boy with my feet even as I work the hair still wrapped around my ankle and now also looped through my hands. Desperately I tug, pleading with the hair to shorten. I whip it and rein it in, whip it and pull it, and quickly wade towards my babies as they sink one at a time beneath the surface - the first pulling down the second and so on.

Rocks continuously hit the lake, but we are too far out.

Finally I reach a sunken baby. I'm up to my waist. Have not found the boy yet. The powder is slick and the slope steep. It is Idunno I pull above the surface out of the powder (my feet slip downhill in reaction to the tug) and I sob into her face. She breathes. I jam her feet into the hair now wrapped around my waist so she is standing mostly out of the powder. For the first time ever, she reaches for me, wraps her arms around me. Her eyes are wide and frightened. I whimper her name.

I whip the hair and pull in the hair and wade forward with searching feet, mind still split in two. I am finding them faster now; the hair - precious hair, cherished hair - stays intact and is retracting with undulations of its own, which is good, because I have waded so deep I

286

cannot manage to whip it and keep my rescued babies from falling off my shoulders and keep myself upright on my feet. I have Wanna. I have Hissie. I have my hand on Eggee's arm. It's limp. I'm whimpering non-stop.

Where is that boy? He was not out this far - unless he slid downhill after going under. I am sliding downhill. He could have slid anywhere. I have Eggee. I gather in Whaddle. I have them all, my babies. But am up to my sternum and two are below surface - Idunno and Wanna. Every inch of me burns. The blinded-Innar-boy could not have slid this far, I missed him. I bob on my toes and turn and try to get traction back uphill. Feet keep slipping. The babies desperately claw at me; unbalance me. The ones at my waist cannot breathe. They've been under too long. Under too long. The boy, too, has been under too long. I must get back.

Holding onto the hair I grab two, Hissie and Eggee, from my shoulders and throw them out in front of me. The hair zings across my palms so quickly it cuts me – burns a sharp streak. The looks of surprise on my little one's faces are heartbreaking. Then I grab hold of them and pull myself forward, toes grabbing at rock or dirt or any purchase. The lake bed gives up ground. I make progress a precious two inches. Then throw the two ahead again; I strain; we gain half a foot and now they know what this is about and do not fight me. Now I am up to my ribs and feet are again searching for the blind-Innar-boy. I take my first two out from the hair at my waist and beg them to breathe. It seems like forever, but they breathe and open their eyes and cling to me. Now my own precious babies are all out of the powder, but the burning continues and so do their cries. What do I do? Let them burn or abandon the Innar-boy? I am completely blind, the powder so compromising my sight I can no longer position me to any reference except the height of the powder against my body.

Shoulders slump. I pause then burst out a cry of rage because I cannot find him. He has been under too long.

I tumble to shore, wrapped like a mummy in a hairbag with my five. At least the hail of rocks has stopped. No sounds but our own cries. The Innar children gone. No powder on the shore; just dirt. But there is no relief. The burning continues on our skin, in our eyes, up our noses, in our minds. My mind burns - I did not save that Innar boy who was playing with the horrible children. The thought burns, burns.

Other minds burn, too, my babies' minds, my precious loads. Their minds burn - they are wrong, feared; they don't feel wrong; how could they be wrong?

"We monsters?" The oldest whimpers. Confused they look; haunted visages, vulnerable little fingers cling to me; trying to make sense of the violence and the screams of hate and rage.

Gently I dab spit across their eyes and clean out their mouths and wipe their delicate limbs with the blood flowing constantly from my chest wound. Their poor little bodies are red and blistered. There are alarming bruises and gashes from unfair rocks. I rub my eyes and realize I am whimpering at their wounds. And then, finally, finally, my throat relaxes enough to force words out, "You are not monsters," I croon. "Ah, na na, there there shh, shh sweet sweet, ah no, no - you are not monsters." I do not flinch from their anguish or tell them to buck-up. I just hold them until they fall asleep, limp from exhaustion, jumbled up together in my arms and lap.

When did I begin to love them so? Hell, when did I even accept them? How could they have become so dear to me and I not know? I look down at them, each so different. And watch them breathe through their blistered lips. Then, for the second time since my parents died, I cry. I cry softly so as not to wake them, but I cry to break my heart.

I want the old heart broken. The old heart understood nothing that a heart needs to know. It tears open, my heart, and grief unfolds in my stomach - swelling, unfurling, reaching-out-like-a-fist-to-plug-my-throat-and-clamp-my-heart grief.

I unhinge my lower jaw and breathe roughly through my mouth to control the harsh sobs. My tears water the ones in my lap. Shaking fingers brush little cheeks.

The terrible griefLove grips my heart again and again; each time the grip tightens, pierces me. What keeps my heart from bursting? Only love does and this grief. They feel much the same – love and grief. Almost the same.

I have no defense against what my heart sees and knows and accepts and loves. I never knew love made one vulnerable. My God, dear God must be the most vulnerable creature in existence.

Love is almost grief; here is another thing I never knew. I always thought love offered protection, but I was wrong. There is no shield in love. Love unreservedly offers its tenderest shoots to the sun. Now I realize my three deaths had nothing to do with earning heaven, love, or connection. I needed to learn to give love. I will run from love no more.

There! I have made my decision. I am sure finally about something and then, in an instant, the hairs attached to my neck lift and wave in the air acting as tiny feelers. Something feels different. My eyes roll searching and my neck swivels and my arms tighten in a protective gesture. There, on our back trail is a glow. Not yellowish, not Grama Ans with her torch-eyes. It looks like heaven's white light and it's moving my way.

My heart squeezes again, from fear. This is no time to leave my babies. I gather them in a hairbag sling and get to my feet, one end of the hairbag pushing up on my rear end (lending a hand, so to speak). We need to vacate Lake Purpus, get lost from that advancing white light. It's coming at me. Coming fast.

The hair pulls at my arms - towards the light - hell, no! I take off running the other way. EyeLight turned on full illuminates my way. I've got to get us out of here.

I'm panting, so scared. My legs pound, pound, pound out a rhythm of escape. It's a rough ride, I imagine. I glance down at my precious cargo. Only Idunno is looking at me. I fall into those eyes and am scared, scared of leaving her - leaving any of them. I cannot be taken from them.

They need me. I have purpose. There are five reasons I exist. Finally I understand. Finally, I know I am correct.

Throwing a quick glance over my shoulder causes me to stumble. My God! The light is almost upon me. I run. I bound. Time slows down so that even though every muscle strains ahead, I feel as if I am running in white lake-powder again, up to my neck. Around me, the rock shimmers with an unearthly white glow.

"Oh God. Oh, no. Oh God, no," I chant, pant, reject what is happening. My shadow runs out far in front of me stark black because the light is bright and directly behind. My back feels warm. It is upon me. I leap out of it. *<Oh, God, no!>*

I will stay in this dark and harsh and un-nourishing death and make it a good home for my babies. My back is warm again. No. It is faster than I. I feel it fold over me like a warm bright tunnel. I leap out. Am caught. It pulls me in and seems to scrape off the hair. The Hair falls from me, releases me; for the first time I am the one grabbing at it.

Suddenly Soldier leaps from the shadows. He leaps towards me, leaps up at me, leaps grasping with hands held like claws. He grabs my legs and sinks his nails into my skin. I wrap my feet around his hands. "Pull me down," I yell. "Draw me back to the ground. Help me!"

My babies fall away one by one. I feel Idunno's delicate little wrist bone break as I tighten my grasp - I will not let go. The hair falls heavily on Soldier, which causes him to stumble. I taste the sound of Idunno's despairing cry as she falls away from me.

Soldier leaps again, but I am too far away. He can no longer reach me. He opens his 'muzzle' but the hair wraps around it, around him, entangling him with my little ones. He cannot scream his rage.

I feel as if a tunnel is moving backwards over me absorbing me into its center. I see joy - reject it. Reach towards Idunno and away from the light with every fibrous aspect of me. Resist the light.

My two friends are there - I rage at them - so angry at too much. My rage is so huge I can eat it. "Let me go," I am, I say, I taste, I hear.

They are trying to calm me, my friends-who-are-no-friends-of-mine-who-want-me-to-think-I-am-wrong-in-my-wanting-to-stay-in-my-dark-and-rocky-place.

"Let me go, let me go, go, go, let go. I wanna go, I wanna, me, me, me, let me go ..." I sound just like all of my babies at the same time. "No to the light." All I see is light, movement, moving away...ssssssstop!

Then stillness - maybe even a pause - and I am before a gate. Behind the gate is everyone I have ever loved and lost before this third death. They are speaking, I see their lips move, but hear nothing. Momma reaches out an imploring arm between the bars. "No!" I deny her.

A man takes one step towards me. I've never seen, heard, or felt this man, but I know him. He will judge me.

"I will ask you one question," he says, his voice and visage fearful and yet his eyes so gentle I could ... almost ... get lost in them.

"No." I say again. "No to any question you ask me."

He unrolls the scroll, glances at it then back to me.

"No." I resist again.

"I have not yet asked..."

"No. I choose to go back."

"You don't understand," he says so beautifully I ... almost ... agree.

So I close my non-eyes against any drawing power, against God, and Momma, and Da, and friends, and life, and heaven, and white light. I close myself against any pull or urge or drawing or enlightenment. And then, then, then, the white light ever-so-gently, wistfully releases me. All of me is relieved.

I taste, feel, am more than relieved as the white light allows me to pull back out of it. Beyond relieved and beyond grateful, I may be in an ecstatic state. Am highly aware of the last fingers of light letting me go. Am falling back down into rocky darkness. My non-legs twitch as they tap, tap, tap for my babies, for the hair, for the ground of this third death, for the boy still missing in the lake, and for me. In my ecstasy I hear my heart beating again.

I am in touch, in touch with love finally and understand what it all has been about. Love of my babies is more than enough. *Tha-thump Tha-thump Tha-thump* drums out my new start to deadly life. *Tha-thump Tha-thump Tha-thump* I welcome whole heartedly my blessed connections.

~

About the Author

Dayna Hubenthal graduated with a Masters of Fine Arts degree from San Jose State University after fifteen years of college. She loves to learn and is passionate about being at the frontier of knowledge. She is a writer, an artist, an innovator and a researcher.

For many years, Dayna made her living as a technical writer in Silicon Valley. She helped brilliant people at bleeding-edged start-ups transform esoteric ideas into assessable and usable knowledge.

She is fascinated by heroes who have the courage to live an examined life (and those willing to enter uncharted territory). It takes a special kind of person to go where no one has gone before. She writes for these 'heroes' as they embark upon (or resist) their own journey of self-discovery. She also writes for those who create a safe place for the transformed-hero to come back to.

Many cultures interest Dayna, especially the ancient cultures of Hawaii. She enjoys discovering archetypal patterns and subtle differences throughout societies past and present and is fascinated by great human achievements.

Dayna and husband, Scott Burr, have lived all over the West Coast, from Northern Washington (Omak) to Southern California (Imperial Beach). They live with Rumi - possibly the cutest dog in the world.

Persephone's Seeds is Dayna's first novel.

www.ingramcontent.com/pod-product-compliance
Lightning Source LLC
Chambersburg PA
CBHW021211250626
47155CB00008B/2765